Torchy, Private Sec.

Sewell Ford

Illustrated by F. Foster Lincoln

Esprios.com

By SEWELL FORD

TORCHY
TRYING OUT TORCHY
ON WITH TORCHY
TORCHY, PRIVATE SEC.
ODD NUMBERS
  "Shorty McCabe"
SHORTY McCABE ON THE JOB

"Why didn't you tell me before that you had such a grand name?"

TORCHY, PRIVATE SEC.

BY

SEWELL FORD

AUTHOR OF
TORCHY, TRYING OUT TORCHY,
ON WITH TORCHY, ETC.

ILLUSTRATIONS BY
F. FOSTER LINCOLN

NEW YORK
GROSSET & DUNLAP
PUBLISHERS

1914

CONTENTS

CHAPTER

I.	The Up Call for Torchy
II.	Torchy Makes the Sir Class
III.	Torchy Takes a Chance
IV.	Breaking It to the Boss
V.	Showing Gilkey the Way
VI.	When Skeet Had His Day
VII.	Getting a Jolt from Westy
VIII.	Some Guesses on Ruby
IX.	Torchy Gets an Inside Tip
X.	Then Along Came Sukey
XI.	Teamwork with Aunty
XII.	Zenobia Digs Up a Late One
XIII.	Sifting Out Uncle Bill
XIV.	How Aunty Got the News
XV.	Mr. Robert and a Certain Party
XVI.	Torchy Tackles a Short Circuit
XVII.	Mr. Robert Gets a Slant
XVIII.	When Ella May Came By
XIX.	Some Hoop-la for the Boss

CHAPTER I

THE UP CALL FOR TORCHY

Well, it's come! Uh-huh! And sudden, too, like I knew it would, if it came at all. No climbin' the ladder for me, not while they run express elevators. And, believe me, when the gate opened, I was right there with my foot out.

It was like this: One mornin' I'm in my old place behind the brass rail, at the jump-end of the buzzer. I'm everybody's slave in general, and Piddie's football in particular. You know—head office boy of the Corrugated Trust.

That's description enough, ain't it? And I'd been there so long—— Honest, when I first went on the job I used to sneak the city directory under the chair so my toes could touch. Now my knees rub the under-side of the desk. Familiar with the place? Say, there are just seventeen floor cracks between me and the opposite wall; it's fifty-eight steps through into Old Hickory's roll-top and back; and the ink I've poured into all them desk-wells would be enough to float a ferry-boat.

At 8.30 on this special mornin' there I am, as I said; and at 2.21 P. M. the same day I'm—— Well, of course, there was a few preliminaries, though I didn't tag 'em as such when they come along. I expect the new spring costume helped some. And the shave—oh, I was goin' it strong! No cut-price, closing-out, House-of-Smartheimer bargain, altered free to fit—not so, Lobelia! Why, I pawed over whole bales of stuff in a sure-enough Fifth-ave. tailor works; had blueprint plans of the front and side elevations drawn, even to the number of buttons on the cuffs, and spent three diff'rent noon hours havin' it modeled on me before they could pull a single bastin' thread.

But it's some stream line effect at the finish, take it from me! Nothing sporty or cake-walky, you understand: just quiet and dignified and rich-like, same as any second vice or gen'ral manager would wear.

Torchy, Private Sec.

Two-button sack with wide English roll and no turn-up to the trousers—oh, I should ripple!

The shave was an afterthought. I'd worked up to it by havin' some of my lurid locks trimmed, and as Giuseppe quits shearin' and asks if there'll be anything else I rubs my hand casual across my jaw and remarks:

"Could you find anything there to mow with a razor?"

Could he? He'd go through the motions on a glass doorknob!

Then it's me tilted back with my heels up and the suds artist decoratin' my map until it looks like a Polish weddin' cake. Don't it hit you foolish the first time, though? I felt like everybody in the shop, includin' the brush boy and the battery of lady manicures, was all gathered around pipin' me off as a raw beginner. So I stares haughty at the ceilin' and tries to put on a bored look.

I'd been scraped twice over, and was just bein' unwrapped from the hot towel, when I turns to see who it is has camped down in the next chair, and finds Mr. Robert gazin' at me curious.

"Why!" says he, chucklin'. "If it isn't Torchy! Indulging in a shave, eh?"

"Oh, no, Sir," says I. "Been havin' my eye teeth tested for color blindness, that's all."

Mr. Robert grins amiable and reaches out for the check. "This is on me then," says he. "I claim the privilege."

As he comes in after luncheon he has to stop and grin again; and later on, when I answers the buzzer, he makes me turn clear around so he can inspect the effect and size up the new suit.

"Excellent, Torchy!" says he. "Whoever your tailor may be, you do him credit."

"This trip I paid cash, though, " says I. "It's all right, is it? "

"In every particular, " says he. "Why, you look almost grown up. May I ask the occasion? Can it be that Miss Verona is on the point of returning from somewhere or other? "

"Uh-huh, " says I. "Bermuda. Got in yesterday. "

"And Aunty, I trust, " goes on Mr. Robert, "is as well as usual? "

"I'm hoping for the worst, " says I; "but I expect she is. "

We swaps merry expressions again, and Mr. Robert pats me chummy on the shoulder. "You're quite all right, Torchy, " says he, "and I wish you luck. " Then the twinkle fades out of his eyes and he turns serious. "I wish, " he goes on, "that I could do more than just— well, some time, perhaps. " And with another friendly pat he swings around to his desk, where the letters are stacked a foot high.

Say, he's the real thing, Mr. Robert is, no matter if he does take it out in wishin'! It ain't every boss would do that much, specially with the load he's carryin'. For you know since Old Hickory's been down South takin' seven kinds of baths, and prob'ly cussin' out them resort doctors as they was never cussed before, Mr. Robert Ellins has been doin' a heap more than give an imitation of bein' a busy man. But he's there with the wallop, and I guess it's goin' to take more'n a commerce court to put the Corrugated out of business.

Too bad, though, that Congress can't spare the time from botherin' about interlockin' directors to suppress a few padlockin' aunties. Say, the way that old girl does keep the bars up against an inoffensive party like me is something fierce! I tries to call Vee on the 'phone as soon as I've discovered where she is, and all the satisfaction I get is a message delivered by a French maid that "Miss Hemmingway is otherwise engaged. " Wouldn't that crust you?

But I've been up against this embargo game before, you know; so the first chance I gets I slips uptown to do a little scoutin' at close range.

Torchy, Private Sec.

It's an apartment hotel this time, and I hangs around the entrance, inspectin' the bay trees out front for half an hour, before I can work up the nerve to make the Brodie break. Fin'lly I marches in bold and calls for Aunty herself.

"Is she in, Cephas?" says I to the brunette Jamaican in the olive-green liv'ry who juggles the elevator.

"I don't rightly know, Suh," says he; "but you can send up a call, Suh, from the desk there, and——"

"Ah, let's not disturb the operator," says I. "Give a guess."

"I'm thinking she'll be taking her drive, Suh," says Cephas, blinkin' stupid.

"Then I'll have to go up and wait," says I. "She'd be mighty sore on us both if she missed me. Up, Cephas!"

"Yes, Suh," says he, pullin' the lever.

I should have known, though, from one look at that to-let expression of his, that his ideas on any subject would be vague. And this was a bum hunch on Aunty. Out? Why, she was propped up in an easy-chair with a sprained ankle, and had been for three days! And you should have seen the tight-lipped, welcome-to-our-grand-jury-room smile that she greets me with.

"Humph!" she says. "You! Well, young man, what is your excuse this time?"

I grins sheepish and shuffles my feet. "Same old excuse," says I.

"Do you mean to tell me," she gasps, "that you have the impudence to try to see my niece, after all I have——"

"Uh-huh," I breaks in. "Don't you ever take a sportin' chance yourself?"

She gurgles somethin' throaty, goes purple in the gills, and prepares to smear me on the spot; but I gives her the straight look between the eyes and hurries on.

"Oh, I know where you stand, all right, " says I; "but ain't you drawin' it a little strong? Say, where's the harm in me takin' Verona out for a half-hour walk along the Drive? We ain't had a chat for over two months, you know, not a word, and I'd kind of like to — —"

"No doubt, " says Aunty. "Are you quite certain, however, that Verona would like it too? "

"I'm always guessin' where Vee is concerned, " I admits; "but by the latest dope I had on the subject, I expect she wouldn't object strenuous. "

Aunty sniffs. "It is quite possible, " says she. "Verona is a whimsical, willful girl at times, just as her poor mother was. Keeping up this pretense of friendship for you is one of her silly notions. "

"Thanks awfully, Ma'am, " says I.

"Let me see, " goes on Aunty, squintin' foxy at me, "you are employed in Mr. Ellins's office, I believe? "

I nods.

"As office boy, still? " says she.

"No, as a live one, " says I. "Anybody that stays still very long at the Corrugated gets canned. "

"Please omit meaningless jargon, " says Aunty. "Does my niece know just how humble a position you occupy? Have you ever told her? "

"Why, " says I, "I don't know as I've ever gone into details. "

"Ah-h-h!" says she. "I was certain that Verona did not fully realize. Perhaps it would be as well that she——" and here she breaks off sudden, like she'd been struck with a new idea. For a second or so she gazes blank over the top of my head, and then she comes to with a brisk, "That will do, young man! Verona is not at home. You need not trouble to call again. The maid will show you out. Celeste!"

And the next thing I knew I was ridin' down again with Cephas. I'm some shunter myself; but I dip the colors to Aunty: she does it so neat and sudden! It must be like the sensation of havin' a flight of trick stairs fold up under you, —one minute you're most to the top, the next you're pickin' yourself up at the bottom.

What worries me most, though, is this hint she drops about Vee. Looks like the old girl had something up her sleeve; but what it is I can't dope out. So all I can do is keep my eyes open and my ear stretched for the next few days, watchin' for something to happen.

Course, I had one or two other things on my mind meanwhile; for down at the gen'ral offices we wa'n't indulgin' in any spring-fever symptoms, —not with three big deals under way, all this income mess of deductin' at the source goin' on, and Mr. Robert's grand scheme for dissolvin' the Corrugated—on paper—bein' worked out. Oh, sure, that's the easiest thing we do. We've split up into nineteen sep'rate and distinct corporations, with a diff'rent set of directors for each one, and if the Attorney General can sleuth out where they're tied together he's got to do some high-class snoopin' around.

Maybe you think too, that little Sunny Haired Hank, guardin' the brass gate, ain't wise to every move. Say, I make that part of my job. If I didn't, I'd be towin' a grouchy bunch of minority kickers in where the reorganization board was cookin' up a new stock-transfer game, or make some other fool break that would spill the beans all over the pantry floor.

"Torchy," says Mr. Robert, chewin' his cigar nervous and pawin' through pigeonholes, "ask Mr. Piddie what was done with those Mesaba contracts."

"Filed under Associated Developments, " says I.

"Oh, yes, so they were, " says he. "Thanks. And could you find out for me when we organized General Transportation? "

"Wa'n't that pulled off the day you waited for that Duluth delegation to show up, just after Easter? " says I.

"That's it, " says he, "the fifteenth! Has Marling of Chicago been called up yet? "

"Nope, " says I. "He'll be waitin' for the closing quotations, won't he? But there's that four-eyed guy with the whiskers who's been hangin' around a couple of hours. "

"Ah! " says Mr. Robert, huntin' out a card on his desk. "That Rowley person! I'd forgotten. What does he want? "

"Didn't say, " says I. "Got a roll of something under one arm — crank promoter, maybe. Will I ditch him? "

"Not without being heard, " says Mr. Robert. "I haven't time myself, though. Perhaps Mr. Piddie might interview him and — — "

"Ah, Piddie! " says I. "He'd take one look at the old gink's round cuffs and turn him down haughty. You know Piddie? "

Mr. Robert smiles. "Then suppose you do it, " says he. "Go ahead — full powers. Only remember this: My policy is to give everyone who has a proposition to submit to the Corrugated a respectful and adequate hearing. Get the idea? "

"I'm right behind you, " says I. "The smooth stuff goes; and if we must spill 'em, grease the skids. Me for Rowley! "

And, say, you should have heard me shove over the diplomacy, tellin' how sorry Mr. Robert was he couldn't see him in person; but wouldn't he please state the case in full so no time might be lost in actin' one way or the other? Inside of three minutes too, he has his papers spread out and is explainin' his by-product scheme for mill tailings, with me busy takin' notes on a pad. He had it all figured out into big money; but of course I couldn't tell whether he had a sure thing, or was just exercisin' squirrels in the connin' tower.

"Ten millions a year, " says he, "and I am offering to put this process in operation for a five-per-cent. royalty! I've been a mine superintendent for twenty years, young man, and I know what I'm talking about. "

"Your spiel listens like the real thing, Mr. Rowley, " says I; "only we can't jump at these things offhand. We have to chew 'em over, you know. "

Rowley shakes his head decided. "You can't put me off for six months or a year, " says he. "I've been through all that. If the Corrugated doesn't want to go into this — —"

"Right you are! " I breaks in. "Ten days is enough. I'll put this up to the board next Wednesday week and get a decision. Much obliged to you, Mr. Rowley, for givin' us first whack at it. We 're out for anything that looks good, and we always take care of the parties that put us next. That's the Corrugated way. Good afternoon, Mr. Rowley. Drop in again. Here's your hat. "

And as he drifts out, smilin', pleased and hopeful, I glances over the spring-water bottle, to see Mr. Robert standin' there listenin' with a grin on.

"Congratulations! " says he. "That peroration of yours was a classic, Torchy; the true Chesterfield spirit, if not the form. I am tempted to utilize your talent for that sort of thing once more. What do you say? "

"Then put it over the plate while I'm on my battin' streak, " says I. "Who's next? "

"A lady this time, " says he; "perchance two ladies. " And he develops that eye twinkle of his.

"Huh! " says I, twistin' my neck and feelin' of my tie. "You ain't springin' any tea-pourin' stunt, are you? "

"Strictly business, " says he; "at least, " he adds, chucklin', "that is the presumption. As a matter of fact, I've just been called over the 'phone by Miss Verona Hemmingway's aunt. "

"Eh! " says I, gawpin'.

"She holds some of our debenture bonds, you know, " says Mr. Robert, "and I gather that she has been somewhat disturbed by these reorganization rumors. "

"But she ought to know, " says I, "that our D. B.'s. are as solid as——"

"The feminine mind, " cuts in Mr. Robert, "does not readily grasp such simple facts. But I haven't half an hour or more to devote to the process of soothing her alarm; besides, you could do it so much more gracefully. "

"Mooshwaw! " says I. "Maybe I could. But she's only one. Who's the other? "

"She failed to state, " says Mr. Robert. "She merely said, 'We shall be down about three o'clock. '"

"We? " says I. Then I whistles. So that was her game! It was Vee she was bringin' along!

"Well? " says Mr. Robert.

I expect I was some pinked up, and fussed, too, at the prospect. "Excuse me, " says I, "but I got to sidestep. "

"Why, " says he, "I rather thought this assignment might be somewhat agreeable. "

"I know, " says I. "You mean well enough; but, honest, Mr. Robert, if that foxy old dame's comin' down here with Miss Vee, I'm—well, I don't stand for it, that's all! I'm off; with a blue ticket or without one, just as you say. "

I was reachin' for my new lid too, when Mr. Robert puts out his hand.

"Wouldn't that be—er—rather a serious breach of office discipline? " says he. "Surely, without some good reason——"

"Ah, say! " says I. "You don't think I'm springin' any prima donna whim, do you? It's this plot to show me up through the wrong end of the telescope that gets me sore. "

"Scarcely lucid, " says he, lookin' puzzled. "Could you put it a little simpler? "

"I'll make it long primer, " says I. "How do I stand here in the Corrugated? You know, maybe, and sometimes I give a guess myself; but on the books, and as far as outsiders go, I'm just plain office boy, ain't I, like 'steen thousand other four-dollar-a-week kids that's old enough to have work papers? I've been here goin' on four years now, and I ain't beefed much about it, have I? That's because I've been used white and the pay has been decent. Also I'm strong for you and Mr. Ellins. I expect you know that, Mr. Robert. Maybe I ain't got it in me to be anything but an office boy, either; but when it comes to goin' on exhibition before certain parties as the double cipher on the east side of the decimal—well, that's where I make my foolish play. "

"Ah! " says he, rubbin' his chin thoughtful. "Now I fully understand. And, as you suggest, there has been for some time past something—er—equivocal about your position here. However, just at this moment I have hardly time to—— By Jove! " Here he breaks off and glances at the clock. "Two-fifteen, and a general council of our attorneys called for half-past in the directors' room! Someone else must attend to Miss Verona's estimable aunt—positively! Now if there was anyone who could relieve you from the gate——"

"Heiny, the bondroom boy," says I.

"Why not?" says Mr. Robert. "Then, if you should choose to stay and prime yourself with facts about those debentures, there is that extra desk in my office, you know. Would you mind using that?"

"But see here, Mr. Robert," says I, "I wa'n't plannin' any masquerade, either."

"Quite so," says he; "nor I. It so happens, though, that the gentleman whose name appears as president of our Mutual Funding Company is—well, hardly in active business life. It is necessary that he be represented here in some nominal capacity. The directors are now meeting in Room 19. I have authority to name a private secretary pro tem. Do you accept the position?"

"With a pro-tem. salary, stage money barred?" says I.

"Oh, most certainly," says he.

"Then I'm the guy," says I.

"Good!" says Mr. Robert. "These debentures come in your department. I will notify Mr. Piddie that——"

"Say, Mr. Robert," says I, grinnin' once more, "I'd break it gentle to Piddie."

I don't know whether he did or not; for five minutes after that Heiny has my old seat, and I'm inside behind the ground-glass door, sittin' at a reg'lar roll-top, with a lot of file cases spread out, puzzlin' over this incorporation junk that makes the Fundin' Comp'ny the little joker in the Corrugated deck.

And next thing I know in comes Heiny, gawpin' foolish, and trailin' behind him Aunty and Vee. I wa'n't throwin' any bluff about tryin' to look busy, either. I was elbow-deep in papers, with a pen behind one ear and ink on three fingers.

You should have heard the gasp that comes from Aunty as she pipes off who it is at the desk. My surprise as I'm discovered is the real thing too.

"Chairs, Boy! " says I, snappin' my fingers at Heiny.

But Aunty catches her breath, draws herself up stiff, and waves away the seats. "Young man, " says she, "I came here to consult with Mr. Robert Ellins about——"

"Yes'm, " says I, "I understand. Debenture six's, ain't they? Not affected by the reorganization, Ma'am. You see, it's like this: Those bonds were issued in exchange for——"

"Young man, " she breaks in, aimin' her lorgnette at me threatenin', "I prefer to discuss this matter with Mr. Robert. "

"Sorry, " says I, "but as he's very busy he asked me to——"

"And who, pray, " snaps the old girl, "are you? "

"Representin' the president of the Mutual Funding Comp'ny, " says I.

"Just how? " she demands.

"Private secretary, Ma'am, " says I.

"Humph! " she snorts. "This is too absurd of Mr. Robert—wholly absurd! Come, Verona. "

And as she sails out I just has time for a glance at Vee, and catches a wink. Believe me, though, a friendly wink from one of them gray eyes is worth waitin' for! She follows Aunty through the door with a handkerchief stuffed in her mouth like she was smotherin' a snicker; so I guess Vee was on. And I'm left feelin' all warmed up and chirky.

Mr. Robert comes in from his lawyer session just before closin' time; rubbin' his hands sort of satisfied too.

"Well, " says I, jumpin' up from the swing-chair, "it was some jolt you slipped Aunty. I expect I can resign now? "

"Oh, I trust not, " says he. "The board indorsed your appointment an hour ago. Keep your desk, Torchy. It is to be yours from now on. "

"Wh-a-a-at? " says I, my eyes bugged. "Off the gate for good, am I? "

"We are hoping, " says he, "that the gate's loss will be the Funding Company's gain. "

I gurgles gaspy a couple of times before I catches my breath. "Will it? " says I. "Say, just watch me! I'm goin' to show you that fundin' is my long suit! "

CHAPTER II

TORCHY MAKES THE SIR CLASS

Say, it's all right, gettin' the quick boost up the ladder, providin' you don't let it make you dizzy in the head. And, believe me, I was near it! You see, bein' jumped from office boy to private sec, all in one afternoon, was some breath-takin' yank.

I expect the full force of what had happened didn't hit me until here the other mornin' when I strolls into the Corrugated gen'ral offices on the new nine o'clock schedule and finds this raw recruit holdin' down my old chair behind the rail. Nice, smooth-haired, bright-eyed youngster, with his ears all scoured out pink and his knickerbocker suit brushed neat. He hops up and opens the gate real respectful for me.

"Well, Son, " says I, "what does Mother call you? "

"Vincent, Sir, " says he.

"Some class to that, too, " says I. "But how do you know, Vincent, that I'm one of the reg'lar staff and not canvassin' for something? "

"I don't, Sir, " says he, "until I see if you know where to hang your hat. "

"Good domework, Vincent, " says I. "On that I'm backin' you to hold the job. "

"Thank you, Sir, " says he. "I told Mother I'd do my best. "

And with that he springs a bashful smile. It was the "Sir" every time that caught me, though. For more'n four years I'd been just Torchy or Boy to all hands in the shop, from Old Hickory down; and now all of a sudden I finds there's one party at least that rates me in the Sir class. Kind of braced me for swingin' past all that row of giggly lady typists and on into Mr. Robert's private office.

Thrill No. 2 arrived half an hour later. In postin' myself as to what this Mutual Fundin' Company really is that I'm supposed to be workin' for, I needed some papers from the document safe. And for the first time I pushes the buzzer button. Prompt and eager in comes Vincent, the fair haired.

"Know which is Mr. Piddie, do you? " says I.

"Oh, yes, Sir, " says he.

"Well, " says I, "tell him I need those—no, better ask him to step in here a minute. "

Honest, I wa'n't plannin' to rub it in, either. Course, I'd done a good deal of trottin' for Piddie, and a lot of it wa'n't for anything else than to let him show his authority; but I didn't hold any grudge. I'd squared the account in my own way. How he was goin' to take it now I was the one to send for him, I didn't know; but there wa'n't any use dodgin' the issue.

And you should have seen Piddie make his first official entrance! You know how stiff and wooden he is as a rule? Well, as he marches in over the rug and comes to a parade rest by the desk, he's about as limber as a length of gas pipe. And solemn? That long face of his would have soured condensed milk!

"Yes, Sir? " says he. And to me, mind you! It come out a little husky, like it was bein' filtered through strong emotions; but there it is. Piddie has sirred me his first "Sir. "

He knows a roll-top when he sees one, Piddie does, and he ain't omittin' any deference due. You know the type? He's one of the kind that was born to be "our Mr. Piddie"; the sort that takes off his hat to a vice-president, and holds his breath in the presence of the big wheeze. But, say, I don't want any joss-sticks burned for me.

Torchy, Private Sec.

"Ditch it, Piddie, " says I, "ditch it! "

"I—er—I beg pardon? " says he.

"The Sir stuff, " says I. "Just because I'm behind the ground glass instead of the brass rail don't make me a sacred being, or you a lobbygow, does it? I guess we've known each other too long for that, eh? " And I holds out the friendly mitt.

Honest, he's got a human streak in him, Piddie has, if you know where to strike it. The cast-iron effect comes out of his shoulders, the wooden look from his face. He almost smiles.

"Thank you, Torchy, " says he. "I—er—my congratulations on your new——"

"We'll spread 'em on the minutes, " says I, "and proceed to show the Corrugated some teamwork that mere salaries can't buy. Are you on? "

He was. Inside of three minutes he'd chucked that stiff-necked, flunky pose and was coachin' me like a big brother, and by the time he'd beat into my head all he knew about the Fundin' Comp'ny we was as chummy as two survivors of the same steamer wreck. Simple, I know; but this little experience made me feel like I'd signed a gen'ral peace treaty with the world at large.

I hadn't, though. An hour later I runs up against Willis G. Briscoe. He's kind of an outside development manager, who makes preliminary reports on new deals. One of these cold-eyed, chesty parties, Willis G. is; tall and thin, and with a big, bowwow voice that has a rasp to it.

"Huh! " says he, as he discovers me busy at the desk. "I heard of this out in Chicago three days ago; but I thought it must be a joke. "

"Them reporters do get things straight now and then, don't they? " says I.

"Reporters!" he snorts. "Philip wrote me about it."

"Oh!" says I. "Cousin Philip, eh?"

And that gave me the whole plot of the piece. Cousin Phil was a cigarette-consumin' college discard that Willis G. had been nursin' along in the bondroom, waitin' for a better openin'; and this jump of mine had filled a snap job that he'd had his eyes on for Cousin.

"I suppose you're only temporary, though," says he.

"That's all," says I. "Mr. Ellins will be resignin' in eight or ten years, I expect, and then they'll want me in his chair. Nice mornin', ain't it?"

"Bah!" says he, registerin' deep disgust, as they say in the movie scripts. "You'll do well if you last eight or ten days."

"How cheerin'!" says I, and as he swings off with a final glare I tips him the humorous wink.

Why not? No young-man-afraid-of-his-job part for me! Briscoe might get it away from me, or he might not; but I wa'n't goin' to get panicky over it. Let him do his worst!

He didn't need any urgin'. With a little scoutin' around he discovers that about the only assignment on my hook so far is this Rowley matter: you know, the old inventor guy with the mill-tailings scheme. And the first hint I had that he was wise to that was when Mr. Robert calls me over after lunch and explains how this Rowley business sort of comes in Mr. Briscoe's department.

"So I suppose you'd better turn it over to him," says he.

"Just as you say," says I. "The old gent is due at two-fifteen, and I'll shunt him onto Briscoe."

Which I did. And at two-thirty-five Briscoe breezes in with his report.

"Nothing to it, " says he. "This Rowley person has a lot of half-baked ideas about briquets and retort recoveries, and talks vaguely of big profits; but he's got nothing practical. I shipped him off. "

"But, " says Mr. Robert, "I think he was promised that his schemes should have a consideration by the board. "

"Very well, " says Willis G. jaunty. "I'll give 'em a report next meeting. Wednesday, isn't it? Hardly worth wasting their time over, though. "

And here I'd been boostin' the Rowley proposition to Mr. Robert good and hard, almost gettin' him enthusiastic over it! I was smeared, that's all! My first stab at makin' myself useful in my new swing-chair job has been brushed aside as a beginner's bungle; and there sits Mr. Robert, prob'ly wonderin' if he hadn't made a mistake in takin' me off the gate!

I stares at a row of empty pigeonholes for a solid hour after that, not doin' a blamed thing but race my thinkin' gears tryin' to find out where I was at. This dummy act that I'd been let in for might be all right for some; but it didn't suit me. I've got to have action in mine.

So, long before quittin' time, I slams the desk cover down and pikes out on Rowley's trail. He might be a dead duck; but I wanted to know how and why. I had his address all right, and it didn't take me long to locate him in a fifth-story loft down on lower Sixth-ave. It's an odd joint too, with a cot bed in one corner, a work bench along the avenue side, a cook-stove in the middle, and a kitchen table where the coffeepot was crowded on each side by a rack of test tubes. Old Rowley himself, with his sleeves rolled up, is sittin' in a rickety arm chair peelin' potatoes. He's grouchy too.

"Oh, it's you, is it? " says he. "Well, you might just as well trot right back to the Corrugated Trust and tell 'em that Old Hen Rowley don't give two hoots for their whole outfit. "

"I take it you didn't get on so well with Mr. Briscoe? " says I.

"Briscoe! " he grunts savage. "Who could talk business to a smart Alec like that! He knew it all before I'd begun. You'd think I was trying to sell him a gold brick. All right! We'll see what the Bethlehem people have to say. "

"What? " says I. "Before you get the final word from us? "

"I've had it, " says he. "Briscoe is final enough for me. "

"You're easy satisfied, " says I, "or else you're easy beat. I didn't take you for a quitter, either. "

Say, that got to him. "Quitter, eh! " says he. "See here, Son, how long do you think I've been plugging at this thing? Nine years. And for the last four I've been giving it all my time, day in and day out, and many a night as well. I've been living with it, in this loft here, like a blessed hermit; testing and perfecting, trying out my processes, and fighting the Patent Office sharks between times. Nine years—the best of my life! Call that quitting, do you? "

"Well, that is sticking around some, " says I. "Think you've got your schemes so they'll work? "

"I don't think, " says he; "I know. "

"But what's the good, " I goes on, "if you can't make other folks see you've got a good thing? "

"I can, though, " he says. "Why, any person with even ordinary intelligence can——"

"That's me, " says I. "My nut is just about a stock pattern size, six and seven-eighths, or maybe seven. Come, try it on me, if it's so simple. Now what about this retort business? "

That got him goin'. Rowley drops the potatoes, and in another minute we're neck-deep in the science of makin' an ore puddin', doin' stunts with the steam, skimmin' dividends off the pot, and coinin' the slag into dollars.

I ain't lettin' him slip over any gen'ral propositions on me, either. I'm right there with the Missouri stuff. He has to go clear back to first principles every time he makes a statement, and work up to it gradual. Course, I was keepin' him jollied along too, and while it must have been sort of hopeless at the start, inoculatin' a cauliflower like mine with higher chemistry, I fin'lly showed one or two gleams that encouraged him to keep on. Anyway, we hammered away at the subject, only stoppin' to make coffee and sandwiches, until near two o'clock in the mornin'.

"Help! " says I, glancin' at the nickel alarm clock. "My head feels like a stuffed sausage. A little more, and I won't know whether I'm a nitrous sulphide or a ferrous oxide of bromo seltzer. Let's take the rest in another dose. "

Rowley chuckles and agrees to call it a day, I didn't let on anything at the office next morning; but by eight A. M. I was planted at the roll-top with my elbows squared, tryin' to write out as much of that chemistry dope as I could remember. And it's surprising ain't it, what a lot of information you can sop up when you do the sponge act in earnest? I found there was a lot of points, though, that I was foggy on; so I makes an early getaway and puts in another long session with Rowley.

And, take it from me, by Tuesday I was well loaded. Also I had my plan of campaign all mapped out; for you mustn't get the idea I was packin' my bean full of all this science dope just to see if it would stand the strain. Not so, Clarice! I'd woke up to the fact that I was bein' carried along by the Corrugated as a sort of misfit inner tube stowed in the bottom of the tool-box, and that it was up to me to make good.

So the first openin' I has I tackles Mr. Robert on the side.

"About that Rowley proposition? " says I.

"Oh, yes, " says he. "I fear Mr. Briscoe thinks unfavorably of it. "

"Then he's fruity in the pan, " says I.

"We have been in the habit of accepting his judgment in such matters, " says Mr. Robert.

"Maybe, " says I; "but here's once when he's handin' you a stall. And you're missin' out on something good too. "

Mr. Robert smiles skeptical. "Really? " says he. "Perhaps you would like to present a minority report? "

"Nothin' less, " says I. "Oh, it may listen like a joke, but that's just what I got in mind. "

"H-m-m-m! " says Mr. Robert. "You realize that Briscoe is one of the leading mining authorities in the country, I suppose, and that we pay him a large salary as consulting engineer? "

I nods. "I know, " says I. "And the nearest I ever got to seein' a mine was watchin' 'em excavate for the subway. I'm admittin' all that. "

"I may add too, " goes on Mr. Robert, "that he has a way of stating his opinions quite convincingly. "

"Yep, " says I, "I should judge that. But if I think he's bilkin' you on this, is it my play to sit behind and chew my tongue? "

"By Jove! " says Mr. Robert, his sportin' instincts comin' to the top. "You shall have your chance, Torchy. The directors shall hear your views; to-morrow, at two-thirty. You will follow Briscoe. "

"Let's not bill it ahead, then, " says I, "if it'll be fair to spring it on him. "

"Quite, " says Mr. Robert; "and rather more amusing, I fancy. I will arrange it. "

"I'd like to have old Rowley on the side lines, in case I get stuck," says I.

"Oh, certainly," says he. "Bring Mr. Rowley if you wish. And if there are any preparations you would like to make——"

"I got one or two," says I, startin' for the door; "so mark me off until about to-morrow noon."

Busy? Well, say, a kitten with four feet stuck in the flypaper didn't have anything on me. I streaks it for Sixth-ave. and lands in Rowley's loft all out of breath.

"What's up?" says he.

"The case of Briscoe *et al. vs.* Rowley," says I. "It's to be threshed out before the full Corrugated board to-morrow at two-thirty. I'm the counsel for the defense."

"Well, what of it?" says he.

"I want to use you as Exhibit A," says I, "in case of an emergency."

"All right," says he. "I'll go along if you say so."

"Good!" says I. And then came the hard part. "Rowley," I goes on, "what size collar do you wear?"

"But what has that to do with it?" says he.

"Now don't get peeved," says I; "but you know the kind our directors are,—flossy, silk-lined old sports, most of 'em; and they're apt to size up strangers a good deal by their haberdashery. So I was wonderin' if I couldn't blow you to a neat, pleated bosom effect with attached cuffs."

"Oh, I see," says Rowley, glancin' at his gray flannel workin' shirt. "Anything else?"

"I don't expect you'd want to part with that face shrubbery, or have it landscaped into a Vandyke, eh? " says I. "You know they ain't wearin' the bushy kind now in supertax circles. "

"Would you insist on my being manicured too? " says he, chucklin' easy.

"It would help, " says I. "And this would be my buy all round. "

"That's a generous offer, Son, " says he, "and I don't know how long it's been since anyone has taken so much personal interest in Old Hen Rowley. Seems nice too. I suppose I am rather a shabby old duffer to be visiting the offices of great and good corporations. Yes, I'll spruce up a bit; and if I find it costs more than I can afford—now let's see how my cash stands. "

With that he digs into a hip pocket and unlimbers a roll of corn-tinted kale the size of your wrist. Maybe they wa'n't all hundreds clear to the core, but that's what was on the outside.

"Whiffo! " says I. "Excuse me for classin' you so near the bread line; but by your campin' in a loft, and the longshoreman's shirt, and so on——"

"Very natural, Son, " he breaks in. "And I see your point all the clearer. I've no business going about so. The whiskers shall be trimmed. But your people up at the Corrugated have evidently made up their minds to turn us down. "

"Maybe, " says I; "but if they do, it won't be on any snap decision of Briscoe's. And unless I get tongue tied at the last minute we're goin' to have a run for our money. "

That was what worried me most, —could I come across with the standin' spiel? But, believe me, I wa'n't trustin' to any offhand stuff! I'd got to know in advance what I meant to feed 'em, line for line and word for word. By ten o'clock that night I had it all down on paper too—and perhaps I didn't chew the penholder and leak some from the brow while I was doin' it!

Then came the rehearsin'. Say, you should have seen me risin' dignified behind the washstand in my room, strikin' a Bill Bryan pose, and smilin' calm at the bedposts as I launched out on my speech. Not that I was tryin' to chuck any flowers of oratory. What I aimed to do was to tell 'em about Rowley's schemes as simple and straight away as I could, usin' one-syllable words for the most part, cannin' the slang, and soundin' as many final G's as my tongue would let me. Before I turned in too, I had it almost pat; but I hardly dared to go to sleep for fear it would get away from me.

Say, but it ain't any cinch, this breakin' into public life, is it? The obscure guy with the dinner pail and the calloused palms thinks he has hard lines; but when the whistle blows he can wipe his trowel on his overalls and forget it all until next day. But here I tosses around restless in the feathers, and am up at daybreak goin' over my piece again, trembly in the knees, with a vivid mental picture of how cheap I'd feel if I should go to pieces when the time came.

A good breakfast pepped me up a lot, though, and by noon I had them few remarks of mine so I could say 'em backwards or forwards. How they was goin' to sound outside of my room was another matter. I had my doubts along that line; but I was goin' to give 'em the best I had in stock.

It was most time for the session to begin when Vincent boy trots in with a card announcin' Mr. Henry Clay Rowley. And, say, when this smooth-faced party in the sporty Scotch tweed suit and the new model pearl gray lid shows up, I has to gasp! He's had himself tailored and barbered until he looks like an English investor come over huntin' six per cent. dividends for a Bank of England surplus.

"Zowie! " says I. "Some speed to you, Mr. Rowley. And class? Say, you look like you was about to dump a trunkful of Steel preferred on the market, instead of a few patents. "

Torchy, Private Sec.

"I'm giving your advice a thorough trial, you see, " says he.

"That's the stuff! " says I. "It's the dolled up gets the dollars these days. Be sure and sit where they'll get a good view. "

Then we went into the directors' room and heard Willis G. Briscoe deliver his knock. He does it snappy and vigorous, and when he's through it didn't listen like anything more could be said. He humps his eyebrows humorous when Mr. Robert announces that perhaps the board might like to hear another view of the subject.

"Torchy, " goes on Mr. Robert, "you have the floor. "

For a second or so, though, I felt like spreadin' out so I wouldn't slip through a crack. All of a sudden too, my mouth had gone dry and I had a panicky notion that my brain had ossified. Then I got a glimpse of them shrewd blue eyes of Rowley's smilin' encouragin' at me, the first few sentences of my speech filtered back through the bone, I got my tongue movin', and I was off.

Funny how you can work out of a scare that way, ain't it? Why, say, the first thing I knew I'd picked out old D. K. Rutgers, the worst fish-face in the bunch, and was throwin' the facts into him like I was shovelin' coal into a cellar chute. Beginnin' with Rowley's plan for condensin' commercial acids from the blast fumes, explainin' the chemical process that produced 'em, and how they could be caught on the fly and canned in carboys for the trade, I galloped through the whole proposition, backin' up every item with figures and formulas; until I showed 'em how the slag that now cost 'em so much to get rid of could be sold for road ballastin' and pressed into buildin' blocks at a profit of twenty dollars a ton. I didn't let anything go just by statin' it bald. I took Briscoe's objections one by one, shot 'em full of holes with the come-backs Rowley had coached me on, and then proceeded to clinch the argument until I had old Rutgers noddin' his head.

"And these, Gentlemen, " I winds up with, "are what Mr. Briscoe calls the vague, half-baked ideas of an unpractical inventor. He's an expert, Mr. Briscoe is! I'm not. I wouldn't know a supersaturated solution of methylcalcites from a stein of Hoboken beer; but I'm willin' to believe there's big money in handling either, providing you don't spill too much on the inside. Mr. Rowley claims you're throwing away millions a year. He says he can save it for you. He wants to show you how you can juggle ore so you can save everything but the smell. He's here on the spot, and if you want to quiz him about details, go as deep as you like. "

Did they? Say, that séance didn't break up until six-fifteen, and before the board adjourns Rowley had a whackin' big option check in his fist, and a resolution had gone through to install an experiment plan as soon as it could be put up. An hour before that Willis G. Briscoe had done the silent sneak, wearin' his mouth droopy.

Mr. Robert meets me outside with the fraternal grip and says he's proud of me.

"Thanks, Mr. Robert, " says I. "It was a case of framin' up a job for myself, or else four-flushin' along until you tied the can to me. And I need the Corrugated just now. "

"No more, I'm beginning to suspect, " says he, "than the Corrugated needs you. "

Which was some happy josh for an amateur private sec to get from the boss! Eh?

CHAPTER III

TORCHY TAKES A CHANCE

Say, I expected that after I got to be a salaried man, with a swing-chair in Mr. Robert's private office, I'd be called on only to pull the brainy stuff, calm and dignified, without any outside chasin' around. I had a soothin' idea it would be a case of puttin' in my mornin's dictatin' letters to gen'ral managers, and my afternoons to holdin' interviews with the Secretary of the Treasury, and so on. I was lookin' for plenty of high-speed domework, but nothin' more wearin' on the arms than pushin' a call button or usin' a rubber stamp.

But somehow I can't seem to do finance, or anything else, without throwin' in a lot of extra pep. No matter how I start, first thing I know I'm mixed up with quick action, and as likely as not gettin' my clothes mussed. This last stunt, though—believe me I couldn't have got more thrills if I'd joined a circus!

It opens innocent enough too. I was moochin' around the bondroom when I happens to glance over the transfer book and notices that a big block of our debenture 6's are listed as goin' to the Federated Tractions. And the name of the party who's about to swap the 6's for Tractions preferred is a familiar one. It's Aunty's. Uh-huh—Vee's!

Maybe you remember how Aunty played up her skittish symptoms about them same bonds a few weeks back, the time she planned to exhibit me to Vee in my office boy job and got so badly jolted when she finds me posin' as a private sec instead? Went away real peeved, Aunty did that time. And now it looks like she was takin' it out by unloadin' her bond holdin's. It's to be some swap too, runnin' up into six figures.

"Chee! " thinks I. "That's an income, all right, with Tractions payin' between 7 and 9, besides cuttin' a melon now and then. "

Torchy, Private Sec.

They have their gen'ral offices three floors below us, you know. Not that I wouldn't have had a line on 'em anyway; for whatever that bunch of Philadelphia live wires gets hold of is worth watchin'. Say, they'd consolidate city breathin' air if they could, and make it pay dividends. It's important to note too, that they're buyin' into Corrugated so deep. I mentions the fact casual to Mr. Robert.

"Really, " says he, liftin' his eyebrows surprised. "Federated Tractions! Are you certain? "

"Unless our registry clerk has had a funny dream, " says I. "The notice was listed yesterday. And you know how grouchy the old girl was on us. "

"H-m-m-m! " says he, drummin' his fingers nervous. "Thanks, Torchy. I must look into this. "

Seemed to worry Mr. Robert a bit; so maybe that's why I had my ears stretched wider'n usual. It wa'n't an hour later that I runs across Izzy Budheimer down in the Arcade. He's on the Curb now, Izzy is, and by the size of the diamond horseshoe decoratin' the front of his silk shirt he must be tradin' some in wildcats. Hails me like a friend and brother, Izzy does, tries to wish a tinfoil Fumadora on me, and gives me the happy josh about bein' boosted off the gate.

"You'll be gettin' wise to all the inside deals now, eh? " says he, winkin' foxy. "And maybe we might work off something together. Yes? "

"Sure! " says I. "I'll come down every noon with the office secrets and let you peddle 'em around Broad street from a pushcart. Gwan, you parrot-beaked near-broker! Why, I wouldn't trust tellin' you the time of day! "

Izzy grins like I'd paid him a compliment. "Such a joker! " says he. "But listen! Which side do the Tractions people come down on? "

"Federated? " says I. "North corridor, just around the corner. Sleuthin' around that bunch, are you? What's doing in Tractions? "

"How should I know? " protests Izzy, openin' his eyes innocent. "Maybe I got a customer on the general staff, ain't it? "

"You'd be scoutin' up here at this time of day after a ten-dollar commission, wouldn't you? " says I. "And with that slump in Connecticut Gas in full blast! Can it, Izzy! I know a thing or two about Tractions myself. "

"Yes? " he whispers persuasive, almost holdin' his breath. "What do you hear, now? "

"Don't say I told you, " says I, "but they're thinkin' of puttin' in left-handed straps for south-paw passengers. "

Izzy looks pained and disgusted. He's got a serious mind, Izzy has, and if you could take a thumbprint of his brain, it would be all fractions and dollar signs.

"I have to meet my cousin Abie Moss, " says he, edgin' away. "He has a bookkeeper's job with Tractions for a month now, and I promised his aunt I would ask how he's comin'. "

"How touchin'! " says I as he moves off.

I gazes after him curious a minute, and then follows a sudden hunch. Why not see just how much of a bluff this was about Cousin Abie? So I slips around by the cigar stand, steps behind a pillar, and keeps him in range. Three or four minutes I watched Izzy waitin' at the elevator exit, without seein' him give anyone the fraternal grip. Then he seems to quit. He drifts back towards the Arcade with the lunch crowd, and I was about to turn away when I lamps him bein' slipped a piece of paper by a short, squatty-built guy who brushes by him casual. Izzy gathers it in with never a word and strolls over to the 'phone booths, where he lets on to be huntin' a number in the directory. All he does there, though, is spread out that paper, read it through hasty, and then tear it up and chuck it in the waste basket.

"Huh! " says I, seein' Izzy scuttle off towards Broadway. "Looks like there was a plot to the piece. I wonder? "

And just for the fun of the thing I collected them twenty-eight pieces of yellow paper, carried 'em over to my lunch place, and spent the best part of my noon-hour piecin' 'em together. What I got was this, scribbled in lead pencil:

Grebel out. Larkin melding. Teg morf rednu.

"Whiffo! " thinks I. "What kind of a Peruvian dialect is this? "

Course the names was plain enough. Everybody knows Grebel and Larkin, and that they're the big wheezes in that Philly crowd. But what then? Had Grebel gone out to lunch? And was Larkin playin' penuchle? Thrillin', if true. Then comes this "Teg morf rednu" stuff. Was that Russian, or Chinese?

"Heiney, " says I, callin' the dough-faced food juggler. "Heiney, " I repeats solemn, "Teg morf rednu. "

Not a smile from Heiney. He grabs the bill of fare and begins to hunt through the cheese list panicky.

"Never mind, " says I, "you won't find it there. But here's another: What do you do when you meld a hundred aces, say? "

A look of almost human intelligence flickers into Heiney's face. "*Ach!* " says he. "By the table you pud 'em—so! "

"Thanks, Heiney, " says I. "That helps a little. "

So Larkin was chuckin' something on the table, was he! But this other dope, "Teg morf rednu? " Say, I'd come back to that after every bite. I wrote it out on an envelope, tried runnin' it together and splittin' it up diff'rent, and turned it upside down. Then in a flash I got it.

When Mr. Robert sails in from the club I was waitin' for him. He'd heard a rumor that Grebel was to retire soon. Also he'd met young Larkin in the billiard room, and found that the fam'ly was goin' abroad for the summer.

"But all that may mean nothing at all, you know, " says Mr. Robert.

"And then again, " says I. "Study that out and see if it don't tally with your dope, " and I produces a copy of Izzy's wireless.

Mr. Robert wrinkles his forehead over it without any result. "What is it? " says he.

"An inside tip on Tractions, " says I, and sketches out how I'd got it

"Oh, I see now, " says he. "That about Grebel? But what is melding? And this last—'Teg morf rednu'? I can make no sense of that. "

"Try it backwards, " says I.

"Why—er—by Jove! " says he. "Get from under, eh? Then—then there is a slump coming. And with all that new stock issue, I'm not surprised. But that hits Miss Vee's aunt rather heavily, doesn't it? That is, if the deal has gone through. "

"Who's her lawyers? " says I. "They ought to know. "

"Of course, " says Mr. Robert, reachin' for the 'phone. "Winkler, Burt & Winkler. Look up the number, will you? Eh? Broad, did you say? "

And inside of three minutes he has explained the case and got the verdict. "They don't know, " says he. "The transfer receipts were sent for her to sign last night. If she's signed them, there's nothing to be done. "

"But if she hasn't?" says I.

"Then she mustn't," says Mr. Robert. "It would mean letting that crowd get a foothold in Corrugated, and a loss of thousands to her. See if the tape shows any recent fluctuations."

"Bluey-ooey!" says I, runnin' over the mornin' sales hasty. "Opened at seven-eighths, then 500 at three-quarters, another block at a half, 300 at a quarter—why, it's on the toboggan!"

"She must be found and warned at once," says Mr. Robert.

"Am I the guy?" says I.

"You are," says he. "And minutes may count. I'll get the address for you. It's in that ——"

"Say," I throws over my shoulder on my way to the door, "whose aunt is this, anyway?"

Looked like a simple matter for me to locate Aunty. And if she was out takin' her drive or anything—why, I could be explainin' to Vee while I waited. That would be tough luck, of course; but I could stand it for once.

At their apartment hotel I finds nobody home but Celeste, the maid, all dolled up like Thursday afternoon. She hands it to me cold and haughty that Madame and Ma'mselle are out.

"I could almost guess that from the lid you're wearin'," says I. "One of Miss Vee's, ain't it?"

She pinks up and goes gaspy at that. "Please," she begins pleadin', "if you would not mention——"

"I might forget to," I breaks in, "if you'll tell me where I can find 'em quickest."

And Celeste gets the information out rapid. They're house-partyin' at the Morley Beckhams, over at Quehassett, Long Island. "Rosemere" is the name of the joint.

"Me for Quehassett!" says I, dashin' for the elevator.

But, say, I needn't have lost my breath. Parts of Long Island you can get to every half-hour or so; but Quehassett ain't one of 'em. Huntin' it up on the railroad map, I discovers that it's 'way out to the deuce and gone on the north shore, and the earliest start I can get is the four o'clock local.

Ever cruise around much on them Long Island branch lines? Say, it must be int'restin' sport, providin' you don't care whether you get there this week or next. I missed one connection by waitin' for the brakeman to call out the change. And when I'd caught another train back to the right junction I got the pleasin' bulletin that the next for Quehassett is the theater train, that comes along somewhere about midnight.

So there I was hung up in a rummy little commuter town where the chief industry is sellin' bungalow sites on the salt marsh. Then I tackles the 'phone, which results in three snappy conversations with a grouchy butler at sixty cents a throw, but no real dope on the Beckhams or their guests.

Well, it's near two A. M. when I fin'lly lands in Quehassett, which is no proper time to call on anybody's aunt. Everything is shut tight too; so I spreads out an evenin' edition on a baggage truck and turns in weary. I'd overlooked pullin' down the front shades to the station, though, and the next thing I knew the sun was hittin' me square in the face.

I wanders around Quehassett until a Dago opens up a little fruitstand. He sold me some bananas and a couple of muskmelons for breakfast, and points out which road leads to Rosemere. It's down on the shore about a mile and a half, and I strolls along, eatin' fruit and enjoyin' the early mornin' air.

Torchy, Private Sec.

Some joint Rosemere turns out to be, —acres of lawn, and rows of striped awnin's at the windows. The big iron gates was locked, with nobody in sight; so I has plenty of time to write a note to Vee, beggin' her for the love of soup, if Aunty hasn't signed the transfer papers, not to let her do it until she hears from me. My scheme was to get one of the help to take the message to Vee before she got up.

Must have been near seven o'clock when I gets hold of one of the gardeners, tips him a dollar, and drags out of him the fact that cook says how all the folks are off on the yacht, which is gen'rally anchored off the dock. He don't know if it's there now or not. It was last night. I can tell by goin' down. The road follows that little creek.

So I gallops down to the shore. No yacht in sight. There's a point of land juts out to the left. Maybe she's anchored behind that. Comin' down along the creek too, I'd seen an old tub of a boat tied up. Back I chases for it.

Looked simple for me to keep on; but when I get started on a trail I never know when to stop. I was paddlin' down the creek, bound for nowhere special, when along comes a sporty-dressed young gent, wearin' puttee leggin's and a leather cap with goggles attached. He's luggin' a five-gallon can of gasoline, and strikes me for a lift down the shore a bit.

"Keepin' your car in the Sound, are you? " says I, shovin' in towards the bank.

"It's an aërohydro, " says he.

"Eh? " says I. "A—a which? "

"An air boat, you know, " says he. "I'm going to try her out. Bully morning for a flight, isn't it? "

"Maybe, " says I. "Get aboard. Always have to cart your gas down this way? "

At that he grows real chatty. Seems this is a brand-new machine, just delivered the night before, and he's keepin' it a dead secret from the fam'ly, so Mother won't worry. He says that's all nonsense, though; for he's been takin' lessons on the quiet for more than a year, has earned his pilot's license, and can handle any kind of a plane.

"Just straight driving, of course, " he goes on. "I don't attempt spiral dips, or exhibition work. I've never been up more than five hundred feet. And this is such a safe type. Oh, the folks will come around to it after they've seen me up once or twice. I want to surprise 'em. There she is, up the shore. See! "

Hanged if I hadn't missed it before, when I was lookin' for the yacht! Spidery lookin' affairs, ain't they, when you get close to, with all them slim wire guys? And the boat part is about as substantial as a pasteboard battleship. While he's pourin' in the gasoline I paddles around and inspects the thing.

"Five hundred feet up? " says I. "Excuse me! "

He grins good natured. "Think you wouldn't like it, eh? " says he. "Why? "

"Too cobwebby, " says I. "Why, them wings are nothin' but cloth. "

"Best quality duck, two layers, " says he. "And the frame has a tensile strength of three hundred and fifty pounds to the square foot. Isn't that motor a beauty? Ninety-horse. "

"Guess I'll take my joy ridin' closer to the turf, though, " says I. "Course, I've always had a batty notion I'd like to fly some time; but——"

"Hello! " he breaks in. "There goes the Katrina! " and he points out a big white yacht that's slippin' along through the water about half a mile off. "It's the Beckhams', " he goes on. "They're our neighbors here at Rosemere, you know. They have guests from town, and my folks are aboard. By Jove! Here's my chance to surprise 'em. I say, would you mind paddling around and giving me a shove off?"

But I stands gawpin' out at the yacht. "The Morley Beckhams?" says I.

"Yes, yes!" says he. "But hurry, please. I want to catch them."

"You—you——?" But I was thinkin' too rapid to talk much. Vee and Aunty was out on that boat, and maybe at the next landin' Aunty would mail them transfers. If it was goin' to hit her alone, I might have stood it calmer; but there was Vee.

"Say," I sputters out, "ain't there room for two?"

"Why, ye-e-e-es," says he sort of draggy. "I've never taken up a passenger, though; but I've thought that——"

"Then why not now?" says I. "I want to go the worst way."

"But a moment ago," he protests, "you——"

"It's different now," says I. "There's a party on that yacht I want to get word to,—Miss Hemmingway. I got to, that's all! And what's a neck more or less? I'll take the chance if you will."

"By Jove!" says he. "I'll do it. Shove off. Here, stick your oar into the mud and push. That's it! Now climb in and give that old tub of yours a shove so she'll clear that left plane. Good work! Here's your seat, beside me. Don't get your knees in the way of that lever, please, or put your feet on that cross bar. That's my rudder control. Now! Are you ready? Then I'll start her."

Say, I didn't have time to work up any spine chills, or even say a "Now-I-lay-me." He reaches up behind him, gives the crank a whirl, and the next thing I know we're shootin' over the water like an express train, with the spray flyin', the wind whistlin' in my ears, and eight cylinders exhaustin' direct within two feet of the back of my neck. Talk about speedin'! When you're travelin' through the water at a forty-mile-an-hour gait, and so close you can trail your fingers, you know all about it. Although it's a calm mornin', with hardly a ripple, the motion was a little bumpy. No wonder!

Then all of a sudden I has a sinkin' sensation somewhere under my vest, the bumpin' stops, and I feels like I'd shuffled off somethin' heavy. I had—a billion tons or more! Glancin' over the side, I sees the water ten or a dozen feet below us. We were in the air. And, believe me, I reaches out for something solid to hold onto! All I could find was a two-inch upright, and I takes a fond grip on that. If it had been a telephone pole, I'd felt better.

My sporty-dressed friend smiles encouragin' over his shoulder. I hope I smiled back; but I wouldn't swear to it. Not that I'm scared. Hush, hush! But I wa'n't used to bein' shot through the air so impetuous. I takes another glance overboard. Hel-lup! Someone's pullin' Long Island Sound from under us. The water must have been fifty or sixty feet down, and gettin' more so. For a while after that I looks straight ahead. What's the use keepin' track of how high you are, anyway? You'll only bore just so big a hole in the water if you fall.

But it's funny how soon you can get over feelin's like that. Inside of three minutes I'd quit grippin' the stanchion and was sittin' there peaceful, enjoyin' the ride. We seemed to be sailin' along on a level now, about housetop high, and so far as I could see we was as steady as if we'd been on a front veranda. There's no sway or rock to the machine at all. I'd been holdin' myself as rigid as if I'd been in a tippy canoe; but now I took a chance on shiftin' my position a little. I even leaned over the side. Nothing happened. That was comfortin'. How easy and smooth it was, glidin' along up there!

Meanwhile we'd taken a wide sweep and was leavin' the yacht far behind.

"Say," I shouts to my aviatin' friend, "how do we get to her?"

Torchy, Private Sec.

But it's no use tryin' to converse with that roar in your ears. I points back to the boat. He nods and smiles.

"Wait!" he yells at me.

With that he pulls his plane lever and we begins to climb some more. You hardly know you're doin' it, though. Up or down don't mean anything in the air, where the goin' is all the same. Only as we gets higher the Sound narrows and Long Island stretches further and further. And, take it from me, that's the way to view scenery! Up and up we slid, just soarin' free and careless. He turns to me with another grin, to see how I'm takin' it. And this time I grins back.

"About three hundred!" he shouts, puttin' his mouth close. "Eighty an hour too!"

"Zippy stuff!" says I.

Then he gives me a nudge, juggles his deflectors, and down we shoots. I never had any part of the map come at me so fast. Seemed like the Sound was just rushin' at us, and I was tryin' to guess how far into the bottom we'd go, when he pulls the lever again and we skims along just above the surface. Shootin' the chutes—say, that Coney stunt seems tame compared to this!

In no time at all we've made a circle around the yacht and are comin' up behind her once more. We could see the people pilin' out on deck to rubber at us. In a minute more we'd be even with 'em. And how was I goin' to deliver that message to Vee? Just then I looks in my lap, where I was grippin' my straw lid between my knees, and discovers that I've lugged along one of them muskmelons in a paper bag. That gives me my hunch.

Fishin' out the note I'd written, I slits the melon with my knife and jabs it in. Then I shows the breakfast bomb to my friend and points to the yacht. He nods. Some bean, that guy had!

"I'll sail over her," he howls in my ear. "You can drop it on the deck."

There was no time for gettin' ready or takin' practice shots. Up we glides into the air right over the white wake she was leavin'. The folks on her was wavin' to us. First I made out Vee, standin' on the little bridge amidships, lookin' cute and classy in white serge. Then I spots Aunty, who's tumbled out in her boudoir cap and kimono. I leans over and waves enthusiastic.

"Hey, Vee! " I shouts. "Watch this! "

I'd picked out the widest part of the deck forward, where there's no awnin' up, and when it was exactly underneath I lets the melon go, hard as I could shoot it. Some shot that was too! I saw it smash on the deck, watched one of the sailors stare at it stupid, and then caught a glimpse of Vee rushin' towards the spot. Course I wa'n't sure she knew me at that distance, or had heard what I said; but trust her for doin' the right thing at the right time!

"There's Mother! " I hears my sporty friend roar out. "I say! Mother! It's Billy, you know. "

No doubt about Mother's catchin' on. Maybe she'd suspicioned, anyway; but the last I saw of her she was slumpin' into the arms of a white-haired old gent behind her.

Another minute and we'd left the Katrina behind like she had seven anchors out. On we went and up once more, turnin' with a dizzy swoop and skimmin' past her, back towards where we started from. And just as I was wishin' he'd go faster and higher we settles down on the water, dashes in behind the dock, the motor slows up, the plane floats drag in the mud, and it's all over.

Took the yacht near an hour to get back to us. Mother had insisted, and when she found Billy all safe and sound she fell on his neck and forgave him.

As for me? Well, maybe I didn't have some swell report to turn in to Mr. Robert! I had him listenin' with his mouth open before I got through too.

"Aunty was mighty suspicious first off, " says I; "but after she'd used the long distance and got a line on how Tractions was waverin', she warms up quite a lot, for her. Uh-huh! Gives me a vote of thanks, and says she'll call off the deal. "

"Torchy, " says Mr. Robert, "I am speechless with admiration. Your business methods are certainly advanced. I had not thought of flying as a modern requisite for a commercial career. "

"The real thing in high finance, eh? " says I. "And, say, me for the air after this! I've swallowed the bug. I know how a bloomin' seagull feels when he's on the wing; and, believe me, it's got everything else in the sport line lookin' like playin' tag with your feet tied! "

CHAPTER IV

BREAKING IT TO THE BOSS

I don't admit it went to my head, —not so bad as that, —only maybe my chest measure had swelled an inch or so, and I wouldn't say my heels wa'n't hittin' a bit hard as I strolls dignified up and down the private office.

You see, Mr. Robert was snitchin' a couple of days off for the Newport regatta, and he'd sort of left me on the lid, as you might say. So far as there bein' any real actin' head of the Corrugated Trust for the time being—well, I was it. Anyway, I'd passed along some confidential dope to our Western sales manager, stood by to take a report from the special audit committee, and had an interview with the president of a big bond house, all in one forenoon. That was speedin' up some for a private sec, wa'n't it?

And now I was just markin' time, waitin' for what might turn up, and feelin' equal to pullin' off any sort of a deal, from matchin' Piddie for the lunches to orderin' a new stock issue. What if the asphalt over on Fifth-ave. was softenin' up, with the mercury hittin' the nineties, and half the force off on vacations? I had a real job to attend to. I was doin' things!

And as I stops by the roll-top to lean up against it casual I had that comf'table, easy feelin' of bein' the right man in the right place. You know, I guess? You're there with the goods. You ain't the whole works maybe; but you're a special, particular party, one that can push buttons and have 'em answered, paw over the mail, or put your initials under a signature.

And right in the midst of them rosy reflections the door to the private office swings open abrupt and in pads a stout old party wearin' a generous-built pongee suit and a high-crowned Panama. Also there's something familiar about the bushy eyebrows and the lima bean ears. It's Old Hickory himself. I chokes down a gasp and straightens up.

"Gee, Mr. Ellins!" says I. "I thought you was down at the Springs?"

"Didn't think I'd been banished for life, did you?" says he.

"But Mr. Robert," I goes on, "didn't look for you until——"

"No doubt," he breaks in. "Robert and those fool doctors would have kept me soaking in those infernal mud baths until I turned into a crocodile. I know. I'm a gouty, rheumatic old wreck, I suppose; but I'll be dad blistered if I'm going to end my days wallowing in medicated mud! I've had enough. Where is everybody?"

So I has to account for Mr. Robert, tell how Mrs. Ellins and Marjorie and Son-in-Law Ferdie are up to Bar Harbor, and hint that they're expectin' him to come up as soon as he lands.

"That's their programme, is it?" he growls. "Think I'm going to spend the rest of the season sitting on a veranda taking pills, do they? Well, they're mistaken!"

And off he goes into his own room. I don't know what he thought he was goin' to do there. Just habit, I expect. For we've been gettin' along without Old Hickory for quite some time now, while he's been away. First off he tried to keep in touch with things by night letters, then he had a weekly report sent him; but gradually he lost the run of the new deals, and for the last month or so he'd quit firin' over any orders at all.

Through the open door I could see him sittin' at his big, flat-topped mahogany desk, starin' around sort of aimless. Then he pulls out a drawer and shuffles over some old papers that had been there ever since he left. Next he picks up a pen and starts to make some notes.

"Boy!" he sings out. "Ink!"

Course I could have pushed the buzzer and had Vincent do it; but seein' how nobody had put him wise to the change, I didn't feel like announcin' it myself. So I fills the inkwell, chases up a waste basket for him, and turns on the electric fan.

"Now bring the mail! " says he snappy.

He was back to; so it was safe to smile. You see, I'd attended to all the mornin' deliveries, sorted out what I knew had to be held over for Mr. Robert, opened what was doubtful, and sent off a few answers accordin' to orders. But, after all, he was the big boss. He had a right to go through the motions if he wanted to. So I lugs in the mail, dumps it in the tray, and leaves him with it.

Must have been half an hour later, and I was back at my own desk dopin' out a schedule I'd promised to fix up for Mr. Robert, when I glances up to find Old Hickory wanderin' around the room absent-minded. He's starin' hard at a letter he holds in one paw. All of a sudden he discovers me at the roll-top. For a second he scowls at me from under the bushy eyebrows, and then comes the explosion.

"Boy! " he sings out. "What the hyphenated maledictions are you doing there? "

Well, I broke it to him as gentle as I could.

"Promoted, eh? " he snorts. "To what? "

And I explains how I'm private secretary to the president of the Mutual Funding Company.

"Never heard of such an organization, " says he. "What is it, anyway? "

"Dummy concern mostly, " says I, "faked up to stall off the I. C. C. "

"Eh? " he gawps.

"Interstate Commerce Commission, " says I. "We beat 'em to it, you know, by dissolvin'—on paper. Had to have somebody to use the rubber stamp; so they picked me off the gate. "

"Humph! " he grunts. "So you're no longer an office boy, eh? But I had you hopping around like one. How was that? "

"Guess I got a hop or two left in me, " says I, "specially for you, Mr. Ellins. "

"Hah! " says he. "Also more or less blarney left on the tongue. Well, young man, we'll see. As office boy you had your good points, I remember; but as——" Then he breaks off and repeats, "We'll see, Son. " And he goes to studyin' the letter once more.

Fin'lly he sends for Piddie. They confabbed for a while, and as Piddie comes out he's still explainin' how he's sure he don't know, but most likely Mr. Robert understands all about it.

"Hang what Robert understands! " snaps Old Hickory. "He isn't here, is he? And I want to know now. Torchy, come in here! "

"Yes, Sir, " says I, scentin' trouble and salutin' respectful.

"What about these Universal people refusing to renew that Manistee terminal lease? " he demands.

And if he'd asked how many feathers in a rooster's tail I'd been just as full of information. But from what Piddie's drawn by declarin' an alibi, it didn't look like that was my cue.

"Suppose I get you the correspondence on that? " says I, and rushes out after the copybook.

But the results wa'n't enlightenin'. We'd applied for renewal on the old terms, the Universal folks had sent back word that in due course the matter would be taken up, and that's all until this notice comes in that there's nothin' doin'. "Inexpedient under present conditions, " was the way they put it.

"I expect Mr. Robert will be back Monday, " I suggests cautious.

"Oh, do you? " raps out Old Hickory. "And meanwhile this lease expires to-morrow noon, leaving us without a foot of ore wharf anywhere on the Great Lakes. What does Mr. Robert intend to do then—transport by aëroplane? Just asked pleasant and polite for a renewal, did he? And before I could make 'em grant the original I all but had their directors strung up by the thumbs! Hah! "

He settles back heavy in his chair and sets them cut granite jaws of his solid. He don't look so much like an invalid, after all. There's good color in his cheeks, and behind the droopy lids you could see the fighting light in his eyes. He glances once more at the letter.

"Hello! " says he. "I thought their main offices were in Chicago. This is from Broadway, International Utilities Building. Perhaps you can tell me what they're doing down there? "

"Subsidiary of I. U., " says I. "Been listed that way all summer. "

"Then, " says Old Hickory, smilin' grim, "we have to do once more with no less a personage than Gedney Nash. Well, so be it. He and I have fought out other differences. We'll try again. And if I'm a back number, I'll soon know it. Now get me a list of our outside security holdings. "

That was his first order; but, say, inside of half an hour he had everybody in the shop, from little Vincent up to the head of the bond department, doin' flipflops and pinwheels. Didn't take 'em long to find out that he was back on the job, either.

"Breezy with that now! " I'd tell 'em. "This is a rush order for the old man. Sure he's in there. Can't you smell the sulphur? "

Torchy, Private Sec.

In the midst of it comes a hundred-word code message from Dalton, our traffic superintendent, sayin' how he'd been notified to remove his wharf spurs within twenty-four hours and askin' panicky what he should do about it.

"Tell him to hold his tracks with loaded ore trains, and keep his shirt on, " growls Old Hickory over his shoulder. "And 'phone Peabody, Frost & Co. to send up their railroad securities expert on the double quick. "

That's the way it went from eleven A. M. until two-thirty, and all the lunch I indulged in was two bites of a cheese sandwich that Vincent split with me. At two-thirty-five Old Hickory jams on his hat and signals for me.

"Gather up those papers and come along, " says he. "I think we're ready now to talk to Gedney Nash. "

I smothered a gasp. Was he nutty, or what? You know you don't drop in offhand on a man like Gedney Nash, same as you would on a shrimp bank president, or a corporation head. You hear a lot about him, of course, —now givin' a million to charity, then bein' denounced as a national highway robber, —but you don't see him. Anyway, I never knew of anyone who did. He's the man behind, the one that pulls the strings. Course, he's supposed to be at the head of International Utilities, but he claims not to hold any office. And you know what happened when Congress tried to get him before an investigatin' committee. All that showed up was a squad of lawyers, who announced they was ready to answer any questions they couldn't file an exception to, and three doctors with affidavits to prove that Mr. Nash was about to expire from as many incurable diseases. So Congress gave it up.

Yet here we was, pikin' downtown without any notice, expectin' to find him as easy as if he was a traffic cop on a fixed post. Well, we didn't. The minute we blows into the arcade and begins to ask for him, up slides a smooth-talkin' buildin' detective who listens polite what I feed him and suggests that if we wait a minute he'll call up the gen'ral offices. Which he does and reports that they've no idea where Mr. Nash can be found. Maybe he's gone to the mountains, or over to his Long Island place, or abroad on a vacation.

"Tommyrot! " says Old Hickory. "Gedney Nash never took a vacation in his life. I know he's in New York now. "

The gentleman sleuth shrugs his shoulders and allows that if Mr. Ellins ain't satisfied he might go up to Floor 11 and ask for himself. So up we went. Ever in the Tractions Buildin'? Say, it's like bein' caught in a fog down the bay, —all silence and myst'ry. I expect it's the headquarters of a hundred or more diff'rent corporations, all tied up some way or other with I. U. interests; but on the doors never the name of one shows: just "Mr. So-and-So, " "Mr. Whadye Callum, " "Mr. This-and-That. " Clerks hurry by you with papers in their hands, walkin' soft on rubber heels. They tap respectful on a door, it opens silent, they disappear. When they meet in the corridors they pass without hailin', without even a look. You feel that there's something doin' around you, something big and important. But the gears don't give out any hum. It's like a game of blind man's bluff played in the dark.

And the sharp-eyed, gray-haired gent we talked to through the brass gratin' acted like he'd never heard the name Gedney Nash before. When Old Hickory cuts loose with the tabasco remarks at him he only smiles patient and insists that if he can locate Mr. Nash, which he doubts, he'll do his best to arrange an interview. It may take a day, or a week, or a month, but——

"Bah! " snorts Old Hickory, turnin' on his heel, and he cusses eloquent all the way down and out to the taxi.

"Seems to me I've heard how Mr. Nash uses a private elevator, " I suggests.

"Quite like him, " says Old Hickory. "Think you could find it? "

"I could make a stab, " says I.

But at that I knew I was kiddin' myself. Why not? Ain't there been times when whole bunches of live-wire reporters, not to mention relays of court deputies, have raked New York with a fine-tooth comb, lookin' for Gedney Nash, without even gettin' so much as a glimpse of his limousine rollin' round a corner.

"Suppose we circle the block once or twice, while I tear off a few Sherlock Holmes thoughts? " says I.

Mr. Ellins sniffs scornful; but he'd gone the limit himself, so he gives the directions. I leaned back, shut my eyes, and tried to guess how a foxy old guy like Nash would fix it up so he could do the unseen duck off Broadway into his private office. Was it a tunnel from the subway through the boiler basement, or a bridge from the next skyscraper, or—— But the sight of a blue cap made me ditch this dream stuff. Funny I hadn't thought of that line before—and me an A. D. T. once myself!

"Hey, you! " I calls out the window. "Wait up, Cabby, while we take on a passenger. Yes, you, Skinny. Hop in here. Ah, what for would we be kidnappin' a remnant like you? It's your birthday, ain't it? And the gentleman here has a present for you—a whole dollar. Eh, Mr. Ellins? "

Old Hickory looks sort of puzzled; but he forks out the singleton, and the messenger climbs in after it. A chunky, round-faced kid he was too. I pushed him into one of the foldin' front seats and proceeds to apply the pump.

"What station do you run from, Sport? " says I.

"Number six, " says he.

"Oh, yes, " says I. "Just back of the Exchange. And is old Connolly chief down there still? "

"Yes, Sir, " says he.

"Give him my regards when you get back, " says I, "and tell him Torchy says he's a flivver. "

The kid grins enthusiastic.

"By the way, " I goes on, "who's he sendin' out with the Nash work—Gedney Nash's, you know? "

"Number 17, " says he, "Loppy Miller. "

"What! " says I. "Old Loppy carryin' the book yet? Why, he had grown kids when I wore the stripes. Well, well! Cagy old duffer, Loppy. Ever ask him where he delivers the Nash business? "

"Yep, " says the youngster, "and he near got me fired for it. "

"But you found out, didn't you? " says I.

He glances at me suspicious and rolls his eyes. "M-m-m-m, " says he, shakin' his head.

"Ah, come! " says I. "You don't mean that a real sure-fire like you could be shunted that way? There'd be no harm in your givin' a guess, and if it was right—well, we could run that birthday stake up five more; couldn't we, Mr. Ellins? "

Old Hickory nods, and passes me a five-spot prompt.

"Well? " says I, wavin' it careless.

The kid might have been scared, but he had the kale-itch in his fingers. "All I know, " says he, "is that Loppy allus goes into the William Street lobby of the Farmers' National. "

"Go on! " says I. "That don't come within two numbers of backin' against the Traction Buildin'. "

Torchy, Private Sec.

"But Loppy allus does, " he insists. "There's a door to the right, just beyond the teller's window. But you can't get past the gink in the gray helmet. I tried once. "

"Secret entrance, eh? " says I. "Sounds convincin'. Anyway, I got your number. So here's your five. Invest it in baby bonds, and don't let on to Mother. You're six to the good, and your job safe. By-by! "

"What now? " says Old Hickory. "Shall we try the secret door? "

"Not unless we're prepared to do strong arm work on the guard, " says I. "No. What we got to frame up now is a good excuse. Let's see, you can't ring in as one of the fam'ly, can you? "

"Not as any relative of Gedney's, " says Old Hickory. "I'm not built right. "

"How about his weak points? " says I. "Know of any fads of his? "

"Why, " says Mr. Ellins, "he is a good deal interested in landscape gardening, and he goes in for fancy poultry, I believe. "

"That's the line! " says I. "Poultry! Ain't there a store down near Fulton Market where we could buy a sample? "

I was in too much of a rush to go into details, and it must have seemed a batty performance to Old Hickory; but off we chases, and when we drove up to the Farmers' National half an hour later I has a wicker cage in each hand and Mr. Ellins has both fists full of poultry literature displayed prominent. Sure enough too, we finds the door beyond the teller's window, also the gink in the gray helmet. He's a husky-built party, with narrow-set, suspicious eyes.

"Up to Mr. Nash's, " says I casual, makin' a move to walk right past.

"Back up! " says he, steppin' square across the way. "What Mr. Nash? "

"Whadye mean, what Mr. Nash? " says I. "There ain't clusters of 'em, are there? Mr. Gedney Nash, of course. "

"Wrong street, " says he. "Try around on Broadway. "

"What a kidder! " says I. "But if you will delay the champion hen expert of the country, " and I nods to Old Hickory, "just send word up to Mr. Nash that Mr. Skellings has come with that pair of silver-slashed blue Orpingtons he wanted to see. "

"Blue which? " says the guard.

"Ah, take a look! " says I. "Ain't they some birds? Gold medal winners, both of 'em. "

I holds open the paper wrappings while he inspects the cacklers. And, believe me, they was the fanciest poultry specimens I'd ever seen! Honest, they looked like they'd been got up for the pullets' annual costume ball.

"And Mr. Nash, " I goes on, "said Mr. Skellings was to bring 'em in this way. "

The guard takes another glance at Old Hickory, and that got him; for in his high-crowned Panama the boss does look more like a fancy farmer than he does like the head of the Corrugated.

"I'll see, " says he, openin' a little closet and producin' a 'phone. He was havin' some trouble too, tellin' someone just who we was, when I cuts in.

"Ah, just describe the birds, " says I. "Silver-slashed blue Orpingtons, you know. "

Does it work? Say, in less than two minutes we was being towed through a windin' passage that fin'lly ends in front of a circular shaft with a cute little elevator waitin' at the bottom.

Torchy, Private Sec.

"Pass two," says the guard.

Another minute and we're bein' shot up I don't know how many stories, and are steppin' out into the swellest set of office rooms I was ever in. A mahogany door opens, and in comes a wispy, yellow-skinned, dried-up little old party with eyes like a rat. Didn't look much like the pictures they print of him, but I guessed it was Gedney.

"Some prize Orpingtons, did I understand?" says he, in a soft, purry voice. "I don't recall having——" Then he gets a good look at Old Hickory, and his tone changes sudden. "What!" he snaps. "You, Ellins? How did you get in here?"

"With those fool chickens," says the boss.

"But—but I didn't know," goes on Mr. Nash, "that you were interested in that sort of thing."

"Glad to say I'm not," comes back Old Hickory. "Just a scheme of my brilliant-haired young friend here to smuggle me into the sacred presence. Great Zacharias, Nash! why don't you shut yourself in a steel vault, and have done with it?"

Gedney bites his upper lip, annoyed. "I find it necessary," says he, "to avoid interruptions. I presume, however, that you came on some errand of importance?"

"I did," says Old Hickory. "I want to get a renewal of that Manistee terminal lease."

Say, of all the scientific squirmin', Gedney Nash can put up the slickest specimen. First off he lets on not to know a thing about it. Well, perhaps it was true that International Utilities did control those wharves: he really couldn't say. And besides that matter would be left entirely to the discretion of——

"No, it won't," breaks in Old Hickory, shakin' a stubby forefinger at him. "It's between us, Nash. You know what those terminal privileges mean to us. We can't get on without them. And if you take 'em away, it's a fight to a finish—that's all!"

"Sorry, Ellins," says Mr. Nash, "but I can do nothing."

"Wait," says Old Hickory. "Did you know that we held a big block of your M., K. & T.'s? Well, we do. They happen to be first lien bonds too. And M., K. & T. defaulted on its last interest coupons. Entirely unnecessary, I know, but it throws the company open to a foreclosure petition. Want us to put it in?"

"H-m-m-m!" says Mr. Nash. "Er—won't you sit down?"

Now if it had been two common, everyday parties, debatin' which owned a yellow dog, they'd gone hoarse over it; but not these two plutes. Gedney Nash asks Old Hickory only three more questions before he turns to the wicker cages and begins admirin' the fancy poultry.

"Excellent specimens, excellent!" says he. "And in the pink of condition too. I have a few Orpingtons on my place; but—oh, by the way, Ellins, are these really intended for me?"

"With Torchy's compliments," says Old Hickory.

"By Jove!" says Gedney. "I—I'm greatly obliged—truly, I am. What plumage! What hackles! And—er—just leave that terminal lease, will you? I'll have it renewed and sent up. Would you mind too if I sent you out by the Broadway entrance?"

I didn't mind, for one, and I guess the boss didn't; for the last office we passes through was where the gray-haired gent camped watchful behind the brass gratin'.

"Well, wouldn't that crimp you?" I remarks, givin' him the passin' grin. "Our old friend Ananias, ain't it?"

And he never bats an eyelash.

But Gedney wa'n't in that class. Before closin' time up comes a secretary with the lease all signed. I was in the boss's room when it's delivered.

"Gee, Mr. Ellins! " says I. "You don't need any more mud baths, I guess. "

All the rise that gets out of him is a flicker in the mouth corners. "Young man, " says he, "whose idea was it, taking you off the gate? "

"Mr. Robert's, " says I.

"I am glad to learn, " says he, "that Robert had occasional lapses into sanity while I was away. What about your salary? Any ambitions in that direction? "

"I only want what I'm worth, " says I.

"Oh, be reasonable, Son, " says he. "We must save something for the stockholders, you know. Suppose we double what you're getting now? Will that do? "

And the grin I carries out is that broad I has to go sideways through the door.

CHAPTER V

SHOWING GILKEY THE WAY

I got to say this about Son-in-Law Ferdie: He's a help! Not constant, you know; for there's times when it seems like his whole scheme of usefulness was in providin' something to hang a pair of shell-rimmed glasses on, and givin' Marjorie Ellins the right to change her name. But outside of that, and furnishin' a comic relief to the rest of the fam'ly, blamed if he don't come in real handy now and then.

Last Friday was a week, for a sample. I meets up with him as he's driftin' aimless through the arcade, sort of caromin' round and round, bein' bumped by the elevator rushers and watched suspicious by the floor detective.

"What ho, Ferdie!" I sings out, grabbin' him by the elbow and swingin' him out of the line of traffic. "This ain't no place to practice the maxixe."

"I—I beg—oh, it's you, Torchy, is it?" says he, sighin' relieved. "Where do I go to send a telegram?"

"Why," says I, "you might try the barber shop and file it with the brush boy, or you could wish it on the candy-counter queen over there and see what would happen; but the simple way would be to step around to the W. U. T. window, by the north exit, and shove it at Gladys."

"Ah, thanks," says he, "North exit, did you say? Let's see, that is—er——"

"'Bout face!" says I, takin' him in tow. "Now guide right! Hep, hep, hep—parade rest—here you are! And here's the blank you write it on. Now go to it!"

Torchy, Private Sec.

"I—er—but I'm not quite sure, " protests Ferdie, peelin' off one of his chamois gloves, "I'm not quite sure of just what I ought to say. "

"That bein' the case, " says I, "it's lucky you ran into me, ain't it? Now what's the argument? "

Course it was a harrowin' crisis. Him and Marjorie had got an invite some ten days ago to spend the week-end at a swell country house over on Long Island. They'd hemmed and hawed, and fin'lly ducked by sendin' word they was so sorry, but they was expectin' a young gent as guest about then. The answer they got back was, "Bring him along, for the love of Mike! " or words to that effect. Then they'd debated the question some more. Meanwhile the young gent had canceled his date, and the time has slipped by, and here it was almost Saturday, and nothin' doing in the reply line from them. Marjorie had thought of it while they was havin' lunch in town, and she'd chased Ferdie out to send a wire, without tellin' him what to say.

"And you want someone to make up your mind for you, eh? " says I. "All right. That's my long suit. Take this: 'Regret very much unable to accept your kind invitation'—which might mean anything, from a previous engagement to total paralysis. "

"Ye-e-es, " says Ferdie, hangin' his bamboo stick over his left arm and chewin' the penholder thoughtful, "but Marjorie'll be awfully disappointed. I think she really does want to go. "

"Ah, squiffle! " says I. "She'll get over it. Whose joint is it, anyway? "

"Why, " says he, "the Pulsifers', you know. "

"Eh? " says I. "Not the Adam K. 's place, Cedarholm? "

Ferdie nods. And, say, it was like catchin' a chicken sandwich dropped out of a clear sky. The Pulsifers! Didn't I know who was there? I did! I'd had a bulletin from a very special and particular party, sayin' how she'd be there for a week, while Aunty was in the

Berkshires. And up to this minute my chances of gettin' inside Cedarholm gates had been null and void, or even worse. But now—say, I wanted to be real kind to Ferdie!

"One or two old friends of Marjorie's are to be there, " he goes on dreamy.

"They are? " says I. "Then that's diff'rent. You got to go, of course. "

"But—but, " says he, "only a moment ago you——"

"Ah, mooshwaw! " says I. "You don't want Marjorie grumpin' around for the next week, do you, wishin' she'd gone, and layin' it all to you? "

Ferdie blinks a couple of times as the picture forms on the screen. "That's so, " says he. "She would. "

"Then gimme that blank, " says I. "Now here, how's this, 'Have at last arranged things so we can come. Charmed to accept'? Eh? "

"But—but there's Baby's milk, " objects Ferdie. "Marjorie always watches the nurse sterilize it, you know. "

"Do up a gallon before you leave, " says I.

"It's such a puzzling place to get to, though, " says Ferdie. "I'm sure we'd never get on the right train. "

"Whadye mean, train, " says I. "Ah, show some class! Go in your limousine. "

"So we could, " says Ferdie. "But then, you know, they'll be expectin' us to bring an extra young man. "

"They needn't be heartbroken over that, " says I. "You didn't say who he was, did you? "

"Why, no, " says Ferdie; "but——"

"Since you press me so hard, " says I, "I'll sub for him. Guess you need me to get you there, anyway. "

"By Jove! " says Ferdie, as the proposition percolates through the hominy. "I wonder if——"

"Never waste time wonderin', " says I. "Take a chance. Here, sign your name to that; then we'll go hunt up Marjorie and tell her the glad news. "

Ferdie was still in a daze when we found the other three-quarters of the sketch, and Marjorie was some set back herself when I springs the scheme. But she's a good sport, Marjorie is, and if she was hooked up to a live one she'd travel just as lively as the next heavyweight.

"Oh, let's! " says she, clappin' her hands. "You know we haven't been away from home overnight for an age. And Edna Pulsifer's such a dear, even if her father is a grouchy old thing. We'll take Torchy along too. What do you say, Ferdie? "

Foolish question! Ferdie was still dazed. And anyhow she had said it herself.

So that's how it happens I'm one of the chosen few to be landed under the Cedarholm porte-cochère that Saturday afternoon. Course the Pulsifers ain't reg'lar old fam'ly people, like Ferdie's folks. They date back to about the last Broadway horse-car period, I understand, when old Adam K. begun to ship his Cherryola dope in thousand-case lots. Now, you know, it's all handled for him by the drug trust, and he only sits by the safety-vault door watchin' the profits roll in. But with his name still on every label you could hardly expect the Pulsifers to qualify for Mrs. Astor's list.

Seems Edna went to the same boardin' school as Marjorie and Vee, though, and neither of 'em ever thinks of throwin' Cherryola at her.

And as far as an establishment goes, Cedarholm is the real thing. Gave me quite some thrill to watch two footmen in silver and baby blue pryin' Marjorie out of the limousine.

"Gee! " thinks I, glancin' around at the deep verandas, the swing seats, and the cozy corner nooks. "If Vee and I can't get together for a few chatty words among all this, then I'm a punk plottist! "

These country house joints are so calm and peaceful too! It's a wonder anybody could work up a case of nerves, havin' this for a steady thing. But Edna and Mrs. Pulsifer acted sort of restless and jumpy. She's a tall, thin, hollow-eyed dame, Mrs. Pulsifer is, with gray hair and a smooth, easy voice. Miss Edna must take more after her Pa; for she's filled out better, and while she ain't what you'd call mug-mapped, she has one of these low-bridge noses and a lot of oily, dark red hair that she does in a weird fashion of her own with a side part. Seems shy and bashful too, except when she snuggles up on the lee side of Marjorie and trails off with her.

The particular party I was strainin' my eyesight for ain't in evidence, though, and all the hint I gets of her bein' there was hearin' a ripply laugh at the far end of the hallway when she and Marjorie go to a fond clinch. That was some comfort, though, —she was in the house!

As I couldn't very well go scoutin' around whistlin' for her to come out, I does the next best thing. After bein' shown my room I drifts downstairs and out on the lawn where I'd be some conspicuous. Course I wa'n't suggestin' anything, but if somebody should happen to see me and judge that I was lonesome, they might wander out that way too. Sure enough somebody did, —Ferdie.

"I thought you had to take a nap before dinner, " says I, maybe not so cordial.

"Bother! " says he. "There's no such thing as that possible with those three girls chattering away in the next room. "

"Well, they ain't been together for some time, I expect, " says I.

"It's worse than usual, " says Ferdie. "A man in the case, you might know. "

"Eh? " says I, prickin' up my ears. "Whose man? "

"Oh, Edna Pulsifer's absurd ditch digger, " says Ferdie. "He's a young engineer, you know, that she's been interested in for a couple of years. Her father put a stop to it once; kept her in Munich for ten months—and that's a perfectly deadly place out of season, you know. But it doesn't seem to have done much good. "

I grins. Surprisin' how cheerful I could be so long as it was a case of Miss Pulsifer's young man. I pumps the whole tale out of Ferdie, — how this Mr. Bert Gilkey—cute name too—had been writin' her letters all the time from out West, how he'd been seized with a sudden fit, wired on that he must see her once more, and had rushed East. Then how Pa Pulsifer had caught 'em lalligaggin' out by the hedge, had talked real rough to Gilkey, and ordered him never to muddy his front doormat again.

"And now, " goes on Ferdie, "he sends word to Edna that he means to try it once more, no matter what happens, and everyone is all stirred up. "

"So that accounts for the nervous motions, eh? " says I. "What does Pa Pulsifer have to say to this defi? "

"Goodness! " says Ferdie, shudderin'. "He doesn't know. No one dares tell him a word. If he found out—well, it would be awful! "

"Huh! " says I. "One of these fam'ly ringmasters, is he? "

That was it, and from Ferdie's description I gathered that old Adam K. was a reg'lar domestic tornado, once he got started. Maybe you know the brand? And it seems Pa Pulsifer was the limit. So long as things went his way he was a prince, —right there with the jolly haw-haw, fond of callin' wifey pet names before strangers, and posin' as an easy mark, —but let anybody try to pull off any programme that didn't jibe with his, and black clouds rolled up sudden in the West.

"I do hope, " goes on Ferdie, "that nothing of that sort occurs while we are here. "

So did I, for more reasons than one. What I wanted was peace, and plenty of it, with Vee more or less disengaged.

Nothin' could have been more promisin' either than the openin' of that first dinner party. Pa Pulsifer had showed up about six o'clock from the Country Club, with his rugged, hand-hewed face tinted up cheery. Some of it was sunburn, and some of it was rye, I expect, but he was glad to see all of us. He patted Marjorie on the cheek, pinched Vee by the ear, and slapped Ferdie on the back so hearty he near knocked the breath out of him. So far as our genial host could make it, it was a gay and festive scene. Best of all too, I'd been put next to Vee, and I was just workin' up to exchangin' a hand squeeze under the tablecloth when, right in the middle of one of Pa Pulsifer's best stories, there floats in through the open windows a crash that makes everybody sit up. It sounds like breakin' glass.

"Hah! " snorts Pulsifer, scowlin' out into the dark. "Now what in blazes was that? "

"I—I think it must have been something in the kitchen, Dear, " says Mrs. Pulsifer. "Don't mind. "

"But I do mind, " says he. "In the first place, it wasn't in the kitchen at all, and if you'll all excuse me, I'll just see for myself. "

Meanwhile Edna has turned pale, Marjorie has almost choked herself with a bread stick, and Ferdie has let his fork clatter to the floor. Ma Pulsifer is bitin' her lip; but she's right there with the soothin' words.

"Please, Dear, " says she, "let me go. They want you to finish your story. "

It was a happy touch, that last. Pa Pulsifer recovers his napkin, settles back in his chair, and goes on with the tale, while Mother slips out quiet. She comes back after a while, springs a nervous little laugh, and announces that it was only the glass in one of the hotbed frames.

"Some stupid person taking a short cut across the grounds, I suppose," says she.

Didn't sound very convincin' to me; but Pulsifer had got started on another boyhood anecdote, and he let it pass. I had a hunch, though, that Mrs. Pulsifer hadn't told all. I caught a glance between her and Edna, and some flashes between Edna and Vee, and I didn't need any sixth sense to feel that something was in the air.

No move was made, though, until after coffee had been served in the lib'ry and Pa Pulsifer was fittin' his fav'rite Harry Lauder record on the music machine.

First Mrs. Pulsifer slips out easy. Next Edna follows her, and after them Marjorie and Vee, havin' exchanged some whispered remarks, disappears too. Maybe it was my play to stick it out with Ferdie and the old boy, but I couldn't see any percentage in that, with Vee gone; so I wanders casual into the hall, butts around through the music room, follows a bright light at the rear, and am almost run down by Marjorie hurrying the other way sleuthy.

"Oh!" she squeals. "It's you, is it, Torchy? S-s-s-sh!"

"What you shushin' about?" says I.

"Oh, it's dreadful!" puffs Marjorie. "He—he's come!"

"That Gilkey guy?" says I.

"Ye-e-es," says she. "But—but how did you know?"

"I'm a seventh son, born with a cowlick, " says I. "Was it Gilkey made his entrance through the cucumber frame? "

It was. Also he'd managed to cut himself in the ankles and right wrist. They had him in the kitchen, patchin' him up now, and they was all scared stiff for fear Pa Pulsifer would discover it before they could send him away.

"He'll be a nut if he don't, " says I, "with all you women out here. Your game is to chase back and keep Pulsifer interested. "

"I suppose you're right, " says Marjorie. "Let's tell them. "

So I follows into the big kitchen, where I finds the disabled Romeo propped up in a chair, with the whole push of 'em, includin' the fat cook, a couple of maids, and the butler, all tryin' to bandage him in diff'rent spots. He's a big, gawky-lookin' young gent, with a thick crop of pale hair and a solemn, serious look on his face, like he was one of the kind that took everything hard. As soon as Marjorie gives 'em my hint about goin' back to Father there's a gen'ral protest.

"Oh, I can't do it! " says Edna.

"He would notice at once how nervous I am, " groans Mrs. Pulsifer.

"But you don't want him walking out here, do you? " demands Marjorie.

That settled 'em. They bunched together panicky and started back for the lib'ry.

"I'll stay and attend to the getaway, " says I. "Nobody'll miss me. "

"Thank you, " says Gilkey; "but I'm not sure I wish to go away. I came to see Edna, you know. "

"So I hear, " says I. "Unique idea of yours too, rollin' in the hotbeds first. "

"I—I was only trying to avoid meeting Mr. Pulsifer, " says he; "exploring a bit, you see. I could hear voices in the dining-room; but I couldn't quite look in. There was a little shed out there, though, and by climbing on that I could get a view. That was how I lost my balance. "

"Before you go callin' again, " says I, "you ought to practice roostin' in the dark. Say, the old man must have thrown quite a scare into you last time. "

"I am not afraid of Mr. Pulsifer, not a bit, " says he.

"Well, well! " says I. "Think of that! "

"Anyway, " says he, "I just wasn't goin' to be driven off that way. It—it isn't fair to either of us. "

"Then it's a clear case with both of you, is it? " says I.

"We are engaged, " says Gilkey, "and I don't care who knows it! It's not her money I'm after, either. We don't want a dollar from Mr. Pulsifer. We—we just want each other. "

"Now you're talkin'! " says I; for, honest, the simple, slushy way he puts it across sort of wins me. And if that was how the case stood, with Edna longin' for him, and him yearnin' for Edna, why shouldn't they? If I'm any judge, Edna wouldn't find another right away who'd be so crazy about her, and anyone who could discover charms about Gilkey ought to be rewarded.

"See here! " says I. "Why not sail right in there, look Father between the eyes, and hand that line of dope out to him as straight as you gave it to me? "

He gawps at me a second, like I'd advised him to jump off the roof. "Do—do you think I ought? " says he.

Torchy, Private Sec.

I has to choke back a chuckle. Wanted my advice, did he? Well, say, I could give him a truckload of that!

"It depends, " says I, "on how deep the yellow runs in you. Course it's all right for you to register this leader about not bein' scared of him. You may think you ain't, but you are all the same; and as long as you're in that state you're licked. That's the big trouble with most of us, —bein' limp in the spine. We're afraid of our jobs, afraid of what the neighbors will say, afraid of our stomachs, afraid of tomorrow. And here you are, prowlin' around on the outside, gettin' yourself messed up, and standin' to lose the one and only girl, all because an old stuff like Pulsifer says 'Boo! ' at you and tells you to 'Scat! ' Come on now, better let me lead you out and see you safe through the gate. "

Course that was proddin' him a little rough, but I wanted to bring this thing to a head somehow. Made Gilkey squirm in his chair too. He begins rollin' his trousers down over the bandages and struggles into his coat.

"I suppose you're right, " says he. "I—I think I will go in and see Mr. Pulsifer. "

"Wha-a-at? " says I. "Now? "

"Why not? " says he, pushin' through the swing door.

"Hey! " I calls out, jumpin' after him. "Better let me break it to 'em in there. "

"As you please, " says Gilkey; "only let's have no delay. "

So I skips across the hall and into the lib'ry, where they're all makin' a stab at bein' chatty and gay, with Pa Pulsifer in the center.

"Excuse me, " says I, "but there's a young gent wants a few words with Mr. Pulsifer. "

"What's that? " growls Adam K., glarin' about suspicious at the gaspy circle. "What young man? "

"Why, " says I, "it's——" But then in he stalks.

"Oh, Herbert! " sobs Edna, makin' a wild grab at Marjorie for support.

As for Pa Pulsifer, his eyes get stary, the big vein in the middle of his forehead swells threatenin', and his bushy white eyebrows seem to bristle up.

"You! " he snorts. "How did you get in here, Sir? "

"Through the kitchen, " says Gilkey. "I came to tell you that——"

"Stop! " roars Pulsifer, stampin' his foot and bunchin' his fists menacin'. "You can't tell me anything, not a word, you—you good-for-nothing young scoundrel! Haven't I warned you never to step foot in my house again? Didn't I tell you——"

Well, it's the usual irate parent stuff, only a little more wild and ranty than anything Belasco would put over. He abuses Gilkey up and down, threatens him with all kinds of things, from arrest to sudden death, and gets purple in the face doin' it. While Gilkey, he just stands there, takin' it calm and patient. Then, when there comes a lull, he remarks casual:

"If that is all, Sir, I wish to say to you that Edna and I are engaged, and that I intend to marry her early next week. "

Wow! That's the cue for another explosion. It starts in just as fierce as the first; but it don't last so long, and towards the end Pa Pulsifer is talkin' husky and puffing hard.

"Go! " he winds up. "Get out of my house before I—I——"

"Oh, I say, " breaks in Gilkey, "before you do what? "

"Throw you out!" bellows Pulsifer.

"Don't be absurd," says Gilkey, statin' it quiet and matter of fact. "You couldn't, you know. Besides, it isn't being done."

And it takes Pa Pulsifer a full minute before he can choke down his temper and get his wind again. Then he advances a step or so, points dramatic to the door, and gurgles throaty:

"Will—you—get—out?"

"No," says Gilkey. "I came to see Edna. I've had no dinner either, and I'd like a bite to eat."

Pulsifer stood there, not two feet from him, glarin' and puffin', and tryin' to decide what to do next; but it's no use. He'd made his grand roarin' lion play, which had always scared the tar out of his folks, and he'd responded to an encore. Yet here was this mild-eyed young gent with the pale hair and the square jaw not even wabbly in the knees from it.

"Come, Edna," says Gilkey, holdin' out a hand to her. "Let's go into the dining-room."

"But—but see here!" gasps Pa Pulsifer, makin' a final effort. "I—I——"

"Oh, hush up!" says Gilkey, turnin' away weary. "Come, Edna."

And Edna, she went; also Mrs. Pulsifer; likewise Vee and Marjorie. Trust women for knowin' when a bluff has been called. I expect they was wise, two or three minutes before either me or Gilkey, that Pa Pulsifer was beat. I stayed long enough to see him slump into an easy-chair, his under lip limp and a puzzled look in his eyes, like he was tryin' to figure out just what had hit him. And over by the fireplace is Ferdie, gawpin' at him foolish, and exercisin' his gears, I expect, on the same problem. Neither of them had said a word up to the time I left.

Torchy, Private Sec.

It took the women half an hour or more to feed Herbert up proper with all the nice things they could drag from the icebox. Then Mother Pulsifer patted him on the shoulder and shooed Edna and him through the French doors out on the veranda.

And what do you guess is Mrs. Pulsifer's openin' as we drifts back towards the scene of the late conflict?

"Why, Deary! " says she. "You haven't your cigars, have you? Here they are—and the matches. There! Now for the surprise. Our young people have decided—that is, Edna has—not to be married until two weeks from next Wednesday. "

Does Pa Pulsifer rant any more rants? No. He gets his perfecto goin' nicely, blows a couple of smoke rings up towards the ceilin', and then remarks in sort of a weak growl:

"Hanged if I'll walk down a church aisle, Maria—hanged if I do! "

"I told them you wouldn't, " says Ma Pulsifer, smoothin' the hair back over his ears soothin'; "so they've agreed on a simple home wedding, with only four bridesmaids. "

"Huh! " says he. "It's lucky they did. "

But, say, take it from me, his days of crackin' the whip around that joint are over. I'm beginnin' to believe too how some of that dope I fed to Herbert must have been straight goods. Vee insists on talkin' it over later, as we are camped in one of them swing seats out on the veranda.

"Wasn't he just splendid, " says she: "standing up to Mr. Pulsifer that way, you know? "

"Some hero! " says I. "I wonder would he give me a few lessons, in case I should run across your Aunty some day? "

"Which was one of the reasons I turned the porch light off."

"Pooh!" says Vee. "Just as though I didn't go back to see if he'd gone and hear you putting him up to all that yourself! It was fine of you to do it too, Torchy."

"Right here, then!" says I. "Place the laurel wreath right here."

"Silly!" says she, givin' me a reprovin' pat. "Besides, that porch light is on."

Which was one of the reasons why I turned it off, and maybe accounts for our sudden break when Marjorie comes out to tell us it's near twelve o'clock.

Yes, indeed, though he may not look it, Ferdie is more or less of a help.

Torchy, Private Sec.

CHAPTER VI

WHEN SKEET HAD HIS DAY

There's one thing about bein' a private sec, —you stand somewhere on the social list. It may be down towards the foot among the discards; but you're in the running.

Not that I'm thinkin' of havin' a fam'ly crest worked on my shirt sleeves, or that I'm beginnin' to sympathize with the lower clawsses. Nothing like that! Only it does help, when Marjorie, the boss's married daughter, has planned some social doin's, to get an invite like a reg'lar guy.

What do you know too? It's dance! Not out at their country place, either. She'd dragged Ferdie into town for a couple of weeks, and they'd been stayin' at the Ellins's Fifth-ave. house, just visitin' and havin' a good time. That is, Marjorie had. Ferdie, he spends his days mopin' about the club and taggin' Mr. Robert.

"Better sneak off up to the Maison Maxixe with me, " says I, "and brush up on your hesitation. "

A look of deep disgust from Ferdie. "I'm not a dancing man, you know, " says he.

"Both feet Methodists, eh? " says I.

Ferdie stares puzzled. "It's only that I'm sure I'd look absurd, " says he.

"For once, " says I, "you ain't so far from wrong. I expect you would. "

Even that don't seem to please him, and he refuses peevish to trail along and watch me blow myself to a pair of dancin' pumps. Gee! but this society life runs into coin, don't it? I'd dropped into one of them swell booterers and was beefin' away at the clerk about havin'

Torchy, Private Sec.

to pay six-fifty just for a pair of tango moccasins, when I hears someone on the bench back of me remark casual:

"Nine dollars? Very well. Send them up to my hotel. Here's my card."

And as there's somethin' familiar about the voice I takes a peek over my shoulder. But neither the braid-bound cutaway fittin' so snug at the waist, nor the snappy fall derby snuggled down over the lop ears, suggested any old friends. Not until he swings around and I gets a view of that nosy profile do I gasp any gasps.

"Sizzlin' Stepsisters!" says I. "If it ain't Skeet Keyser!"

"I—ah—I beg pardon?" says he, doin' it cold and haughty. Blamed if I don't think he meant to hand me the mistaken identity dope first off; but after another glance he thinks better of it. "Oh, yes," says he, sort of languid, "Torchy, isn't it?"

"Good guess, Skeet," says I, "seein' it's been all of two years since you used to shove me my coffee reg'lar at the——"

"Yes, yes," he breaks in hasty; "but—I—ah—I have an appointment. Glad to have seen you again."

"You act it," says I. And then, grabbin' him by the sleeve as he's backin' off, I whispers, "What's the disguise, Skeet?"

"Really, now!" he protests indignant.

"Oh, very well, very well!" says I. "But how should I know if someone has wished a life income on you? Congrats."

"Ah—er—thanks," says he. "I—I'll see you again—perhaps."

I loved the way he puts that last touch on too, and you could almost hear the sigh of relief as he fades down the aisle, leavin' me in one stockin' foot gawpin' after him.

Torchy, Private Sec.

No wonder I'm left open faced! Skeet Keyser in a tail coat, orderin' nine-dollar pumps sent to his hotel! Why, say, more'n once I've staked him to the price of a twenty-cent lodgin', and the only way I ever got any of it back was by tippin' him off to this vacancy on the coffee urn at the dairy lunch. Used to be copy boy on the Sunday, Skeet did; but that was 'way back. It didn't last long either; for he was just as punk a performer at that as he ever was at any of the other things he's tackled.

Gettin' the can tied to him was always Skeet's specialty. No mystery about that, either; for of all the useless specimens that ever grafted cigarettes he was about the limit. All he lacks is pep and bean and a few other trifles. You wouldn't exactly call him ornamental, either. No, him and that Apolloniris guy was quite diff'rent in their front and side elevation. Mostly arms and legs, Skeet is, and sort of swivel-jointed all over, with a back slope to his forehead and an under-cut chin. Nothin' reticent about his beak, though. It juts out from the middle of his face like the handle of a lovin' cup, and with his habit of stretchin' his neck forward he always seems to be followin' a scent, like one of these wienerwurst retrievers.

Brought up somewhere back of Jefferson Market, down in old Greenwich Village—if you know where that is. He's the only boy in a fam'ly of five, and I understand all the Keyser girls have done first rate; one bein' forelady in a big hair-dressin' joint, another married to the lieutenant of a hook and ladder company, and two well placed in service.

It was through bein' in on a little mix-up Skeet had with one of his sisters that I got so well posted on the fam'ly hist'ry. Must have been more'n a year ago, while Old Hickory was laid up at home there for a spell, and I was chasin' back and forth from the Corrugated to the Ellins house most every day. This time I hears a debate goin' on down at the area door, and the next thing I knows out comes Skeet, assisted active by the butler.

Seems that one of the new maids is his sister Maggie, and he'd just been callin' friendly in the hopes of sep'ratin' her from a dollar or so.

Torchy, Private Sec.

It wa'n't Maggie's day for contributin' to the prodigal son fund, though, and Skeet was statin' his opinion of her reckless when the butler interfered. Come near losin' Maggie her job, that little scene did; but she promises faithful it sha'n't happen again, and was kept on.

"Blast her!" says Skeet to me later. "She's just as bad as the rest of 'em. They're all tightwads. Why, even the old lady runs me out now when I happen to be carryin' the banner and can't come across with my little old five of a Saturday night! I might starve in the streets for all they care. But I'll show 'em some day. You'll see!"

Hanged if it don't look like he'd turned the trick too; for, as I've hinted, Skeet is costumed like a lily of the field. But how he'd managed to do it is what gets me. And for two days after that I wasted valuable time tryin' to frame up just where in the gen'ral scheme of things a party like Skeet Keyser could connect with real money. After that I gave up the myst'ry and spent my spare minutes wonderin' if I could do this "One-two-three—hold!" business as successful in public as I could while them dancin' school fairies was drillin' it into my nut at one-fifty per throw.

That's right, grin! But if you're billed to mingle in the merry throng at a dance fest, you ain't goin' to trot out on the floor with any such antique act as last season's Boston dip, are you? Might as well spring the minuet. And specially when I'd had word that among others was to be a certain party. Uh-huh! You can play it both ways too that Vee would be up on the very latest, and if it was in me I meant to be right behind her.

Was I? Say, maybe if I wa'n't so blamed modest I could give you an idea of how Vee and I just naturally—but I can't do it. Besides, there's other matters; the grand jolt that come early in the evenin', for instance. It was after the second number, and I'd made a dash into the gents' dressin' room to see if my white tie showed any symptoms of ridin' up in the back, and I'd just strolled out into the entrance hall again, watchin' the push straggle in, when who should show up through the double doors but a tall, lanky young chap with lop ears and a nose one was bound to remember.

It's Skeet Keyser; Skeet in shiny, thin-soled pumps, a pleated dress shirt, black silk vest, and a top hat! He's bein' bowed in dignified by the same butler, and is passed on to—well, it's a funny world, ain't it? The maid on duty just inside the door happens to be Sister Maggie. She has the respectful bow all ready when she gets a full-face view.

"Aloysius! " says she, scared and husky.

I got to hand it to Skeet, though, that he bears up noble. All he does is to try to swallow his throat apple a couple of times, and then he stares at her stern and distant. Also Maggie makes a quick recovery.

"Gentlemen this way, Sir, " says she, and waves Skeet into the dressin' room.

I wanted to follow him up and tip him off that there's one or two other reasons why this was the wrong house to put over any sporty bluff in; but as it was I'm overdue in another quarter. You see, Marjorie has been sittin' out on the side lines, as usual, and Vee has hinted how it would be nice and charitable of me to brace her for a spiel. I'd sort of been workin' myself up to the sacrifice, for you know Marjorie's some hefty partner for anybody not in trainin' to steer around a ballroom floor; but I'd figured out that the longer I put it off the worse it would be. So off I trails with my heels draggin' a little heavy.

"Why, thanks ever so much, Torchy, " says she, "but I think I have a partner for the first four or five. After that, though — — "

"Don't mention it, " says I. "I mean, much obliged, " and I backs off hasty before she can change her mind.

Torchy, Private Sec.

I had to kill time while Vee was dividin' a couple dances between two young shrimps; so I sidles into a corner where Ferdie sits behind his shell-rimmed glasses, lookin' bored and lonesome.

"Now don't you wish you'd gone and had your feet educated? " says I.

Ferdie yawns. "I think it quite sufficient, " says he, "that one of us intends making an exhibition. Marjorie has been taking lessons, you know. "

"So I hear, " says I. "And it's all right if she don't tackle the maxixe. Hello! There it goes. Now you will see some stunts! "

Yep, we did! And among the first couples to sail out on the floor, if you'll believe it, was none other than Marjorie and our lop-eared young hero, Skeet Keyser.

"Oh, Gosh! " I groans. "Don't look, Ferdie! "

I meant well too; It was goin' to be bad enough to see a corn-fed young matron the size of Marjorie, who can spin the arrow well up to the hundred and eighty mark, monkey with them twisty evolutions; but to have her get let in for it with a roughneck ringer like Skeet—well, that was goin' to be a real tragedy. How he'd worked it, or what his excuse was for bein' here at all, was useless questions to ask then. What was comin' next was the thing to watch for.

As for Ferdie, he just sits there and blinks, followin' 'em through his spare panes. Course I could guess he wa'n't hep to any facts about Skeet. He was just a strange young gent to him, and it wa'n't up to me to add any details. So I settles back and watches 'em too.

And, say, you know how surprised you'd be to see any fat friend of yours buckle on a pair of ice skates and do the double grapevine up and down the rink? Well, that's the identical kind of jar I got when Marjorie begins that willowy bendy figure. It ain't any waddly caricature of it, either. It's the real thing. Honest, she's as light on her feet as if her middle name was Pavlowa!

At the same time it's lucky Skeet has arms, long enough to reach 'way round when he's steerin' her. If they'd been an inch or so shorter, he'd have had to break his clinch in some of them whirls, and then there'd been a big dent in the floor. He seems just built for the job, though. In and out, round and round, through the Parisienne, the flirtation, and all the other frills, he pilots her safe, bendin' and swayin' to the music, his number ten feet glidin' easy, and kind of a smirky, satisfied look on that sappy mug of his; while Marjorie, she simply lets herself go for all she's worth, her eyes sparklin', and the pink and white in her cheeks showin' clear and fresh.

Take it from me too, it's some swell exhibit! There was four or five other couples on at the same time, the girls all slender, wispy young things, that never split out a waist seam in their lives; but Marjorie and her partner had the gallery right with 'em. Two or three times durin' the dance they got scatterin' applause, and when the music fin'lly stops, leavin' 'em alone in the middle of the floor, they got a reg'lar big hand.

"I take it all back, " says I to Ferdie. "That was real classy spielin'. Now wa'n't it?. "

"No doubt, " he grunts. "And I suppose I should be thankful that Marjorie didn't try to jump through a paper hoop. I trust, however, that this concludes the performance. "

It did not! Next on the card was a onestep, with Marjorie and her unknown goin' to it like professionals; and if they omitted any fancy waves, you couldn't prove it by me. By this time too, Ferdie was sittin' up and takin' notice. "Oh, I say, " says he, "isn't that the same fellow she danced with before? "

"You don't think a bunch of works like that could be twins, do you? " says I.

"But—but I'm sure I don't remember having met him, you know, " says Ferdie, rubbin' his chin thoughtful.

"Then maybe you ain't, " says I.

When they comes on for a third time, though, and prances through about as flossy a half-and-half as I've ever seen pulled at a private dance, Ferdie is some agitated in the mind. He ain't exactly green-eyed, but he's some disturbed. Yes, all of that!

"I—I think I'd best speak to Marjorie, " says he.

"You'll have plenty of competition, " says I. "Look! "

For the young chappies are crowdin' around her two deep, makin' dates for the next numbers. "Ferdie stares at the spectacle puzzled. He's a persistent messer, though.

"But really, " he goes on, "I think I ought to meet that young fellow and find out who he is. "

"Ah, bottle it up until afterwards! " says I. "Don't rock the skiff. "

But there's a streak of mule in Ferdie a foot wide. "People will be asking me who he is! " he insists, "and if I don't know, what will they think? See, isn't that he, standing just over there? "

And then Mr. Robert has to drift along and complicate matters by joshin' brother-in-law a little. "Congratulations on your substitute, Ferdie, " says he. "Where did he come from? "

Which brings a ruddy tint into Ferdie's ears. "Ask Marjorie, " says he. "I'm sure he's an utter stranger to me. "

"Wha-a-at? " says Mr. Robert, and when he's had the full situation mapped out for him blamed if he don't begin to take it serious too.

"To be sure, Ferdie, " says he. "Everyone seems to think he must be a guest of yours; but as he isn't—well, it's quite time someone discovered. Let's go over and introduce ourselves. "

And somehow that didn't listen good to me, either. Marjorie's done a lot of nice turns for me, and this looked like it was my play to lend a hand.

"With two or three more, " says I, "you could form a perfectly good mob, couldn't you? "

Mr. Robert whirls and demands sarcastic, "Well, what would you suggest, young man? "

"He's got all the earmarks of a reg'lar invited guest, ain't he? " says I. "And unless you're achin' to start somethin', why not let me handle this 'Who the blazes are you? ' act? "

He sees the point too, Mr. Robert does. He shrugs his shoulders and grins. "That's so, " says he. "All right, Torchy. Full diplomatic powers, and if necessary I shall restrain Ferdie by the collar. "

I wa'n't wastin' time on any subtle strategy, though. Walkin' over to Skeet I taps him on the shoulder, and then it's his turn to gawp at my costume.

"Why, " he gasps, "how—er—where did you——"

"Oh, I brought myself out last season, " says I. "But just a minute, if you don't mind, " and I jerks my thumb towards the dressin' room.

"But, you know, " he begins, "I—I——"

"Ah, ditch the shifty stuff! " says I. "This is orders from headquarters. Come! "

And he trots right along. Once I gets him behind the draperies I shoots it at him straight. "Who'd you pinch the invite from? " says I.

"See here, now! " he comes back peevish. "You have no call to say that. I had a bid, all right; got it with me. There! What about that? " And he flashes a card on me.

It's one of Marjorie's!

"Huh! " says I. "Met her at Mrs. Astor's, I expect? "

Skeet shuffles his feet and tries to look indignant.

"Come on, give us the plot of the piece, " says I, "or I'll call up Sister Maggie and put her on the stand. Where was it, now? "

"If you must know, " says Skeet sulky, "it was at Roselle's. "

"The tango factory? " says I. "Oh, I'm beginnin' to get the thread. The place where she's been takin' lessons, eh? "

Skeet nods.

"Is this romance, or business, then? " says I.

"Think I'm a fathead? " says he. "I'm gettin' fifteen for this, and I'm earnin' the money too. It's a regular thing. Last night I was Cousin Harry for an old maid from Washington—went to a swell house dance up on Riverside Drive. She came across with twenty for that, and paid for the taxi. "

"Well, well! " says I. "Then them long legs of yours has turned out a good asset after all. What you pullin' down, Skeet, on an average? "

"Twenty regular, and a hundred or so on the side, " says he, swellin' his chest out. "And, say, I guess I got it some on the rest of the family. You know how they used me, —like dirt, the old lady callin' me a loafer, and Annie so stuck up on livin' in an elevator apartment she wouldn't have me around. Maggie too! Didn't I hand it to her, though? Notice me frost her, eh? But I said I'd show 'em some day. Guess I've delivered the goods. Look at me now, all dolled up every night, and mixin' with the best people! Say, you watch me! Why, I can go out there and pick any queen you want to name. They're crazy about me. I could show you mash notes and photos too. Oh, I'm Winning Willie with the fluffs, I am! "

Well, it was worth listenin' to. He struts around waggin' his silly head, until I can hardly keep from throwin' a chair at him. Course something had to be dealt out. He needed it bad. So I sizes him up rapid and makes the first play that comes into my head.

"You're a wonder, Skeet, " says I. "And it's a great game as long as you can get away with it. But whisper! " Here I glances around cautious. "You know I'm a friend of yours. "

"Oh, sure, " says he careless. "What then? "

"Only this, " says I. "Here's once when I'm afraid you're about to pull down trouble. "

"How's that? " says he, twistin' his neck uneasy.

"Notice the two gents I was just talkin' with, " I goes on, "specially the savage-lookin' one with the framed lamps? Well, that was Hubby. He's got one of these hair-trigger dispositions too. "

"Pooh! " says Skeet. But he's listenin' close.

"I'm only tellin' you, " says I. "Then the big one with the wide shoulders—that's Brother. Reg'lar brute, he is, and a temper——"

That gets him stary eyed. "You—you don't mean, " says he, "that——"

"Uh-huh! " says I. "You know you and the young lady was some conspicuous. There's been talk all round the room. They've both heard, and they're beefin' something awful. Course I ain't sayin' they'll spring any gunplay right in the house; but—why, what's wrong, Skeet? "

Honest, he's gone putty faced and panicky. He begins pawin' around for his overcoat.

"Ain't goin' so soon, are you, " says I, "without breakin' a few more hearts? "

"I—I'm goin' to get out of here! " says he, his teeth chattery. He'd grabbed his silk lid and was makin' a dash for the front door when I stopped him.

"Not that way, for the love of soup! " says I. "They'll be layin' for you there. Why not bluff it out and cut up with some of the other queens? "

"I'm not feeling well, " says he. "I—I'm going, I tell you! "

"If you insist, then, " says I, "perhaps I can sneak you out. Here, this way. Now slide in behind that portière until I find one of the maids. Oh, here's one now. S-s-s-t! That you, Maggie? Well, smuggle Mr. Keyser out the back way, will you? And if you don't want to witness bloodshed, do it quick! "

I tipped her the wink over his shoulder, and the last glimpse I had of Skeet he was bein' hustled and shoved towards the back way by willin' hands.

By the time I gets back into the ballroom I finds Marjorie right in the midst of a fam'ly court martial. She's makin' a full confession.

"Of course I hired him, " she's sayin' to Brother Robert. "Why? Because I've been a wall flower at too many dances, and I'm tired of it. No, I don't know who he is, I'm sure; but he's a perfectly lovely dancer. I wonder where he's disappeared to? "

Which seemed to be my cue to report. "Mr. Keyser presents his compliments, " says I, "and begs to be excused for the rest of the evenin' on account of feelin' suddenly indisposed. He says you can send him that fifteen by mail, if you like. "

"Well, the idea! " gasps Marjorie.

As for Mr. Robert, he chuckles. Takin' me one side, he asks confidential, "What did you use on our young friend, persuasion, or assault with intent? "

"On a fish-face like that? " says I. "Nope. This was just a simple case of spill. "

CHAPTER VII

GETTING A JOLT FROM WESTY

You might call it time out, or suspended hostilities durin' peace negotiations, or anything like that. Anyway, Aunty has softened up to the extent of lettin' me come around once a week without makin' me assume a disguise, or crawl in through the coal chute. Course I'm still under suspicion; but while the ban ain't lifted complete she don't treat me quite so much like a porch climber or a free speech agitator.

"Remember, " says she, "Friday evenings only, from half after eight until not later than ten. "

"Yes'm, " says I, "and it's mighty——"

"Please! " she breaks in. "No grotesquely phrased effusions of gratitude. I am merely indulging Verona in one of her absurd whims. You understand that, I trust? "

"I get your idea, " says I, "and even if it don't swell my chest any, I'm——"

"Kindly refrain from using such patois, " says Aunty.

"Eh? " says I. "You mean ditch the gabby talk? All right, Ma'am. "

Aunty rolls her eyes and sighs hopeless. "How my niece can find entertainment in such——" Here Aunty stops and shrugs her shoulders. "Well, " she goes on, "it is a mystery to me. "

"Me too, " says I; "so for once we're playin' on the same side of the net, ain't we! Say, but she's some girl though! "

Aunty's mouth corners wrinkle into one of them sarcastic smiles that's her specialty, and she remarks careless: "Quite a number of young men seem to have discovered that Verona is rather attractive."

"They'd have to be blind in both eyes and born without ears if they didn't," says I, "believe me!"

Oh, yes, we had a nice confidential little chat, me and Aunty did, — almost chummy, you know, —and as it breaks up and I backs out into the hall, givin' her the polite "Good evenin', Ma'am," I thought I heard a half-smothered snicker behind the draperies. Maybe it was that flossy French maid of theirs. But I floats downtown as gay and chirky as though I'd been promoted to first vice-president of something.

Course I was wise to the fact that Aunty wa'n't arrangin' any duo act with the lights shaded soft. Not her! Even if I had an official ratin' in the Corrugated now, and a few weeks back had shunted her off from a losin' stock deal, she wa'n't tryin' to decoy me into the fam'ly. Hardly! I could guess how she'd set the stage for my weekly call, and if I found myself with anything more than a walk-on part in a mob scene I'd be lucky.

You know she's taken a house for the winter, one of them old-fashioned brownstone fronts up on Madison-ave. that some friends of hers was goin' to close durin' a tour abroad. Nothin' swell, but real comfy and substantial, and as I marches up bold for my first push at the bell button I'm kind of relieved that I don't have to stand in line.

Who should I get a glimpse of, though, as I'm handin' my things to the butler, but the favored candidate, Sappy Westlake? Yep, big as life, with his slick, pale hair, his long legs, and his woodeny face! Looked like his admission card must have been punched for eight P. M., or else he'd been asked for dinner. Anyway, he was right on the ground, thumpin' out a new rag on the piano, and enjoyin' the full glare of the limelight. The only other entry I can discover is a girl.

Torchy, Private Sec.

"My friend Miss Ull, " explains Vee.

A good deal of a queen Miss Ull is too, tall and slim and tinted up delicate, but one of these poutin', peevish beauts that can look you over cold and distant and say "Howdy do" in such a bored, tired tone that you feel like apologizin' for the intrusion.

They didn't get wildly enthusiastic over my entrance, Miss Ull and Westy. In fact, almost before the honors are done they turns their backs on me and drifts to the piano once more.

"Do play that 'Try-trimmer-Träumerei' thing again, " urges Miss Ull, and begins to hum it as Westy proceeds to bang it out.

But there's Vee, her wheat-colored hair fluffin' about her seashell ears and her big gray eyes watchin' me sort of quizzin' and impish. "Well, Mr. Private Secretary? " says she.

"When does the rest of the chorus come on? " says I.

"The what? " says Vee.

"The full panel, " says I. "Aunty's planned to have the S. R. O. sign out on my evenin's, ain't she? "

At which Vee tosses her head. "How silly! " says she. "No one else is expected that I know of. Why? "

"Oh, she might think we'd be lonesome, " says I. "Honest, I was lookin' for a bunch; but if it's only a mixed foursome, that ain't so bad. I got the scheme, though. She counts Westy as better than a crowd. 'Safety First' is her motto. But who's the Peevish Priscilla here, that's so tickled to see me come in she has to turn away to hide her emotion? "

"Doris? " says Vee. "Oh, we got to know her on the steamer coming back from the Mediterranean last winter. Stunning, isn't she? "

"Specially her manners," says I. "Almost paralyzin'."

"Oh, that's just her way," says Vee. "Really, she's very nice when you get to know her. I'm rather sorry for her too. Her home life is—well, not at all congenial. That's one reason why I asked her to visit me for a week or so."

"That's the easiest thing you do, ain't it," says I, "bein' nice to folks that ain't used to it?"

"Thank goodness," says Vee, "someone has discovered my angelic qualities at last! Go on, Torchy, think of some more, can't you?" And she claps her hands enthusiastic.

"Quit your spoofin'," says I, "or I'll ring for Aunty and tell how you've been kiddin' the guest of honor. I might talk easier too, if we could adjourn to the window alcove over there. No rule against that, is there?"

Didn't seem to be. And we'd have had a perfectly good chat if it hadn't been for Doris. Such a restless young female! First she wants to drum something out on the piano herself. Then she must have Vee come show her how it ought to go. Next she wants to practice a new fancy dance, and so on. She keeps Westy trottin' around, and Vee comin' and goin', and things stirred up gen'rally. One minute she's gigglin' hysterical over nothin' at all, and the next she's poutin' sulky.

Anyway, she managed to queer the best part of the evenin', and I'd just settled down with Vee in a corner when the big hall clock starts to chime ten, and in through the draperies marches Aunty. It ain't any accidental droppin' in, either. She glances at me stern and suggestive and nods towards the door. So it was all over!

"Say," I whispers to Vee as I does a draggy exit, "if Doris is to be with us again, would you mind my bringin' a clothesline and ropin' her to the piano?"

Torchy, Private Sec.

Maybe it wa'n't some discouragin' a week later to find the same pair still on the job, with Doris as much of a peace disturber as ever. I got a little more of her history sketched out by Vee that night. Seems that Doris didn't really belong, for all her airs. Her folks had only lived up in the West 70's for four or five years, and before that— —

"Well, you know, " says Vee, archin' her eyebrows expressive, "on the East Side somewhere. "

You see, Father had been comin' strong in business of late, — antiques and house decoratin'. I remember havin' seen the name over the door of his big Fifth-ave. shop, —Leo Ull. You know there's about five hundred per cent, profit in that game when you get it goin', and while Pa Ull might have started small, in an East 14th Street basement, with livin' rooms in the rear, he kept branchin' out, —gettin' to Fourth-ave., and fin'lly to Fifth, jumpin' from a flat to an apartment, and from that to a reg'lar house.

So the two boys went to college, and later on little Doris, with long braids down her back and weeps in her eyes, is sent off to a girls' boardin' school. By the time her turn came too, the annual income was runnin' into six figures. Besides, Doris was the pet. And when Pa and Ma Ull sat down to pick out a young ladies' culture fact'ry for her the process was simple. They discarded all but three of the catalogues, savin' them that was printed on the thickest paper and havin' the most halftone pictures, and then put the tag on the one where the rates was highest. Near Washington, I think it was; anyway, somewhere South, —board and tuition, two thousand dollars and up; everything extra, from lead pencils to lessons in court etiquette; and the young ladies limited to ten new evenin' dresses a term.

Maybe you've seen products of such exclusive establishments? And if you have perhaps you can frame up a faint picture of what Doris was like after four years at Hetherington Hall and a five months' trip abroad chaperoned by the Baroness Parcheezi. No wonder she didn't find home a happy spot after that!

"Her brothers are quite nice, I believe, " says Vee. "They're both married, though. Mr. Ull is not so bad, either, —a little crude perhaps; but he has learned to wear a frock coat in the shop and not to talk to lady customers when he has a cigar between his teeth. But Mrs. Ull—well, she hasn't kept up, that's all."

"Still on East 14th Street, eh? " says I.

Vee admits that nearly states the case. "And of course, " she goes on, "she doesn't understand Doris. They don't get on at all well. So when Doris told me how lonely and unhappy she was at home and begged me to visit her for a week in return—well, what could I do? I'm going back with her Monday."

"Then, " says I, "I see where I cut next Friday off the calendar."

"Unless, " suggests Vee, droppin' her long eyelashes coy, "you were not too stupid to think of——"

"Say, " I breaks in, "gimme that number again, will you? Suppose I could duck meetin' Westy if I came the first evenin'? "

"If you're at all afraid of him, you shouldn't run the risk, " comes back Vee.

"Chance is my middle name, " says I. "Only him stickin' around does make a room so crowded. I didn't know but he might miss a night occasionally."

Vee sticks the tip of her tongue out. "Just two during the last ten days, if you want to know, " says she.

"Huh! " says I. "Must think he holds a season ticket."

I couldn't make out, either, what it was that Vee seems so amused over; for as near as I can judge she was never very strong for Sappy herself. Maybe it was just a string she was handin' me.

Havin' decided on that, I waits patient until eight-fifteen Monday evenin', and then breezes cheery and hopeful through the Ulls' front door and into the front room. No Westy in sight, or anybody else. The maid says the young ladies are in somewhere, and she'll tell 'em I've come.

So I wanders about amongst the furniture, that's set around almost as thick as in a showroom, —heavy, fancy pieces, most likely ones that had been sent up from the store as stickers. The samples of art on the walls struck me as a bit gaudy too, and I was tryin' to guess how it would seem if you had to live in that sort of clutter continual, when out through the slidin' doors from the lib'ry appears Sappy the Constant.

"The poor prune! " thinks I. "I wonder if I've got time to work up some scheme of puttin' the skids under him? "

But instead of givin' me the haughty stare as usual he rushes towards me smilin' and excited. "Oh, I say! " he breaks out. "Torchy, isn't it? Well, I—I've got a big piece of news. "

"I know, " says I. "Someone's told you that the Panama Canal's full of water. "

"No, no! " says he. "It—it's about me. Just happened, you know. And really I must tell someone. "

I had a choky sensation in my throat about then, and my breath came a little short; but I managed to get out husky, "Well, toss it over. "

Westy beams grateful. "Isn't it wonderful? " says he. "I—I've got her! "

"Eh? " I gasps, grippin' a chair back.

"She just told me, " says he, "in there. She's—she's wearing my ring now. "

Got me right under the belt buckle, that did. I felt wabbly and dizzy for a second, and I expect I gawps at him open faced. Then I takes a brace. Had to. I don't know how well I did it either, or how convincin' it sounded, but I found myself shakin' him by the mitt and sayin': "Congratulations, Westlake. You—you've got a girl worth gettin', believe me! "

"Thanks awfully, old man, " says he, still pumpin' my arm up and down. "I can hardly realize it myself. Awfully bad case I had, you know. And now, while I have the courage, I suppose I'd best see her mother. "

"Wha-a-at? " says I, starin' at him.

"I know, " says he, "it isn't being done much nowadays, but somehow I think I ought. You know I haven't even met Mrs. Ull as yet. "

I hope he was so fussed he didn't notice that sigh of relief I let out; for I'll admit it was some able-bodied affair, —a good deal like shuttin' off the air in a brake connection, or rippin' a sheet. Anyway, I made up for it the next minute.

"You and Doris, eh? " says I, poundin' him on the back hearty. "Ain't you the foxy pair, though? Well, well! Here, let's have another shake on that. But why not see Father and tell him about it? Know the old gent, don't you? "

"Ye-e-es, " says Westy, flushin' a bit. "But he—well, he's her father, of course. She can't help that. And it makes no difference at all to me if he isn't really refined—not a bit. But—but I'd rather not talk to him just now. I—I prefer to see Mrs. Ull. "

I can't say just what I felt so friendly and fraternal to him about then; but I did. "Westy, " says I, "take my advice about this hunch of yours to see Mother. Don't! "

"But really," he insists, "I must tell one or the other, don't you see. And unless I do it right away I know I never can at all. Besides I've made up my mind that Mrs. Ull ought to be the first to know. I—I'm going to ring for the maid and ask to see her."

"Good nerve!" says I, slappin' him on the shoulder. "In that case I'll just slip into the back room there and shut the door."

"Oh, I say!" says he, glancin' around panicky. "I—I wish you'd stay. I—I don't fancy facing her alone. Please stay!"

"It ain't reg'lar," says I.

"I don't care," says Westy, pleadin'. "You could sort of introduce me, you know, and—and help me out if I got stuck. You would, wouldn't you?"

And it was amazin' how diff'rent I felt towards Westy from five minutes before. His best friend couldn't have looked on him fonder, or promised to stand by him closer. I calls the maid myself, discovers that Mrs. Ull is in the upstairs sittin' room, and sends the message that Mr. Westlake would like to see her right off about something important.

"But you got to buck up, my boy," says I; "for from all the dope I've had you've got a jolt comin' to you."

That wa'n't any idle rumor, either. He'd hardly begun pacin' restless in and out among the chairs and tables before we hears a heavy pad-pad on the stairs, and the next thing we know the lady is standin' in the door.

Not such an awful stout old party as I'd looked for, nor she didn't have such a bad face; but with the funny way she has her hair bobbed up, and the weird way her dress fits her, like it had been cut out left-handed in a blind asylum—well, she's a mess, that's all. It's an expensive lookin' outfit too, and the jew'lry display around her lumpy neck and on her pudgy fingers was enough to make you blink; but somehow it all looked out of place.

For a second she stands there fingerin' her rings fidgety, and then remarks unexpected: "It's about Doris, ain't it? Well, young feller, what is it you got on your mind? "

And all of a sudden I tumbles to the fact that she's lookin' straight at me. Then it was my turn to go panicky. "Excuse me, Ma'am, " says I hasty, "but that's the guilty party, the one over by the fireplace. Mr. Westlake, Ma'am. "

"Oh! " says she. "That one, eh? Well, let's have it! " and with that she paddles over to a high-backed, carved mahogany chair and settles herself sort of grim and defiant. I almost had to push Westy to the front too.

"I expect you've talked this all over with her father, eh? " she goes on. "I'm always the last to get wise to anything that goes on in this house, specially if it's about Doris. Come, let's have it! "

"But I haven't seen Mr. Ull at all, " protests Westy. "It—it's just happened. And I thought you ought to know first. I want to ask you, Mrs. Ull, if I may marry Doris? "

We wa'n't lookin' for what come next, either of us; her big red face had such a hard, sullen look on it, like she knew we was sizin' her up and meant to show us she didn't give a hoot what we thought. But as Westy finishes and bows real respectful, holdin' out his hand friendly, the change come. The hard lines around her mouth softens, the narrowed eyes widen and light up, and her stiff under jaw gets trembly. A tear or so trickles foolish down the side of her nose; but she don't pay any attention. She's just starin' at Westy.

"You—you wanted me to know first, did you? " says she, with a break in her shrill, cackly voice. "Me? "

"I thought it only right, " says Westy. "You're Doris's mother, you know, and——"

"Good boy! " says she, reachin' out after one of his hands and pattin' it. "I'm glad you did too. Doris, she's got too fine for her old mother. That ain't so much her fault as it is mine, I expect. I'm kind of rough, and a good deal behind the times. I ain't kept up, not even the way Leo has. But then, I ain't had the chance. I've been at home, lookin' after the boys and—and Doris. I saw she was gettin' spoiled; but I didn't have the heart to bring her home and stop it. She's young, though. She'll get over it. You'll help her. Oh, I know about you. Quite a young swell, you are; but I guess you're all right. And I'm glad for Doris. Maybe too, she'll find out some day that her rough old mother, who got left so far behind, thinks a lot of her still. You—you'll tell her as much some time perhaps. Won't you? "

Say, take it from me, I was so misty in the eyes about then, and so choky under my collar, that I couldn't have done it myself. But Westy did. There's a heap more to him than shows on the outside.

"Mrs. Ull, " says he, "I shall tell Doris all of that, and much more. And I'm sure that both of us are going to be very fond of you. And if you don't mind, I'm going to begin now to call you Mother. "

Yes, I was gettin' a little uneasy at that stage. I hadn't counted on bein' let in for quite such a close fam'ly scene. And when the two girls showed up with their arms locked about each other, and Vee leads Doris up to Mother Ull, and they goes to a three-cornered clinch, sobbin' on one another's shoulder—well, I faded.

On the way home I was struck by a sudden thought that trickled all the way down my spine like a splinter of ice. "If I ever had the luck to get that far, " thinks I, "would I have to go through any such an act with Aunty? Hel-lup, Hubert! Hel-lup! "

CHAPTER VIII

SOME GUESSES ON RUBY

Well, I'm shocked at Ruby, that's all. Also I'm beginnin' to suspicion I ain't such a human-nature dope artist as I thought, for I've made at least three fruity forecasts on Ruby, and the returns are still comin' in.

My first frame-up was natural enough. When this goose-necked young female with the far-away look in her eyes appeared as No. 7 in our batt'ry of lady typists, and I heard Mr. Robert havin' a séance tryin' to dictate some of the mornin' correspondence to her, I swung round with a grin on my face and took a second look. She was fussed and scared.

No wonder; for Mr. Robert has a shorthand system of his own that he uses in dictatin' letters. He'll reel off the name and address all right, and then simply sketch in what he wants said, without takin' pains to throw in such details as "Replying to yours of even date," or "We are in receipt of yours of the 20th inst." And the connectin' links he always leaves to the stenog.

Course that don't take much bean after they get used to his ways; but this fairy in the puckered black velvet waist and the white linen cuffs hadn't been on the Corrugated staff more 'n three days, and this was her first tryout on private officework. She'd been told to read over the last letter fired at her, and she was doin' it like this:

> BAILY, BANKS & BAKER, Something-or-other Chestnut, Philadelphia. Look up the number, will you? Gentlemen— and so on. Ah—er—what's that note of theirs? Oh, yes! Shipments of ore will be resumed—

Which was where Mr. Robert stops her. "Pardon me," says he, "but before we go any further just how much of that rubbish do you mean to transcribe?"

"Why, " says Ruby, starin' at him vacant, "I—I took down just what you said. "

"Mm-m-m! " says he sarcastic. "My error. And—er—that will be all. " Then, when she's gone, he growls savage: "Delightful, eh? You noticed her, didn't you, Torchy? "

"The mouth breather? " says I. "Sure! That's Ruby. Nobody home, and the front door left open. One of Piddie's finds, I expect. "

"Ring for him, will you? " says Mr. Robert.

Poor Piddie! He was almost as fussed as Ruby had been. He admits takin' her on, but insists that she brought a good letter from some Western mill concern and was a wonder at takin' figures.

"Keep her on them and out of here, then, " says Mr. Robert. "And if you love peace, Mr. Piddie, avoid sending her to the governor. "

Which was a good hunch too. What Old Hickory would have remarked if them letters had got to him it ain't best to imagine. Besides, that stare of Ruby's would have got on his nerves from the start; for it's the weirdest, emptiest, why-am-I-here look I ever saw outside a nut fact'ry. Kind of a hauntin' look too. I couldn't help watchin' for it every time I passes through the front office, just to see if it had changed any. And it didn't—always the same!

Then here one day when I has to cook up some tabulated stuff for the Semiannual me and Ruby had a three-hour session together, me readin' off long strings of numbers, and her thumpin' 'em out on the keys. We got along fine too, and when I says as much at the finish she jars me almost speechless by shootin' over a shy, grateful look and smilin' coy.

From then on it was almost a case of friendly relations between me and Ruby, conducted on the basis of about two smiles a day. Poor thing! I expect them was about the only friendly motions she went through durin' business hours; for she didn't seem to mix at all with the other lady typists, and as for the young sports around the shop — well, to them Ruby was a standin' joke.

And you could hardly blame 'em. Them back-number costumes of hers looked odd enough mixed in with all the harem effects and wired-neck ruffs that the others wore down to work. But when it come to doin' her hair Ruby was in a class by herself. No spit curls or French rolls for her! She sticks to the plain double braid, wound around her head smooth and slick, like the stuff they wrap Chianti bottles in, and with her long soup-viaduct it gives her sort of a top-heavy look. Sort of dull, ginger-colored hair it is too. Besides that she's a tall, shingle-chested female, well along in the twenties, I should judge, and with all the earmarks of bein' an old maid.

So shock No. 2 is handed me when I discovers how the high-shouldered young husk with the wide-set blue eyes, that I'd seen hangin' round the Arcade on and off, was really waitin' for Ruby. Uh-huh! I stood and watched 'em sidle up to each other and go driftin' out into Broadway hand in hand. A swell pair they'd make for a Rube vaudeville act! Honest, with a few make-up touches, they could have walked right on and had the gallery with 'em!

Believe me, I couldn't miss a chance to josh Ruby some on that. I shoves it at her next day when I comes back early from lunch and finds her brushin' her sandwich crumbs into the waste basket.

"Now don't spring any musty first-cousin gag on me, " says I; "for it don't go with the fond, palm-pressin' act. Steady comp'ny, ain't he? "

Which was where you'd expect her to turn pink in the ears and let loose a giggle. But not Ruby. She's a solemn, serious-minded party, Ruby is. "Do you mean Mr. Lindholm? " says she.

"Heavings! " says I. "Do you have relays of 'em? I'm referrin' to the stocky-built young Romeo that picked you up at the door last night. "

"Oh, yes, " says she placid, "Nelson Lindholm. We had Sanskrit together. "

"Eh?" says I. "Sans-which? What kind of a disease is that?"

"It's a language," explains Ruby. "We were in the same class. I thought it might help me in my foreign mission work. I'm sure I don't know why Nelson took it, though. He was studying electrical engineering."

"Maybe it was catchin', at that," says I. "Where was all this?"

"At the Co-ed," says Ruby. "But then I'd known Nelson before. He's from Naukeesha too."

"Come again," says I. "From what?"

"Naukeesha," repeats Ruby, just as if it was some common name like Patchogue or Hoboken.

"Is that an island somewhere," says I, "or just a mixed drink?"

"Why," says she, "it's a town; in Wisconsin, you know."

"Think of that!" says I. "How they do mess up the map! What's it like, this Naukeesha?"

And for the first time Ruby shows some traces of life. "It's nice," says she, "real nice. Not at all like New York."

"Ah come, not so rough!" says I. "What you got special against our burg here?"

Ruby lapses back into her vacant stare and sort of shivers. "It's so big and—and whirly!" says she. "I don't like things to be whirly. Then the people are so strange, and their faces so hard. If—if I should fall down in one of those crowds, I'm sure they would walk right over me, trample on me, without caring."

"Pooh!" says I. "You'll work up a rush-hour nerve in a month or so. Of course, havin' always lived in a place like Naukeesha——"

Torchy, Private Sec.

"But I haven't, " corrects Ruby. "I was born in Kansas. "

"As bad as that! " says I. "And your folks moved up there later, eh? "

"No, " says she. "They—they—I lost them there. A cyclone, you know. "

"You don't mean, " says I, "that—that——"

"Yes, " says she, "Mother, Father, and my two brothers. We were all together when it struck; that is, I was just coming in from the kitchen. I'd been shutting the windows. I saw them all go—whirled off, just like that. The chimney fell, big beams came down, then it was all smoky and dark. I must have been blown through a window. My face was cut a little. I never knew. Neighbors found me in a field by a stump. They found the others too—laid them side by side in the wagon shed. Nothing else was left standing. It's dreadful, being in a cyclone—the roar, you know, and things coming at you in the dark, and that feeling of being lifted and whirled. I was only twelve; but I—I can't forget. And when I'm in big, noisy places it all comes back. I suppose I'm silly. "

Was she? Say, what's your guess about that? And, take it from me, I didn't wonder any more at that stary look of hers. She'd seen 'em all go—four of 'em. Good-night! I talked easy and soothin' to Ruby after that.

"Then I went up to live with Uncle Edward at Naukeesha, " she trails along. "He's a minister there. It was he who suggested my going into foreign mission work. I had to do something, you know, and I'd always been such a good scholar. I love books. So I studied hard, and was sent to the Co-ed. But the languages took so much time. Then I had to skip several terms and work to help pay my expenses. I worked during vacations too, at anything. Now I'm waiting for a field. They send you out when there's a vacancy. "

"How about Nelson? " says I. "He's goin' to be a missionary too? "

"He doesn't want me to go, " says Ruby, shakin' her head. "That is why he came on. He had charge of the electric light plant too, a good place. And here he gets only odd jobs. I tell him he's silly to stay. I can't see why he does. "

"Asked him, have you? " says I.

"Why, no, " says Ruby.

"Shoot it at him to-night, " says I.

But she shakes her head, opens her notebook, and feeds in a copyin' sheet as the clock points to 1. I looks up just in time to catch a couple of them cheap bondroom sports nudgin' each other as they passes by. Thought I'd been joshin' the Standin' Joke, I expect. Well, that's the way I started in, I'll admit.

It's only a day or so later I has the luck to run across Oakley Mills. Something had come up that needed to be passed on by Mr. Robert, and as he was still out lunchin' I scouts over to his club, and finds him stowed away at a corner table with this chatty playwright party.

He's quite a swell, Oakley is, you know; and I guess with one Broadway hit in its second year, and a lot of road comp'nies out, he can afford to flit around under the white lights. Him and Mr. Robert has always been more or less chummy, and every now and then they get together like this for a talkfest. As Mr. Mills seems to be right in the middle of something as I drifts in, Mr. Robert waves me to a chair and signals him to keep on, which he does.

"It's a curious mess, that's all, " says Oakley, spreadin' out his manicured fingers and shruggin' his shoulders under his Donegal Norfolk. "I'm not sure if the new piece will ever go on. "

"Another procrastinating producer? " asks Mr. Robert careless.

"No, a finicky author this time, " says Oakley. "You see, there is one part, a character part, which I'm insisting must be cast right. It seemed easy at first. But these women of our American stage! No training, no facility, no understanding! Not one of them can fill it, and we've tried nearly a dozen. If I could only find the original! "

"Eh? " says Mr. Robert, who's been payin' more attention to manipulatin' the soda siphon than to Oakley's beefin'. "What original? "

"The dumbest, woodenest, most conscientious young female person it has ever been my lot to meet, " goes on Mr. Mills. "Talk about your rare types! You should have known Faithful Fannie (my name for her, you know). It was out in the Middle West last summer. I had two or three weeks' work to do on the new piece, revising it to fit Amy Dean. All stars of that magnitude demand it, you understand.

"Well, I should have stayed right here until it was done, but some Chicago friends wanted me to go with them up into the lake region, promised me an ideal place to work in—all that. So I went. I might have had better sense. You know these bungalow colonies in the woods—where they live in fourteen-room log cabins, fitted with electric lights and English butlers? Bah! It was bridge and tennis and dancing day and night, with a new mob every week-end. Work? As well try it in the middle of the Newport Casino.

"So I hunted up a little third-rate summer hotel a mile or so off, where the guests were few and the food wretched, and camped down with my mangled script and my typewriter. There I met Fannie the Unforgetful. She was the waitress I happened to draw out of a job lot. I suppose it was her début at that sort of thing. For the sake of hungry humanity I hope it was. What she did not know about serving was simply amazing; but her capacity for absorbing suggestions and obeying orders was profound. 'Could I have a warm plate? ' I asked at the first meal. 'Oh, certainly, Sir, ' says Fannie, and from then on every dish she brought me was piping hot, even to the cold-meat platter and the ice cream saucer. It was that way with every wish I was rash enough to express. Fannie never forgot, and she kept to the letter of the law.

"Also she would stand patiently and watch me eat. That is, she would fix her eyes on me intently, never moving, and keep them there for a quarter of an hour at a time. A little embarrassing, you know, to be so constantly observed. She had such big, stary eyes too, absolutely without any expression in them. To break the spell I would order things I didn't want, just to get her out of the way for a moment or so while I snatched a few unwatched bites. You know how it is? There's green corn. Now I like to tackle that with both hands; but I don't care to be closely inspected while I'm at it. I used to fancy that her gaze was somewhat critical. 'Good heavens, Girl! ' I said one day. 'Can't you look somewhere else—at the ceiling, or out of the window? ' She chose the ceiling. It was a bit weird to have her stationed opposite me, her eyes rolled heavenward. Uncanny! It attracted the attention of the other guests. But it was something of a relief. I could watch her then.

"There was something fascinating about Faithful Fannie, though, as there is about all unusually plain persons. Not that she was positively homely. Her features were regular enough, I suppose. But she was such a tall, slim, colorless, neutral creature! And awkward! You've seen a young turkey, all legs and neck, with its silly head bobbing above the tall grass? Well, something like that. And as I never read at my meals I had nothing else to do but study that sallow, unmoving face of hers with its steady, emotionless, upward gaze. Was she thinking? And what about! Who was she? Where had she come from?

"A haunting face, Fannie's was; at least, for me. It became almost an obsession. I could see it as I sat down to my work. And the first thing I knew I was writing Fannie into my play. There was a maid's part in it, —the conventional, table-dusting, note-carrying, tea-serving maid, with not half a dozen words to speak. But before I knew it this insignificant part had become so elaborated, I had sketched in Fannie's personality so vividly, that the whole action and theme of the piece were revolving about her—hinged on her. I couldn't seem to stop, either. I wrote on and on and—well, by Jove! it ended in my turning out something entirely different from that which I had begun. The original skeleton is still there, the characters are the same;

but the values have exchanged places. This is a Fannie play through and through. And it's good, the biggest thing I've done; but——"
Once more Oakley shrugs his shoulders and ends with a deep sigh.

"Rubbish! " says Mr. Robert. "You and your artistic temperament! What's the real trouble, anyway? "

"As I've tried to make clear to your limited and wholly commercialized intelligence, " comes back Mr. Mills, "I have created a character which is too deep and too subtle for any available American actress to handle. If I could only find the original now, with her tractable genius for doing exactly what she was told——"

"Why not send out for her, then? " asks Mr. Robert.

"As though I hadn't! " says Oakley. "Two weeks ago I located the hotel manager in Florida and wired him a full description of the girl. All I got from him was that he'd heard she was somewhere in New York. "

"How simple! " says Mr. Robert. "Here is my young friend Torchy, with wits even more brilliant than his hair. Ask him to find Fannie for you. "

"A girl whose name I don't even know! " protests Oakley. "How in blazes could anyone trace a——"

"I'll bet you the dinners, " cuts in Mr. Robert, "that Torchy can do it. "

"Taken, " says Mr. Mills, and turns to me brisk. "Now, young man, what further details would you like? "

"Don't happen to have a lock of her hair with you? " says I, grinnin'.

"Alas, no! " says he. "She favored me with no such mark of her esteem. "

"Was it kind of ginger-colored, " says I, "and done in a braid round her head? "

"Why—er—I believe it was, " says he.

"And didn't she have sort of droopy shoulders, " I goes on, "and a trick of starin' vague, with her mouth part way open? "

"Yes, yes! " says he eager. "But—but whom are you describing? "

"Ruby Everschott, " says I. "Come down to the Corrugated and take a look. "

Course it seemed like a 100 to 1 chance, but when I got the Wisconsin part of his yarn, and tacked it onto the rest, it didn't seem likely one State could produce two such specimens. Inside of fifteen minutes the three of us was strollin' casual through the front offices.

"Glance down the line of lady typists, " I whispers to Oakley.

"By George! " says he gaspy. "The one at the far end? "

"You win, " says I.

"And you also, my young wizard, " says Oakley.

"I'll have her sent into my private office, " suggests Mr. Robert.

And once more I was lookin' for some startled motions from Ruby when she discovers Mr. Mills. But in she comes, as woodeny and stiff as ever, goes to her little table, and spreads out her notebook, without glancin' at any of us.

"Pardon me, Miss Everschott, " says Mr. Robert, "but—er—my friend Mills here fancies that he—er—ah—oh, hang it all! you say it, Oakley. "

At which Mr. Mills steps up smilin'. I should judge he was a fairly smooth, high-polished gent as a rule; but after Ruby has turned that stupid, stary look on him, without battin' an eyelash or liftin' an eyebrow, the smile fades out. She don't say a word or make a move: just continues to stare. As for Oakley, he shifts uneasy on his feet and flushes up under the eyes.

"Well? " says he. "I trust you remember me? "

Ruby shakes her head slow. "No, Sir, " says she.

"Eh? " says Oakley. "Weren't you a waitress at the Lakeside Hotel last summer? "

"Certainly, Sir, " says Ruby.

"And didn't you bring me my meals three times a day for four mortal weeks? " he insists.

"Did I? " says Ruby, starin' stupider than ever.

"Great Scott, young woman! " breaks out Oakley. "Didn't you look at me long enough and steadily enough to remember? Don't you recall I was disagreeable enough to ask you not to watch me eat? "

"Oh! " says Ruby, a flicker of almost human intelligence in her big eyes. "The one who wanted hot plates! "

"At last, " says Oakley, "I am properly identified. Yes, I am the hot-plate person. "

"You had tea for breakfast too, didn't you? " asks Ruby.

"Always, " says he. "An eccentricity of mine. "

"And you put salt on your muskmelon, and wanted your eggs opened, and didn't like tomato soup, " adds Ruby, like she was repeatin' a lesson.

Torchy, Private Sec.

"Guilty on all three counts," says Mr. Mills.

"I tried to remember," says Ruby, sort of meek.

"Tried!" gasps Oakley. "Why, you made an art of it. You never so much as—— But tell me, was it those foolish little whims of mine you were thinking so hard about while you stood there gazing so intently at me?"

Ruby nods; a shy, bashful little nod.

Mr. Mills makes a low bow. "A thousand pardons, my dear young lady!" says he. "I stand convicted of utter selfishness. But perhaps I can atone."

And with that he proceeds to put his proposition up to her. He tells her about the play, the trouble he's had tryin' to fit one special part, and how he's sure she could do it to a T. He asks her to give it a try.

"Go on the stage!" says Ruby, her big eyes starin' at him like he'd asked her to jump off the Metropolitan Tower. "No, I don't think I could. I'm going to be a foreign missionary, you know."

"A—a what?" gasps Oakley. "Missionary! But see here—that can wait. And in one season on the stage you could make——"

Well, I must say Oakley argued it well and put it strong; but he'd have produced just as good results if he'd been out in the square askin' the bronze statue of Lafayette to hand him down a match. Ruby drops back into her vague gazin' act and shakes her head. So at last he ends by askin' her to think it over for a day, and Ruby goes back to her desk.

"How absurd!" growls Oakley. "But I simply must have her. Why, we would pay her three hundred dollars a week."

I catches my breath at that. "Excuse me if I seem to crash in," says I, "but was that a gust of superheated air, or did you mean it?"

"I should be glad to submit a contract to Miss Everschott on those terms," says he.

"Then leave it to me," says I; "that is, to me and Nelson."

Did we win Ruby? Say, with our descriptions of what three hundred a week might mean in the way of Christmas presents to Uncle Ed, and donations to the poor box, and a few personal frills on the side, we shot that foreign missionary scheme so full of holes it looked like a last year mosquito bar at the attic window.

"But I'm sure I sha'n't like it at all," says Ruby as she signs her name.

I didn't deny that. I knew she was in for a three weeks' drillin' by the roughest stage manager in the business. You know who. But he can deliver the goods, can't he? He makes the green ones act. Look at what he did with Ruby! Only it don't seem like actin' at all. She's just Ruby, in the same puckered waist, her hair mopped around her head in the same silly braid, and that same stary look in her big eyes. But it gets 'em strong. Packed every night!

I meets Nelson here only yesterday, and he was tellin' me. Comin' along some himself, Nelson is. He's opened an office and is biddin' for big jobs.

"I've just landed my first contract," says he.

"Good!" says I. "What's it for?"

"A fifty-foot, twenty-thousand-candle-power sign over the theater," says he, "with Ruby's name in it. She's signed up for another year, you know."

"Well, well!" says I. "Then it's all off with the heathen, eh?"

And Nelson he drifts up the street wearin' a grin.

CHAPTER IX

TORCHY GETS AN INSIDE TIP

There was two commuters, one loaded down with a patent runner sled, the other chewin' a cigar impatient and consultin' his watch; a fat woman with a six-year-old who was teasin' to go see Santa Claus in the window again; a sporty-lookin' old boy with a red tie who was blinkin' googoos out of his puffy eyes; and then there was me, draped in my new near-English top coat and watchin' the swing doors expectant.

So you see they ain't particular who hangs out in these department store vestibules. But I'll bet I had the best excuse! I was waitin' for Vee! She'd gone in at five-twenty-one, sayin' she'd be only a couple of minutes; so she wa'n't really due for half an hour yet.

The commuter with the sled had just been picked up by Wifey, loaded down with more bundles, and rushed off for the five-forty-something for Somewhere, and a new recruit in the shape of a fish-eyed gink with a double-chin dimple had drifted in, when I has the feelin' that someone has sidled up to me from the far door at the left and is standin' there. Then comes the timid hail:

"I beg pardon, Sir. "

You'd naturally look for somebody special after that, wouldn't you? But what I finds close to my elbow is a wispy little girl with a pinched, high-strung look on her thin face, an amazin' collection of freckles, and a pleadin' look in her big, blue-gray eyes. She's costumed mainly in a shaggy tam-o'-shanter that comes down over her ears, and an old plaid cape that must have been some vivid in its color scheme when it was new.

"Eh, Sister? " says I, gawpin' at her.

"Is it true about the work papers, Sir? " says she.

"The which?" says I, not gettin' her for a second. "Oh! Work papers? Sure! They can't take you on unless you're over fourteen and have been to school so many weeks."

"Not anywhere? Wouldn't they?" she insists.

I shakes my head. "Wouldn't dare," says I. "They'd be fined if they did."

"Th-thank you, Sir," says she. "That's what the man said."

She was winkin' both eyes hard to hold the brine back, and her under lip was trembly; but she was keepin' her chin up brave and steady. She'd turned to go when she swings around.

"Please, Sir," says she, "where does one go when one is tired?"

"Why, Sis," says I sort of quizzin', "what's the matter with home?"

"But if one has no home?" she comes back at me solemn.

"The case being that of a little girl," says I, "she wanders around until she's collected by a cop, turned over to the Children's Society, and committed to some home."

"But I mustn't go there," says she, glancin' around scary. "No, not to a home. Daddums said not to."

"Did, eh?" says I. "Then why don't he—— By the way, just where is Daddums?"

"Taken up," says she.

"You mean pinched?" says I.

"I think so," says she. "Cook says the bobbies came for him. He left word with her that I wasn't to worry, as he'd be let out soon, and I was to stay where I was. Three weeks ago that was, and—and I haven't heard from Daddums since."

"Huh!" says I. "Listens like a case of circumstances over which—— But where did you pick up that trick of speakin' of coppers as bobbies?"

"I beg pardon, Sir?" says she.

"That tells it," says I. "English, ain't you?"

"London, Sir, Brompton Road," says she.

"Been over long?" says I.

"A matter of three months, Sir," says she.

"And what's the name?" says I.

"Mine?" says she. "Helma Allston. And yours, please, Sir?"

I wa'n't lookin' for her to send it back so prompt. She ain't at all fresh about it, you know: just easy and natural. I don't know when I've run across a youngster with such nice manners.

"Why," says I, "I guess you can call me Torchy."

"Thank you, Mr. Torchy," says she, doin' a little dancin'-school duck. "And if you don't mind, I'd like to—to stay here for a minute or two while I think what I'd best—— O-o-o-oh!" She sort of moans out this last panicky and shrinks against the wall.

"Well, what's the trouble now?" says I.

"That's the one!" she whispers husky. "The—the man in the blue cap—the one who told me about the work papers. He said I was to clear out too."

And by followin' her scared glances I discovers this low-brow store sleuth scowlin' ugly at her.

"Pooh! " says I. "Only one of them cheap flat-foots. Don't mind him. You're waitin' with me, you know. Here! " And I reaches down a hand to her.

Maybe it wa'n't some grateful look Helma flashes up as she slips her slim, cold little fingers into mine and snuggles up like a lost kitten. The store sleuth he stares puzzled for a second; but the near-English top coat must have impressed him, for he goes sneakin' back down the main aisle.

So here I am, with this freaky little stray under my wing, when Vee comes sailin' out, all trim and classy in her silver fox furs, with a cute little hat to match, and takes in the picture. Maybe you can guess too, how the average young queen in her set would have curled her lip at sight of that faded cape and oversized cap. But not Vee! She just indulges in a flickery smile, then straightens her face out and remarks:

"Well, Torchy, I haven't had the pleasure, have I? "

Say, she's a real sport, Vee is, take it from me!

"Guess not, " says I. "This is Helma, late of London, just now at large. It's a case of one's havin' mislaid one's home. "

"Oh! " says Vee, a little doubtful. "And one's parents too? "

"Painful subject, " says I, shakin' my head warnin'.

But Helma ain't the kind to gloss things over. She speaks right out. "If you please, Miss, " says she, "I've no mother, and Daddums has been taken up—the bobbies, you know. And I fancy the money he left for my board must have been all used; for I heard the landlady say I'd have to go to a home. So before daylight this morning I slipped out the front door. I'm not going back, either. I—I'm looking for work. "

"For work! " says Vee, starin' first at me and then at Helma. "You absurd little thing! Why, how old are you? "

"I was twelve last month, Miss, " says Helma, bobbin' polite.

"And you've been out since daylight? " demands Vee. "Where did you have breakfast and luncheon? "

"I—I didn't have them at all, Miss, " admits Helma.

Vee presses her lips together sudden and then shoots a knowin' look at me. "There! " says she. "That reminds me. I haven't had tea, either. Well, Torchy? "

"My blow, " says I. "I was just goin' to mention it. There's a joint somewhere near, ain't there? "

"Top floor, " says Vee. "Come, Helma, you'll go with us, won't you? "

And you should have seen the admirin' look Vee got back in exchange for the smile she gives Helma! The look never fades, either, all the while Helma is puttin' away a pot of chocolate, a club sandwich, and an order of toasted muffins and marmalade. She just lets them big eyes of hers travel up and down, from Vee's smooth-fittin' gloves to the little wisp of straw-colored hair that curls up over the side of her fur hat. You couldn't blame Helma. I took a peek now and then myself.

Meanwhile we has a good chance to inspect this waif that's been sort of wished on us. Such a sharp, peaked little face she has, and such bright, active eyes, that it gives her a wide-awake, live-wire look, like a fox terrier. Then the freckles—just spattered with 'em, clear across the bridge of her nose and up to where the carroty hair begins. Like rust specks on a knife blade, they were.

"You didn't get all those livin' in London, did you? " says I.

"Oh, no, Sir, " says she. "Egypt mostly, and then down in Devon. You see, Sir Alfred used to let Daddums take me along. Head butler, you know, Daddums was—until the war. Then Sir Alfred went off with his regiment, and Haldeane House was shut up, like so many others. Daddums was too old to enlist, and besides there was no one to leave me with. So he had to try for a place over here. I—I wish he hadn't. It was awful of the bobbies, wasn't it? "

"Looks so from here, " says I. "Was it jew'lry that was missin', or what? "

"Money, Cook said, " says Helma. "Oh, a lot! Fancy! Why, everyone knows Daddums wouldn't do a thing like that. They could ask Sir Alfred. Daddums was with him ever so long—since I was a little, little girl. "

I glances across at Vee, and she glances back. That's all; but them big eyes of Helma's don't miss it.

"You—you don't believe he took the money, do you? " says she, wistful and pleadin'.

At which Vee reaches over and pats her soothin' on the hand. "I don't believe a word of it, " says she.

"He's a good Daddums, " goes on Helma, spreadin' the last of the marmalade on a buttered muffin. "He was going to take me to Australia, where Uncle Verne has a big sheep ranch. And he'd promised to buy me a sheep pony, all for my very own. I love riding, don't you? In Egypt I had a donkey with a white face; but only hired from Hassan, you know. And in Devon there was a cunning little Shetland that Hobbs would sometimes let me take out. But here! I stay in a dark little room alone for hours. I—I don't like it at all. But it costs such a lot to get to Australia, and Daddums hasn't been well, —he's had a cold on his chest, —and he's been afraid he would lose his place and have to go to a hospital. Just before he was taken up, though, he told me we were to sail for Melbourne soon. Daddums had found a way."

This time I took care that Helma wa'n't lookin' before I glances at Vee. I shakes my head dubious, indicatin' I wa'n't so sure about Daddums. But Vee only tosses up her chin and turns to Helma.

"Of course he would!" says she. "What have you in your lap, Child?"

The kid pinks up and produces a battered old doll, —one of these cloth-topped, everlastin' affairs, that looks like it had come from the Christmas tree quite some seasons back.

"This is my dear Arabella," says Helma in her old-maid way. "I suppose I'm too old to play with dolls now; but I—I can't give her up. Only the night before Daddums went off I missed her for a while and thought she was lost. I cried myself to sleep. But what do you think? In the morning I found her again, right beside me on the pillow. I haven't gone a step without her since."

"You dear little goose!" says Vee, reachin' out impetuous and givin' her a hug. "And where do you think you're going, you and your Arabella?"

"I don't know," says Helma. "Only I mustn't let them put me in a home; for then I couldn't go with Daddums when he came out—you see?"

Sure, we saw—that and a lot more. I could tell that Vee was puzzlin' over the situation by the way she was starin' at the youngster and grippin' her muff. Course you might say we wa'n't any Rescue Mission, or anything like that; but somehow this was diff'rent. Here was Helma, right in front of us! And I'm free to admit the proposition was too much for me.

"Gee!" says I. "Handed out rough sometimes, ain't it? What's the answer, Vee?"

"There's only one, " says she. "I'm going to take Helma home with me. "

"What about Aunty? " says I.

At which Vee's lips come together and her shoulders straighten. "I know, " says she, "there'll be a row. Aunty's always saying that such affairs should be handled by institutions. But this time—well, we'll see. Come, Helma. "

"Oh, is it true? " gasps the youngster. "May I go with you? May I? "

And as I tucked 'em into a taxi, Arabella and all, Vee whispers: "Torchy, if you're any good at all, you'll go straight and find out all about Daddums and just make them let him out! "

"Eh? " says I. "Make 'em—say, ain't that some life-sized order? "

"Perhaps, " says she. "But you needn't come to see us until you've found him. Good-by! "

Just like that I got it! And, say, there wa'n't any use tryin' to kid myself into thinkin' maybe she don't mean it. I'd seen how strong this story of little Helma's had got to her; and, believe me, when Vee gets real stirred up over anything she's some earnest party—no four-flushin' about her! And it don't seem to make much diff'rence who blocks the path. Look at her then, sailin' off to go up against a stiff-necked, cold-eyed Aunty, who's a believer in checkbook charity, and mighty little of that! And just so I won't feel out of it she tosses me a job that would keep a detective bureau and a board of pardons busy for a month.

"Whiffo! " says I, gawpin' up the avenue after the cab. "And I pulled this down just by bein' halfway human! Oh, very well, very well! Here's where I strain something! "

Course, if I hadn't knocked around a newspaper office more or less, I wouldn't have known where to begin any more than—well, than the average private sec would. But them two years I spent outside the Sunday editor's door wa'n't all wasted. For instance, that's where I got to know Whitey Weeks. And now my first move is to pike down to old Newspaper Row and locate him. Inside of half an hour we'd done a lot too. We'd called up their headquarters' man on the 'phone and had him sketch off the case against one Allston, a butler.

"Yep, grand larceny, " says Whitey, his ear to the receiver. "We know that. How much? Eh? Twenty thousand! "

"Ah, tell him to turn over: he's on his back! " says I. "Not twenty thousand cash? "

"That's what he says, " insists Whitey, "all in hundreds. Lifted out of a secret wall safe. "

"Ask him where this guy was buttling, —in a bank, " says I, "or at the Subtreasury? "

And Whitey reports that Allston was workin' for a Mrs. Murtha, West 76th Street; "Mrs. Connie Murtha, you know, " he goes on, "the big poolroom backer, and one of the flossiest, foxiest widows in New York. "

"Then that accounts for the husky wad, " says I. "Twenty thousand! No piker, was he? Ask your man who's on the case? "

"Rusitelli & Donahue, " says Whitey. "Mike's a friend of mine too; but he never talks much. "

"Let's have a try, anyway, " says I.

So we runs this partic'lar detective sergeant down, drags him away from a penuchle game, and Whitey begins by suggestin' that we hear how he's done some clever work on the Allston case.

"I got him right, that's all, " says Mike. "And he'd faked up a nice little stall too. "

"Anything on him when you rounded him up?" asks Whitey.

Donahue shakes his head disgusted. "Stowed it," says he.

"Some cute, eh?" says Whitey.

"Bah!" says Mike. "Who was it sprung that tale about his being a big English crook? The Yard never heard of him. I doped him out from the first, though. Plain nut! The Chief wouldn't believe it until I showed him."

"Showed him what?" says Whitey, innocent like.

"This," says the sleuth, haulin' out of his pocket a bulgy envelope. "I found that in his room. Take a look," and he lifts the flap at the end.

"What the deuce!" says Whitey.

"Sawdust," says Mike, "just plain, everyday sawdust. I had it analyzed, —no dope, no nothing. Now tell me, would anyone but a nut do a thing like that?"

We both agreed nobody but a nut would; also we remarks in chorus that Mr. Donahue is some classy sleuth, which he don't object to at all. In fact, after I've explained how a relation of Allston's had asked me to look him up he fixes it so I can get a pass into the Tombs. Followin' which I blows Whitey to one of Farroni's seventy-five-cent spaghetti banquets and then goes home to think a few chunks of thought.

As the case stood it looked bad for Daddums. A party like Mrs. Connie Murtha, with all the police drag she must have, wa'n't goin' to be separated from her reserve roll without makin' somebody squirm good and plenty. He might have known that, if it was him turned the trick. Or was he nutty, like Donahue had said? Before I went any further I had to settle that point, and while I ain't strong for payin' visits through the iron bars I was up early next mornin' and down presentin' my pass.

"You cub lawyers give me shootin' pains in the neck! " grumbles the turnkey that tows me in.

"How'd you guess I wa'n't the new District Attorney? " says I. "Here, have a perfecto for that pain. " And that soothes him so much he loafs against the tier rail while I knocks on the door of Cell 69.

"I beg pardon? " says a deep, smooth voice, and up to the bars steps a tall, round-shouldered gent, with hair a little thin on top and a pair of reddish-gray butler sideboards in front of his ears. Not a bad face either, only the pointed chin is a little weak.

"I'm from Helma, " says I.

That jolts him at the start. His hands go trembly, and twice he makes a stab at speakin' before he can get the words out. "Is—isn't she all right? " says he. "I left her in lodgings, you know. I—I trust she——"

"She quit, " says I. "They was goin' to put her in a home. Picked me up on the street, you might say. But she's safe enough now. "

"Safe? " says he, dartin' over a suspicious look. "Where? "

"Take my word for it, " says I. "Maybe we can swap a little information later on. Now what about this grand larceny charge? "

"All rubbish! " says he. "Why, I hadn't been out of the house! They admit that. If I'd taken the money, wouldn't it have been found on me? "

"Then they pinched you on the premises? " says I. "I rather thought from what Helma said you'd been to see her that night? "

"Not since the night before, " says he. "Helma was down in the kitchen with Cook when they came. "

"Huh! " says I, rubbin' my chin as a help to deep thought. "The night before? "

I don't know why, either, but somehow that makes me think of sawdust, and from sawdust—say, I had it in a flash.

"Sorry, Allston, " says I, "but on account of Helma I was kind of in hopes they was just makin' a goat of you. She's a cute youngster—Helma. "

"She is all I have to live for, Sir, " says he, bowin' his head.

"Then why take such chances as this? " says I. "Twenty thousand! Say, you know this ain't any jay burg. You can't expect to get away with a wad like that. "

"I know nothing about the money, " says he, stiffenin' up. "They'll have to find it to prove I took it. "

"Big mistake No. 2, " says I. "They got to convict somebody, and the arrow points to you. About fifteen years would be my guess. Now come, Allston, what good would you be after fifteen years' hard? "

He shivers, but shrugs his shoulders dogged. "Poor little Helma! " says he. "Where is she? "

"Excuse me, Mr. Allston, " says I, "but that ain't the order of events. It's like this: First off you tell me where the wad is; then I tell you about Helma. "

Makes him groan a bit, that does, and he scowls at me stubborn. "They tried all that on at Headquarters, " says he. "It's no use. "

"You'd get off lighter if you told, " says I.

"I've nothing to tell, " he insists.

"How about swappin' what you know for two tickets to Australia? " I suggests.

"Hah! " says he. "Helma's been talkin'! "

"She's a chatty youngster, " says I, "and she thinks a heap of her Daddums. I ain't sure, though, whether you come first—or Arabella. "

If I hadn't been watchin' for it, I might not have noticed, but the quiver that begins in the fingers grippin' the bars runs clear up to the sagged shoulders. His mouth twitches nervous, and then he gets hold of himself.

"Oh, yes, " says he, forcin' a smile. "Her doll. She—she still has that, has she? "

"Uh-huh! " says I, watchin' him keen. "I'm keepin' close track of both. "

That little touch did the business. He begins pacin' up and down his cell, wringin' his hands. About the fourth lap he stops.

"If I only could take her to Australia, " says he, "and get her out of—of all this, I would be willing to—to——"

"That's enough, " says I. "All I want is your O. K. on any terms I can make with Mrs. Murtha. "

"She's a hard woman, " says he. "And she doesn't come by her money straight. "

"Nor lose it easy, " says I. "She wants it back. Might talk business, though, if I could show her how——"

"Anything! " says Allston. "Anything to get me out! "

"Now you're usin' your bean, " says I. "I'm off. Maybe you'll hear from me later. "

Course I didn't know what could be done, but I 'phones Piddie at the office to tell 'em I won't be in before lunch, and then I boards an uptown subway express. Easy enough findin' Mrs. Connie Murtha too. She's just finished a ten o'clock breakfast. A big, well-built, dashin' sort of party she is, with an enameled complexion and drugged hair. She's brisk and businesslike.

"If you've come to beg me to let up on that sneaking English butler, " says she, "you needn't waste any more breath. He's going to do time for this job. "

"But suppose he could be coaxed into tellin' where the loot was? " says I.

"He's had the third degree good and strong, " says she. "The boys told me so. He won't squeal. Donahue says he ain't right in his head. Anyway, he goes up. "

"He's leavin' a little girl, " I puts in, "without anyone to look after her. "

"Most crooks do, " says she, sniffin'.

"But if you could get the wad back? " says I.

"All of it? " says she quick.

"Every bean, " says I.

She leans forward, starin' at me hard and eager. "He'll tell, then? " says she.

"Said he would, " says I, "providin' him and the little girl could be shipped to Australia. "

She chews that over a minute. "That's cheap enough, " says she. "I could claim I'd remembered putting the money somewhere and forgotten. Young man, it's a bargain. I'll have my lawyer go down and — —"

"Say, " I breaks in, "why fat up a lawyer? Let's settle this between you and me. "

"But how? " says she.

"Just a minute, " says I, lookin' her full in the eyes. "I'm playin' you to give Allston a square deal, you know. "

"You can bank on that, " says she. "Connie Murtha's word was always as good as government bonds. And if you can wish back that twenty thousand, I'll put a quick crimp in this prosecution. "

"What could be fairer than that? " says I. "I'll be back in an hour. "

It was only forty-five minutes, in fact; but Mrs. Connie was watchin' for me.

"Let's have a pair of scissors, " says I, as I sheds my overcoat and produced from under one arm, where it had been buttoned up snug and tight, about the worst-lookin' doll you ever saw. I hadn't figured on Mrs. Murtha goin' huffy so sudden, either.

"You fresh young shrimp you! " she blazes out. "What's that? "

"This is Arabella, " says I. "She's sufferin' from a bad case of undigested securities, and I got to amputate. "

She stands by watchin' the operation suspicious and ready to lam me one on the ear, I expect. But on the way down I'd sounded Arabella's chest, and I was backin' my guess. When I found the coarse stitchin' done with heavy black thread I chuckles.

"More or less the worse for wear, Arabella, eh? " says I. "But how that youngster did hang onto her! Little Helma Allston, you know. And me offerin' to swap a brand-new two-dollar one that could open and shut its eyes! 'It's for Daddums, ' I says at last, and she gives up. There! Now we're gettin' to it. No wonder Arabella was some plump! "

"Well, of all places! " gasps out Mrs. Murtha, and, believe me, it don't take her long to leave Arabella flat as a pancake. "But how did he manage to——"

"It was the night before, " says I. "You didn't miss the roll until the next afternoon. And he ain't a reg'lar crook, you know. It was a case of bein' up against it, —sickness, and wantin' to get away somewhere with the kid. Honest, he don't strike me as such a bad lot: only a little limber in the backbone. Better count it. "

"All there, " she announces after runnin' through the bunch. "And maybe I'm not tickled to get it back! Catch me forgetting to lock that safe again! But I thought no one knew. Allston must have seen me moving the picture and guessed. Well, I'm not sore. Poor devil! I'll call up the District Attorney's office right away. He gets those tickets to Australia, too. Leave that to me. "

Yep! Mrs. Connie wa'n't chuckin' any bluff. She went down herself and had the indictment ditched.

I didn't mean to stage any heart-throb piece, either; but it just happens that yesterday, when we pulls off the final act, Vee tells me that Helma is in the libr'y, playin' nurse and hairdresser to Aunty's chief pet, a big orange Persian that she calls Prince Hal. That's how Helma had won out with Aunty, you know, by makin' friends with the cat.

"You tell her, " says Vee.

So I steps in quiet where the youngster is busy with the comb and brush. "Someone special to see Miss Helma, " says I.

"To see me? " says she, droppin' pussy and gazin' at the door. "Why, who can—— O-o-o-o-o! Daddums! Daddums! "

And as they rush to a fond clinch in one room something happens to me in the other. Uh-huh! I'm caught around the neck quick, and something soft and sweet hits me on the right cheek, and the next minute I'm bein' pushed away just as sudden.

"No, no!" says Vee. "That's enough. You're a dear, all the same. Of course I knew he didn't take it; but how in the world did you ever make them let him go?"

"Cinch!" says I. "I saw through the sawdust, and they didn't."

I couldn't let on, though, about that inside tip I got from Arabella.

CHAPTER X

THEN ALONG CAME SUKEY

It looked like it was Kick-in Day, or something like that; for here was Nutt Hamilton, a sporty young plute friend of Mr. Robert's, that I'm tryin' to entertain, camped in the private office, when fair-haired Vincent comes in off the brass gate to report respectful this new arrival.

"A gentleman to see Mr. Robert, Sir, " says he.

"Well, he's still out, " says I.

"So I told him, Sir, " says Vincent; "but then he asks if Mr. Ferdinand isn't here. I didn't know, Sir. Is there a——"

"Sure, Vincent, sure! " says I. "Brother-in-law Ferdie, you know. What's the gentleman's real name? "

"Mr. Blair Hiscock, " says Vincent, readin' the card.

"Ever hear that one? " I asks Hamilton, and he says he ain't. "Must be some fam'ly friend, though, " I goes on. "We'll take a chance, Vincent. Tell Blair to breeze in. "

I might have had bean enough to have looked for another pair of shell-rimmed glasses too. That's what shows up. Only this party, instead of beamin' mild and foolish through 'em, same as Ferdie does, stares through his sort of peevish. He's a pale-haired, sharp-faced, undersized young gent too, and dressed sort of finicky in one of them Ballyhooly cape coats, an artist necktie, and a two-story soft hat with a striped scarf wound around it.

"Well? " says I, leanin' back in the swing chair and doin' my best to spring the genial smile.

Torchy, Private Sec.

"Isn't Ferdinand here, then?" he demands, glancin' about impatient.

"Good guess," says I. "He ain't. Drifts in about once a month, though, as a rule, and as it's been three weeks or so since he was here last, maybe you'd like to— —"

"How absurd!" snaps Blair. "But he was to meet me here to-day at this time."

"Was, eh?" says I. "Well, if you know Ferdie, you can gamble that he'll be an hour or two behind, if he gets here at all."

"Thanks," says Blair, real crisp. "You needn't bother. I fancy I know Ferdie quite as well as you do."

"Oh, I wa'n't boastin'," says I, "and you don't bother me a bit. If you think Ferdie's liable to remember, you're welcome to stick around as long as— —"

"I'll wait half an hour, anyway," he breaks in.

"Then you might as well meet Mr. Hamilton," says I. "Friend of Mr. Robert's—Marjorie's too, I expect."

The two of 'em nods casual, and then I notices Nutt take a closer look. A second later a humorous quirk flickers across his wide face.

"Well, well!" says he. "It's Sukey, isn't it?"

At which Mr. Hiscock winces like he'd been jabbed with a pin. He flushes up too, and his thin-lipped, narrow mouth takes on a pout.

"I don't care to be called that," he snaps back.

"Eh?" says Nutt. "Sorry, old man; but you know, up at the camp summer before last—why, everyone called you Sukey."

"A lot of bounders they were too!" flares out Blair. "I—I'd asked them not to. And I'll not stand it! So there!"

"Oh!" says Hamilton, grinnin' tantalizin'. "My error. I take back the Sukey, *Mr.* Hiscock."

There's some contrast between the pair as they faces each other, — young Hiscock all bristled up bantam like and glarin' through his student panes; while Nutt Hamilton, who'd make three of him, tilts back easy in the heavy office armchair until he makes it creak, and just chuckles.

He's a chronic josher, Nutt is, —always puttin' up some deep and elaborate game on Mr. Robert, or relatin' by the hour the horse-play stunts he's pulled on others. A bit heavy, his sense of humor is, I judge. His idea of a perfectly good joke is to call up a bald-headed waiter at the club and crack a soft-boiled egg on his White Way, or balance a water cooler on top of a door so that the first party to walk under gets soaked by it, —playful little stunts like that. And between times, when he ain't makin' merry around town, he's off on huntin' trips, killin' things with portable siege guns. You know the kind, maybe.

So we ain't the chummiest trio that could be got together. Blair makes it plain that he has mighty little use for me, and still less for Hamilton. But Nutt seems to get a lot of satisfaction in keepin' him stirred up, winkin' now and then at me when he gets a rise out of Blair; though I must say, so far as repartee went, the little chap had all the best of it.

"Let's see," says Nutt, "what is your specialty? You do something or other, don't you?"

"Yes," says Blair. "Do you?"

"Oh, come!" says Nutt. "You play the violin, don't you?"

"How clever of you to remember! " says Blair. "Sorry I can't reciprocate. " And he turns his back.

But you can't squelch Hamilton that way. "Me? " says he. "Oh, potting big game is my fad. I got three caribou last fall, you know, and this spring I'm—say, Sukey, —I beg your pardon, Hiscock, — but you ought to come along with us. Do you good. Put some meat on your bones. We're going 'way up into Montana after black bear and silver-tips. I'd like to see you facing a nine-hundred-pound she bear with——"

"Would you? " cuts in Blair. "You know very well I'd be frightened half to death. "

"Oh, well, " says Nutt, "we'd stack you up against a cinnamon cub. "

"Any kind of bear I should be afraid of, " says Sukey.

"Not really! " says Hamilton. "Why, say——"

"Please! " protests Blair. "I don't care to talk about such creatures. I'm afraid of them even when I see them caged. I've an instinctive dread of all big beasts. Smile, if you like. But all truly civilized persons feel the same. I'm not a cave man, you know. Besides, I prefer telling the truth about such things to making believe I'm not afraid, as a lot of would-be mighty hunters do. "

"Not meaning me, I hope? " asks Nutt.

"If you're innocent, don't dodge, " says Blair. "And I—I think I'll not wait for Ferdinand any longer. Tell him I was here, will you? " And with a nod to me he does a snappy exit.

"A constant joy, Sukey is, " remarks Hamilton. "Why, when we were up in the Adirondacks that summer, we used to——"

What they used to do to Sukey I'll never know; for just then Mr. Robert sails in, and Nutt breaks off the account. He'd spieled along for half an hour in his usual vein when Mr. Robert flags him long enough to call me over.

"By the way, Torchy, " says Mr. Robert, "before I forget it——" and he hands me one of Marjorie's cards with a date and "Music" written in the southwest corner. I gazes at it puzzled.

"I strongly suspect, " he goes on, "that a certain young lady may be among those present. "

"Oh! " says I, pinkin' up some, I expect. "Much obliged. In that case I'm strong for music. Some swell piano performer, eh? "

"A young violinist, " says Mr. Robert, "a friend of Ferdie's, I believe, who——"

"Bet a million it's Sukey! " breaks in Nutt. "Blair Hiscock, isn't it! "

"That is his name, " admits Mr. Robert. "But this is to be nothing formal, you know: only Marjorie is bringing him down to the house, and has asked in a few people. "

"By George! " says Nutt, slappin' his knee enthusiastic. "Couldn't you get me in on that affair, Bob? "

"Why—er—I might, " says Mr. Robert. "I didn't know, though, that you were passionately fond of violin music. It's to be rather a classical programme, and——"

"Classic be blowed! " says Nutt. "What I want is a fair whack at Sukey. Seen him, haven't you? "

Mr. Robert shakes his head.

"Well, wait until you do, " says Hamilton. "Say, he's a rare treat, Sukey. About as big as a fox terrier, and just as snappy. Oh, you'll love Sukey! If he doesn't hand you something peppery before you've known him ten minutes, then I'm mistaken. Know what he used to call your sister Marjorie, summer before last? Baby Dimple! After a golf ball, you know. That's a sample of Sukey's tongue."

Mr. Robert shrugs his shoulders. "Quite her own affair, I suppose," says he.

"Oh, she didn't mind," says Nutt. "Everyone stands for Sukey—on account of his music. Only he is such a conceited, snobbish little whelp that it makes you ache to cuff him. Couldn't, of course. Why, he'll begin sniveling if you look cross at him! But it would be great sport to— — Say, Bob, who's going to be there—anyone special?"

"Only the family," says Mr. Robert, "and a few of Marjorie's friends, such as Verona Hemmingway and—er—Torchy here, and Josephine Billings, who's just come for the week-end."

"What!" says Hamilton. "Joey Billings? Say, she's a good sort, Joey; bully fun, and always in for anything. You ought to see her shoot! Yes, Sir! Bring down quail with a choke-bore, or knock over a buck deer with a rifle. Plays billiards like a wizard, Joey does, and can swat a golf ball off the tee for two hundred yards. She's a star. Staying at Ferdie's, eh? Must be a great combination, she and Sukey. I'd like to see 'em together. Say, old man, let me in on this musicfest if you can, will you?"

Course there wa'n't much left for Mr. Robert to do but promise, and while he don't do it with any great enthusiasm, Mr. Hamilton don't seem a bit discouraged. In fact, just before he goes he has a chucklin' fit like he'd been struck by some amazin' comic thought.

"I have it, Bob!" says he, poundin' Mr. Robert on the back. "I have it!"

"Anything you're likely to recover from?" remarks Mr. Robert.

"Never mind," says Nutt. "You wait and see! And the first chance you get ask Sukey if he's afraid of bears."

Torchy, Private Sec.

Just to finish off the afternoon too, and make the Corrugated gen'ral offices seem more like a fam'ly meetin' place, about four o'clock in blows Sister Marjorie from the shoppin' district, trailin' a friend with her; a stranger too. First off, from a hasty glimpse at the hard-boiled lid and the man's collar and the loose-fittin' top coat, I thought it was some chappy. So it's more or less of a shock when I discovers the short skirt and the high walkin' boots below. Then I tumbled. It's Joey, the real sport!

Believe me, she looked the part! One of these female good fellows, you know, ready to roll her own dope sticks, or sit in with the boys and draw three to a pair. Built substantial and heavy, Joey was, but not lumpy, like Marjorie. She swings in swaggery, gives Mr. Robert the college hick greetin', and when I'm introduced to her treats me to a grip that I felt the tingle of for half an hour.

"Hello, Kid!" says she. "I've heard of you. Torchy, eh? Well, the name's a fine fit."

"Yes," says I, "I was baptized with my hat off."

"Ripping!" says she. "I like that. Torchy! Couldn't be better."

"Not so poetic as Crimson Rambler," says I, "but easier to remember."

Hearty chuckles from Joey. "You're all right, Torchy," says she, rumplin' my hair playful.

Not at all hard to get acquainted with, Joey. One of the free and easy kind that gets to call men by their front names durin' the first half-hour. But somehow them's the ones that always seem to hang longest on the branch. You've noticed? Take Joey now, —well along towards thirty, so I finds out later, but still untagged and unchosen. Maybe she likes it better that way. Who knows? And, as Nutt Hamilton has suggested, it would be int'restin' to see her and Sukey lined up together.

Torchy, Private Sec.

That ain't exactly why I'm so early showin' up at the Ellins' house the night of the musical—not altogether. But what Vee and I has to say to one another durin' the half-hour we managed to slip over on Aunty don't matter. Vee was supposed to be arrangin' some flowers in the drawin' room, and I—well, I was helpin'. My long suit, arrangin' flowers; that is, when the planets are right.

But it goes quick. Pretty soon others begun buttin' in, and by eight-thirty there was a roomful, includin' Vee's Aunty, who watches me as severe as if I was a New Haven director. Joey Billings floats in too. And I got to admit that in an evenin' gown she ain't such a worse looker. Course her jaw outline is a trifle strong, and she has quite a swing to her hips; but she's so good-natured and cheerful lookin' that you 'most forget them trifles.

And Blair Hiscock, in his John Drew regalia, looks even thinner and whiter than ever; but he struts around as perky and important as if he was Big Bill Edwards. First off he has to have the piano turned the other way. Then, when he goes to unlimber his music rack, it develops that a big vase of American Beauties is too near his elbow. He glares at 'em pettish.

"Can't those things be taken out? " says he. "I detest heavy odors while I'm playin'! "

So the flowers are carted off. Then some draperies just back of him must be pulled together, so he won't feel a draught. After that he has the usual battle with his violin strings, while the audience waits patient, only exchangin' a smile now and then when Blair shows his disposition strongest.

At last, though, after makin' the accompanist take two fresh starts, he's off. Some goulash rhapsody, I believe it was, by a guy whose name sounds like a sneezin' fit. But, take it from me, that sharp-faced little wisp could do things to a violin! Zowie! He could just naturally make it sing, with weeps and laughs, and moans and giggles, and groans and cusswords, all strung along a jumpy, jerky little air that sort of played hide and seek with itself. Music? I should quiver! He had us all sittin' up with our ears stretched, and when he finishes and the applause starts in like a sudden shower on a tin roof what does he do but turn away with a bored look and shoot some spicy remark at the young lady pianist!

Next he gives a lullaby kind of thing, that's as sweet and touchin' as anything Farrar or Gluck could put over. He's just windin' that up and we're gettin' ready with more handclaps, when——

"Woof! Woof-woof!"

Some of the ladies gasps panicky. I got a little start myself, before I tumbled to what it was; for in through the draperies behind Sukey has shuffled about as good an imitation of a black bear as you'd want to see; a big, bulky bear, all complete, even to the dishpan paws and the wicked little eyes. It's scuffin' along on all-fours, waddlin' lifelike from side to side and lettin' out that deep, grumbly "Woof! Woof!" remark.

Blair is so deep in his music that he don't hear it for a minute. Then he must have caught on from the folks in front that something was up. He stops, glarin' indignant through his big glasses. Then he turns.

It wa'n't exactly a scream he lets out, nor a moan. It's the sort of a weird, muffled noise you'll sometimes make in your sleep, after a late welsh rabbit. I didn't think he could turn any whiter; but he does. His face has about as much color left in it as a marshmallow.

Then the thing on the floor rears up on its hind legs until it tops Blair by two feet, and there comes another of them deep "Woofs!"

I was lookin' for him to pass away complete; but he don't. He sets his jaw, tosses his violin on a chair, grabs the music rack, and swings it over his shoulder defiant.

"Come on, you brute!" he breathes husky. "I don't know what you are; but——"

Torchy, Private Sec.

Just what happens next, though, is a cry of "Shame, shame!" Someone dashes from the back row of chairs, and we sees Joey Billings makin' a clutch at the bear's head. It came off too, with a rip of snap hooks, and reveals Nutt Hamilton's big moon face with a wide grin on it.

"You, eh?" says Joey. "I thought as much. Your old masquerade trick! And anyone else would have had better sense. Don't you think you're beast enough without— —"

"Stop!" breaks in Blair, his lips blue and trembly and the tears beginnin' to trickle down his nose. "You—you've no right to interfere. I—I was going to smash him. I'll kill the big brute! I—I'll— —"

Once more Joey does the right thing; for Blair is blubberin' hysterical and the scene is gettin' worse. So she just tucks him under one arm, claps a hand over his mouth, and lugs him kickin' and strugglin' into the lib'ry, givin' Nutt a shove to one side as she brushes by.

You can guess too there was some panicky doin's in the Ellins's drawin' room for the next few minutes; Mr. Robert and Marjorie and others tryin' to tell Hamilton what they thought of him, all at the same time. And Nutt was takin' it sheepish.

"Oh, I say!" he protests. "I was only trying to have a bit of fun with the little runt, you know. I only meant to— —"

"Fun!" breaks in Mr. Robert savage. "This is neither a backwoods barroom nor a hunting camp, and I want to assure you right now, Hamilton, that— —"

But in comes young Blair again. He's had the tear stains swabbed off, and he's got some of his color back; but he's still wabbly in the knees. He pushes right to the front, though.

"I suppose you all think me a great baby," says he, "to get so frightened and to cry over such a silly trick. Perhaps I am a baby. At least I haven't control of my nerves. Would you, though, if you had been an invalid for fifteen years? Well, I have. And a good part of that time, you know, I spent in hospitals and sanatoriums, and traveling around with trained nurses and three or four relatives to wait on me and humor my whims. Even when I was studying music abroad it was that way. And I suppose I'm not really strong now. So I couldn't help being afraid. But I don't want your sympathy. You need not scold Hamilton any more, either. He can't help being a big bully any more than I can help acting like a baby. He doesn't know any better—never will. All beef and no brains! And at that I don't care to change places with him. Some day I shall be well and fairly strong. He'll never have any better sense or manners than he has now. And I prefer to fight my own battles. So let it drop, please."

Well, they did. But for the first time, I expect, a few cuttin' remarks got through Nutt Hamilton's thick hide. He shuffles out of his bear skin and sneaks off with his head down.

He'd hardly gone when Vee slips up beside me and touches me on the arm. "We can't do anything with her," she whispers mysterious. "Don't say a word, but come."

"Can't do anything with who?" says I.

"Joey," says she. "She's in the library, and we can't find out what is the matter."

"Wha-a-at! Joey?" says I.

It's a fact, though. I finds Joey slumped on a couch with her shoulders heavin'. She's doin' the sob act genuine and earnest.

"Well, well!" says I. "Why the big weeps?"

She looks up and sees who it is. "Torchy!" says she between sobs. "Dud-don't tell him. Please!"

"Tell who?" says I.

"B-b-b-blair, " says she. "I—wouldn't have him know for—for anything. But he—he—what he said hurt. He—he called me a meddlesome old maid. It was something I had to do too. I—I thought he'd understand. I—I thought he knew I—I liked him! "

"Eh? " says I gaspy.

"I've never cared so much before—about what the others thought, " she goes on. "I'm just Joey to them, out for a good time. I'll always be Joey, I suppose, to most of them. But I—I thought Blair was different, you know. I—I——"

And the sobs get the best of the argument. I glances over at Vee puzzled, and Vee shrugs her shoulders. We drifts back as far as the door.

"Poor Joey! " says Vee.

"Is it straight, " says I, "about her and Blair? "

Vee nods. "Only he doesn't know, " says she.

"Then it's time he did, " says I.

"There! " says Vee, givin' me a grateful look that tingles clear down to my toes. "I just knew you could help. But how can——"

"Watch! " says I.

I finds him packin' his precious violin and preparin' to beat it.

"See here, Hiscock, " says I. "Maybe you think you're the only one whose feelin's have been hurt this evenin'. "

He stares at me grouchy.

"Ah, ditch the assault and battery! " says I. "It ain't me. But there's someone in the lib'ry you could soothe with a word or two maybe. Why not go in and see her? "

"Her? " says he, starin' pop-eyed. "You—you don't mean Miss Billings? "

"Sure! " says I. "Joey, it's you she wants, and if I was you I'd——" But he's off on the run, with a queer, eager look on his face. I don't expect there's been so many who've wanted Sukey.

But the worst of it was I had to go without hearin' how it all come out. Mr. Robert didn't have much to report next mornin', either. "Oh, we left them in the library, still talking, " says he.

It's near a week later too that I gets anything more definite. Then I was up to the Ellins's on an errand when I discovers Blair waitin' in the front room. He greets me real cordial and friendly, which is quite a jar. A minute later down the stairs floats Marjorie and her friend Miss Billings.

"Oh, there you are, Joey! " says Blair, rushin' out and grabbin' her by the arm impetuous. "Come along. I'm going to take you both to dinner and then to the opera. Come! "

"Isn't he brutal? " laughs Joey, pattin' him folksy on the cheek.

So I take it there's been something doin' in the solitaire and wilt-thou line. Some cross-mated pair they'll make; but I ain't so sure it won't be a good match.

Anyway, when he gets her as a side partner, Sukey needn't do any more worryin' about bears.

CHAPTER XI

TEAMWORK WITH AUNTY

As Mr. Robert hangs up the desk 'phone and turns to me I catches him smotherin' a smile. "Torchy, " says he, "are you a patron of the plastic art? "

"Corns, or backache? " says I.

"Not plasters, " says he; "plastic; in short, sculpture. "

"Never sculped a sculpin, " says I. "What's the joke? "

"On the contrary, " says he, "it's quite serious, —a sculptor in distress; a noble young Belgian at that, one Djickyns, in whose cause, it seems, I was rash enough to enlist at a recent dinner party. And now— —" Mr. Robert waves towards his piled-up desk.

"I'd be a hot substitute along that line, wouldn't I? " says I.

"As I understand the situation, " goes on Mr. Robert, "it is not a matter of giving artistic advice, but of—er—financing the said Djickyns. "

"Oh! " says I. "Slippin' him a check? "

Mr. Robert shakes his head. "Nothing so simple, " says he. "One doesn't slip checks to noble young sculptors. In this instance I am supposed to assist in outlining a plan whereby certain alleged objects of art may be—er— —"

"Wished onto suckers in exchange for real money, eh? " says I. "Ain't that it? "

Mr. Robert nods.

"With so many dividends bein' passed, " says I, "that's goin' to take some strategy. "

"Hence this appeal to us, " says he. "And I might add, Torchy, that one of those most interested is a near relative of a certain young lady who— —"

"Aunty? " says I.

It was. So I grins and grabs my hat.

"That bein' the case, Mr. Robert, " says I, "we'll finance this Djickyns party if we have to bull the sculpture market till it hits the rafters. "

With that I takes the address of the scene of trouble and breezes uptown to a third-rate studio buildin'; where I finds Aunty and Vee and Sister Marjorie all grouped around a stepladder on top of which is balanced a pallid youth with long black hair and a fair white brow projectin' out like a double dormer on a cement bungalow. He seems to be tryin' to drape a fish net across the top of an alcove accordin' to three diff'rent sets of directions; but leaves off abrupt when I blows in.

You'd hardly guess I'd been sent for, either. "Humph! " remarks Aunty, after I've announced how sorry Mr. Robert was he couldn't come himself and that he's detailed me instead. "How perfectly absurd! "

"But, Aunty, " protests Vee, "you know Torchy is a private secretary now and understands all about such things. Besides, he knows such heaps of important business men who— —"

"If he can bring them here Wednesday afternoon, very well, " says Aunty; "but I have my doubts that he can. "

"What's the game? " says I.

"It is not a game at all, young man, " says Aunty. "Our project, if that is what you mean, is to have a studio tea for Mr. Djickyns and to secure the attendance of as many purchasers for his works as possible. Have you any suggestions? "

"Why, " says I, "not right off the bat. Maybe if I could chew over the proposition awhile, I might——"

"I gathers him in on the fly. "

"Oh, I say, " breaks in the noble young gent on the stepladder, "I—I'm getting dizzy up here, you know. I—I'm feeling rather——"

"Mercy! " squeals Marjorie. "He's fainting! "

"Steady there! " I sings out to Djickyns, makin' a jump. "Don't wabble until I get you. Easy! "

I ain't a second too soon, either; for as I reaches up he topples toward me, as limp as a sack of flour. I was fieldin' my position well for an amateur; for I gathers him in on the fly, slides him down head first with only a bump or two, and stretches him out on the rug. It's only a near-faint, though, and after a drink of water and a sniff at Aunty's smellin' salts he's able to be helped onto a couch and propped up with cushions.

"Awfully sorry, " says he, smilin' mushy, "but I fear I can't go on with the decorating to-day. "

"Never mind, " says Aunty, comfortin'. "This young man will help us. "

"Please do, Torchy, " adds Marjorie.

"You will, won't you? " says Vee, shootin' over a glance from them gray eyes that makes me feel all rosy and tingly.

"That's my job in life, " says I, pickin' up the fish net. "Now how does this go? "

And for the next hour or so, when I wa'n't clingin' to the ceilin' with my eyelids, tackin' things up, I was down on all-fours arrangin' rugs, or executin' other merry little stunts. Aunty had collected a whole truckload of fancy junk, —wall tapestries, old armor, Russian tea machines, and such, —with the idea of transformin' this half-bare loft of Djickyns's into a swell studio. And, believe me, we came mighty near turnin' the trick!

"There!" says she. "With a few flowers I believe it will do. Now, young man, have you thought how we can get the right people here? Of course we shall advertise in all the papers."

"As an open show?" says I. "Say, that's nutty! Don't you do it. You'd only get in a bunch of suburban shoppers and cheap-skate art students. My tip is, make it exclusive, — admission by card only. Then if it's done right you can graft a lot of free press agent stuff by playin' up the Belgian part of it strong. See? Lets you ring in on this fund for Belgian sufferers. I take it you want to unload as much of this plaster junk as you can? Well, all you got to do is mark it up twenty per cent. and announce that you'll chip in that much towards the fund. Get me?"

She never bats an eye, Aunty don't. "To be sure," says she. "I think that is precisely what we had in mind all the time; only we — er — —"

"I know," says I. "You hadn't been playin' the relief act strong enough. But that's what'll get you into the headlines. 'Social Leader to the Rescue,'— all that dope. I'll send some of the boys up to see you to-night. Don't let your butler frost 'em, though. Give 'em a clear track to the lib'ry, and if you're servin' after-dinner coffee and frosted green cordials, so much the better. Reporters are almost human, you know. It would help too if you'd happen to be just startin' for the op'ra, with all your pearl ropes on. And whisper, — soft pedal on Djickyns here, but heavy on his suff'rin' countrymen! That's the line."

Aunty shudders a couple of times, and once she starts to crash in with the sharp reproof; but she swallows it. Some little old diplomat, Aunty is! She was gettin' the picture. Havin' planned that part of the campaign, she switches the debate as to who should go on the list of invited guests.

"Leave it to me," says I. "You just pick out about a dozen patronesses. Pick 'em from the top, the ones that are featured oftenest in the society notes. And me, I'll sift out a couple of hundred sound propositions from the corporation lists, —parties that have stayed on the right side of the market and still have cash to spend."

Aunty nods approvin'. She even hands over some names she'd jotted down herself and asks me to put 'em in if they're all right.

"Most of 'em are fine," says I, glancin' over the slip; "but who's this W. T. Wiggins with no address?"

"I particularly want to reach him," says she. "He is a wealthy merchant who is apt to be rather generous, I am told, if properly approached."

"I'll look him up," says I, "and see that he gets an invite—registered."

"Of course," goes on Aunty, "he doesn't belong socially, you understand; but in this instance——"

"Uh-huh!" says I. "You'll be pleased to meet his checkbook. And, by the way, what schedule are you runnin' this on, —doors open at when?"

"The cards will read, 'From half after four until seven,'" says Aunty.

"I see," says I. "Then if I drift in before six a frock coat will pass me."

And for the first time durin' the session she inspects me insultin' through her lorgnette. "Really," says she, "I had not considered that it would be necessary——"

"Eh?" I gasps. "Ah, have a heart! Think how handy I'd be if someone did another flop, or if Miss Vee wanted——"

"Verona will be fully occupied in serving tea," breaks in Aunty. "Besides, we shall try to give this affair the appearance, at least, of a genuine social function. I imagine that the presence of such persons as Mr. Wiggins will make the task sufficiently difficult. Don't you see?"

"I ought to, " says I. "You ain't left much to the imagination. Sort of a blot on the landscape I'd be, would I? "

Aunty shrugs her shoulders. "Please remember, " says she, "that I am not making social distinctions. I merely recognize those which exist. You must not hold me responsible for— —"

"Oh, Aunty, " breaks in Vee, trippin' into our corner impulsive, "we've forgotten the tea things. I must go out and find a store and get them at once. Mayn't Torchy come to carry the bundles? "

"Yes, " says Aunty; "but I think I will go also, to be sure you order the right things. "

Think of carryin' round a disposition like that! She trails right along with us too, and just to make the trip int'restin' for her I strikes for Eighth-ave. through one of them messy cross streets where last week's snow piles and garbage cans was mixed careless along the curb.

"What a wretched district! " complains Aunty.

"I thought you wanted to get to the nearest grocery, " says I. "Hello! Here's one of the Wiggins chain. How about patronizin' this? "

It's one of them cheap, cut-rate joints, you know, with the windows plastered all over with daily bargain hints, —"Three pounds of Wiggins's best creamery butter for 97 cents—to-day only, " "Canned corn, 6 cents—our big Monday special, " and so on. Aunty sniffs a bit, but fin'lly decides to take a chance and sails in in all her grandeur. The one visible clerk was busy waitin' on lady customers, one with a shawl over her head and the other luggin' a baby on her hip. So Aunty raps impatient on the counter.

At that out from behind a stack of Wiggins's breakfast food boxes appears a middle-aged gent strugglin' into a blue jumper three sizes too small for him. He's kind of heavy built and slow movin' for an average grocery clerk, and he's wearin' gold-rimmed specs; but when Aunty proceeds to cross-examine him about his stock of tea he sure showed he was onto his job. He seems to know about every kind of tea ever grown, and produces samples of the best he has in the shop.

Aunty was watchin' him casual as he weighs out a couple of pounds, when all of a sudden she unlimbers her long-handled glasses and takes a closer look. "My good man, " says she, "haven't I seen you somewhere before? "

"Oh, yes, " says he, scoopin' a pinch off the scales so they'd register exactly to the quarter ounce.

"In some other store, perhaps? " says she.

"I think not, " says he.

"Then where? " asks Aunty.

"Cooperstown, " says he, reachin' for a paper bag and shootin' the tea in skillful. "Anything more, Madam? "

"Cooperstown! " echoes Aunty. "Why, I haven't been there since I was a girl. "

"Yes, I know, " says he. "You didn't even finish at high school. Cut sugar, did you say, Madam? "

"A box, " says Aunty, starin' puzzled. "Perhaps you attended the same school? "

He nods.

"Oh, I seem to remember now, " says she. "Aren't you the one they called—er—— What was it you were called? "

"Woodie, " says he. "Will you have lemons too? Fresh Floridas. "

"Two dozen," says Aunty. "Well, well! You used to ask me to skate with you on the lake, didn't you?"

"When my courage was running high," says he. "Sometimes you would; but more often you wouldn't. I lived at the wrong end of town, you know."

"In the Hollow, wasn't it?" says she. "And there was something queer about—about your family, wasn't there?"

He looks her straight in the eye at that, Woodie does. "Yes," says he. "Mother went out sewing. She was a widow."

"Oh!" says Aunty. "I recall your skates—those funny old wooden-topped ones, weren't they?"

"I was lucky to have those," says he.

"Hm-m-m!" muses Aunty. "But you could skate very well. You taught me the Dutch roll. I remember now. Then there was the night we had the big bonfire on the ice."

Woodie lets on not to hear this last, but grabs a sales slip and gets busy jottin' down items.

I nudges Vee, and she smothers a snicker. We was enjoyin' this little peek into their past. Could you have guessed it? Aunty! She orders six loaves of sandwich bread and asks to see the canned caviar.

"You've never found anything better to do," she goes on, "than—than this?"

"No," says Woodie, on his way down from the top shelf.

Once more Aunty levels her lorgnette and gives him the cold, curious look over. "Hm-m-mff!" says she through her aristocratic nose. "I must say that as a boy you were presuming enough."

"I got over that," says he.

"So I should hope," says she. "You manage to make a living at this sort of thing, I suppose?"

"In a way," says he.

"You've no family, I trust?" says Aunty.

"There are six of us all told," admits Woodie humble.

"Good heavens!" she gasps. "But I presume some of them are able to help you?"

"A little," says Woodie.

"Think of it!" says Aunty. "Six! And on such wages! Are any of them girls?"

"Two," says he.

"I must send you some of my niece's discarded gowns," says Aunty impulsive. "You are not a drinking man, are you?"

"Not to excess, Madam," says Woodie.

"How you can afford to drink at all is beyond me," says she. "Or even eat! Yet you are rather stout. I've no doubt, though, that plain food is best. But you show your age."

"I know," says he, smoothin' one hand over his bald spot. "Anything else to-day?"

There's just a hint of an amused flicker behind the glasses that makes Aunty glare at him suspicious for a second. "No," says she. "Put all those things in two stout bags and tie them carefully."

"Yes, Madam," says Woodie.

He was doin' it too, when the other clerk steps up, salutes him polite, and says: "You're wanted at the telephone, Sir."

"Tell them to hold the wire," says Woodie.

We was still tryin' to dope that out when a big limousine rolls up in front of the store, out hops a footman in livery, walks in to Woodie with his cap in his hand, and holds out a bunch of telegrams.

"From the office, Sir," says he.

"Wait," says Woodie, wavin' him one side.

Now was them any proper motions for a grocery clerk to be goin' through? I leave it to you. Vee is watchin' with her nose wrinkled up, like she always does when anything stumps her; and me, I was just starin' open-faced and foolish. I couldn't get the connection at all. But Aunty ain't one to stand gaspin' over a mystery while her tongue's still workin'.

"Whose car is that?" she demands.

Woodie slips the string from between his front teeth, puts a double knot scientific on the end of the package, and peers over his glasses out through the door. "That?" says he. "Oh, that's mine."

"Yours!" comes back Aunty. "And—and this store too?"

"Oh, yes," says he.

"Then—then your name is Wiggins?" she goes on.

"Yes," says he. "Don't you remember,—Woodie Wiggins?"

"I'd forgotten," says Aunty. "And all the other stores like this—how many of them have you?"

"Something less than a hundred, " says he. "Ninety-six or seven, I think. "

Most got Aunty's breath, that did; but in a jiffy she's recovered. "Perhaps, " says she, "you don't mind telling me the reason for this masquerade? "

"It's not quite that, " says Wiggins. "I try to keep in touch with all my places. In making my rounds to-day I found my local manager here too ill to be at work. Bad case of grip. So I sent him home, telephoned for a substitute, and while waiting took off my coat and filled in. Fortunate coincidence, wasn't it? —for it gave me the pleasure of serving you. "

"You mean, " cuts in Aunty, "that it gave you the opportunity of making me appear absurd. Those gowns I promised to send! "

Wiggins grins good natured. "Is this the niece you mentioned? " says he.

Aunty admits that it is, and introduces Vee.

Then Wiggins looks inquirin' at me. "Your son? " he asks.

And you should have seen Aunty's face pink up at that. "Certainly not! " says she.

"Oh! " says Woodie, screwin' up one corner of his mouth and tippin' me the wink.

I knew if I got a look at Vee I'd have to haw-haw; so I backs around with one hand behind me and we swaps a finger squeeze.

Then Aunty jumps in with the quick shift. She asks him patronizin' if he finds the grocery business int'restin'. He admits that he does.

"How odd! " says Aunty. "But I presume that you hope to retire very soon? "

Torchy, Private Sec.

"Eh? " says he. "Quit the one thing I can do best? Why? "

"But surely, " she goes on, "you can hardly find such a business congenial. It is so—so—well, so petty and sordid? "

"Is it, though? " says Wiggins. "With more than five thousand employees on my payroll and a daily expense bill running well over thirty thousand, I find it far from petty. Anyway, it keeps me hustling. I used to think I was a hard worker too, when I had my one little general store at Smiths Corners. "

"And now you've nearly a hundred stores! " says Aunty. "How did you do it? "

"I was kicked into doing it, I guess, " says Wiggins, smilin' grim. "The manufacturers and jobbers, you know. They weren't willing to allow me a fair profit. So I had to go under or spread out. Well, I've spread, —flour mills in Minnesota, canning factories from Portland, Oregon, to Bridgeton, Maine, potato farms in Michigan and the Aroostook, cracker and bread bakeries, creameries, raisin and prune plantations, —all that sort of thing, —until gradually I've weeded out most of the greedy middlemen who stood between me and my customers. They're poor folks, most of 'em, and when they trade with me their slim wages go further than in most stores. My ambition is to give them honest goods at a five per cent. profit.

"If they all knew what was best for them, the Wiggins stores would soon become a national institution, and I could hand it over to the federal government; but they don't. If they did, I suppose they wouldn't be working for wages. So my chain grows slowly, at the rate of two or three stores a year. But every Wiggins store is a center for economic and scientific distribution of pure food products. That's my job, and I find it neither petty nor sordid. I can even get a certain satisfaction and pride from it. Incidentally there is my five per cent. profit to be made, which makes the game fascinating. Retire? Not until I've found something better to do, and up to date I haven't. "

Havin' got this off his mind and the parcels done up, Mr. Wiggins walks back to answer the 'phone.

When he comes out again, in a minute or so, he's shucked the jumper and is buttonin' himself into a mink-lined overcoat.

"As a rule, " says he, "we do not deliver goods; but in this instance I beg leave to make an exception. Permit me, " and he waves toward the limousine.

It's the first time too that I ever saw Aunty stunned for more than a second or two at a stretch. She acts sort of dazed as he leads her out to the car and helps stow Vee and me and the bundles before gettin' in himself. Only when we pulls up in front of the studio buildin' does she come to. She revives enough to tell Wiggins all about this noble young Belgian sculptor and his wonderful work.

"Sculpture! " says Wiggins. "I'd like to see it. "

And inside of three minutes Woodruff T. Wiggins, the chain grocery magnate, is right where we'd been schemin' to get him. He inspects the various groups of plaster stuff ranged around the studio, squintin' at 'em critical like he was a judge of such junk, and now and then he makes notes on the back of an envelope.

Meanwhile Aunty explains all about the tea, namin' over some of the swell dowagers that was goin' to act as patronesses, and invites him cordial to drop around on the big day.

"Thanks, " says he; "but I guess I'd better not. I'm still from the wrong end of the town, you know. But here's a memorandum of four pieces I should like done in bronze for my country house. And suppose I leave Mr. Djickyns a check for five thousand on account. Will that do? "

Would it? Say, Aunty almost pats him fond on the cheek as she follows him to the door.

Must have been something romantic about that bonfire episode back in Cooperstown too; for she mellows up a lot durin' the next few minutes, and when I fin'lly calls a taxi and tucks 'em all in she comes near beamin' on me.

"Remember, young man, " says she, "promptly at five on Wednesday. "

"Wha-a-at? " says I.

"And be sure to wear your best frock coat, " she adds as a partin' shot.

Do you wonder I stands gaspin' on the curb until after they've turned the corner? Think of that from Aunty!

"Well? " says Mr. Robert, as I blows in about quittin' time. "Any new quotations in sculpture? "

"If you think that's a merry jest, " says I, "call up Aunty. Why, say, before we get through with this tea stunt of hers that Djickyns party will be runnin' his studio works day and night shifts and rebuildin' Belgium! We're a great team, me and dear old Aunty. We've just found it out. "

CHAPTER XII

ZENOBIA DIGS UP A LATE ONE

And first off I had him listed in the joke column. Think of that! But when I caught my first glimpse of him, there in the Corrugated gen'ral offices that mornin', there was more or less comedy idea to his get-up; the high-sided, flat-topped derby, for instance. Once in a while you run across an old sport who still sticks to that type of hard-boiled lid. Gen'rally they're short-stemmed old ginks who seem to think the high crown makes 'em loom up taller. Maybe so; but where they find back-number hats like that is beyond me.

Then there was the buff-cochin spats and the wide ribbon to his eyeglasses. Beyond that I don't know as there was anything real freaky about him. A rich-colored old gent he is, the pink in his cheeks shadin' off into a deep mahogany tint back of his ears, makin' his frosted hair and mustache stand out some prominent.

He'd been shown into the private office on a call for Mr. Robert; but as I was well heeled with work of my own I didn't even glance up from the desk until I hears this scrappy openin' of his.

"Bob Ellins, you young scoundrel, what the blighted beatitudes does this mean! " he demands.

Naturally that gets me stretchin' my neck, and I turns just in time to watch the gaspy expression on Mr. Robert's face fade out and turn into a chuckle.

"Why, Mr. Ballard! " says he, extendin' the cordial palm. "I had no idea you were on this side. Really! I understood, you know, that you were settled over there for good, and that——"

"So you take advantage of the fact, do you, to make me president of one of your fool companies? " says Ballard. "My imbecile attorney just let it leak out. What do you mean, eh? "

Torchy, Private Sec.

Mr. Robert pushes him into a chair and shrugs his shoulders. "It was rather a liberty, I admit, " says he; "one of the exigencies of business, however. When a meddlesome administration insists on dissolving into its component parts such an extensive organization as ours— well, we had to have a lot of presidents in a hurry. Really, we didn't think you'd mind, Mr. Ballard, and we had no intention of bothering you with the details. "

"Huh! " snorts Mr. Ballard. "And what is this precious corporation of which I'm supposed to be the head? "

"Why, Mutual Funding, " says Mr. Robert.

"Funding, eh? " comes back Ballard snappy. "What tommyrot! Bob Ellins, you ought to know that I haven't the vaguest notion as to what funding is, —never did, —and at my time of life, Sir, I don't propose to learn! "

"Of course, of course, " says Mr. Robert, soothin'. "Quite unnecessary too. You are adequately and efficiently represented, Mr. Ballard, by a private secretary who has mastered the art of funding, mutual and otherwise, until he can do it backward with one hand tied behind him. Torchy, will you step here a moment? "

I was comin' too; but Mr. Ballard waves me off.

"Stop! " says he. "I'll not listen to a word of it. I'd have you know, Bob Ellins, that I have worried along for sixty-two years without having been criminally implicated in business affairs. The worst I've done has been to pose as a dummy director on your rascally board and to see that my letter of credit was renewed every three months. Use my name if you must; but allow me to keep a clear conscience. I'm going in now for a chat with your father, Bob, and if he mentions funding I shall stuff my fingers in my ears and run. He won't, though. Old Hickory knows me better. This his door? All right. Thanks. Hah, you old freebooter! In your den, are you? Well, well! "

At which he stalks into the other office and leaves Mr. Robert and me grinnin' at each other.

"Listened like you was in Dutch for a minute or so there, " says I. "Case of the cat comin' back, eh? "

"From Kyrle Ballard, " says he, "one expects the unexpected. Only we need not worry about his wanting to become the acting head of your department. To-morrow or next week he is quite likely to be off again, bound for some remote corner of the earth, to hobnob with the native rulers thereof, participate in their games of chance, and invent a new punch especially suitable for that particular climate. "

"Gee! " says I. "That's my idea of a perfectly good boss, —one that gives his job absent treatment. "

I thought too that Mr. Robert had doped out his motions correct; for a week goes by and no Mr. Ballard shows up to take the rubber stamp away from me, or even ask fool questions. I was hopin' too that Ballard had gone a long ways from here, accordin' to custom. Then one night—well, it was at the theater, one of them highbrow Shaw plays that I was chucklin' through with Aunt Zenobia.

Eh? Remember her, don't you? Why, she's one of the pair of aunts that I got half adopted by, 'way back when I first started in with the Corrugated. Yep, I've been stayin' on with 'em. Why not? Course our little side street is 'way down in an old-fashioned part of the town; the upper edge of old Greenwich village, in fact, if you know where that is.

The house is one of a row that sports about the only survivin' specimens of the cast-iron grapevine school of architecture. Honest, we got a double-decked veranda built of foundry work that was meant to look like leaves and vines, I expect. Cute idea, eh? Bein' all painted brick red, though, it ain't so convincing but stragglin' over ours is a wistaria that has a few sickly-lookin' blossoms on it every spring and manages to carry a sprinklin' of dusty leaves through the summer. Also there's a nine-by-twelve lawn, that costs a dollar a square foot to keep in shape, I'll bet.

From that description maybe you'd judge that the place where I hang out is a little antique. It is. But inside it's mighty comf'table, and it's the best imitation of a home I've ever carried a latch-key to. As for the near-aunts, Zenobia and Martha, take it from me they're the real things in that line, even if they did let me in off the street without askin' who or what! The best of it is they never have asked, which makes it convenient. I couldn't tell 'em much, if they did.

There's Martha—well, she's the pious one. It ain't any case of sudden spasms with her. It's a settled habit. She's just as pious Monday mornin' as she is Sunday afternoon, and it lasts her all through the week. You know how she started in by readin' them Delilah and Jona yarns to me. She's kept it up. About twice a week she corners me and pumps in a slice of Scripture readin', until I guess we must be more 'n half through the Book. Course there's a lot of it I don't see any percentage in at all; but I've got so I don't mind it, and it seems to give Aunt Martha a lot of satisfaction. She's a lumpy, heavy-set old girl, Martha, and a little slow; but the only thing that ain't genuine about her is the yellowish white frontispiece she pins on over her own hair when she dolls up for dinner.

But Zenobia—say, she's a diff'rent party! A few years younger than Martha, Zenobia is, —in the early sixties, I should say, —and she's just as active and up to date and foxy as Martha is logy and antique and dull. While Martha is sayin' grace Zenobia is gen'rally pourin' herself out a glass of port.

About once a week Martha loads herself into an old horse cab and goes off to a meetin' of the foreign mission society, or something like that; but almost every afternoon Zenobia goes whizzin' off in a taxi, maybe to hear some long-haired violinist, maybe to sit on the platform with Emma Goldman and Bouck White and applaud enthusiastic when the established order gets another jolt. Just as likely as not too, she'll bring some of 'em home to dinner with her.

Zenobia never shoves any advice on me, good or otherwise, and never asks nosey questions; but she's the one who sees that my socks are kept mended and has my suits sent to the presser. She don't read things to me, or expound any of her fads. She just talks to me like she does to anyone else—minor poets or social reformers—about anything she happens to be int'rested in at the time, —music, plays, Mother Jones, the war, or how suffrage is comin' on, —and never seems to notice when I make breaks or get over my head.

A good sport Zenobia is, and so busy sizin' up to-day that she ain't got time for reminiscin' about the days before Brooklyn Bridge was built. And the most chronic kidder you ever saw. Say, what we don't do to Aunt Martha when both of us gets her on a string is a caution! That's what makes so many of our meals such cheerful events.

You might think, from a casual glance at Zenobia, with her gray hair and the lines around her eyes, that she'd be kind of slow comp'ny for me, especially to chase around to plays with and so on. But, believe me, there's nothin' dull about her, and when she suggests that she's got an extra ticket to anything I don't stop to ask what it is, but just gets into the proper evenin' uniform and trots along willin'!

So that's how I happens to be with her at this Shaw play, and discussin' between the acts what Barney was really tryin' to put over on us. The first intermission was most over too before I discovers this ruddy-faced old party in the back of Box A with his opera glasses trained steady in our direction. I glances along the row to see if anyone's gazin' back; but I can't spot a soul lookin' his way. After he's kept it up a minute or two I nudges Aunt Zenobia.

"Looks like we was bein' inspected from the box seats, " says I.

"How flatterin'! " says she. "Where? "

I points him out. "Must be you, " says I, grinnin'.

"I hope so, " says Zenobia. "If I'm really being flirted with, I shall boast of it to Sister Martha. "

But just then the lights go out and the second act begins. We got so busy followin' the nutty scheme of this conversation expert who plots to pass off a flower-girl for a Duchess that the next wait is well under way before I remembers the gent in the box.

"Say, he's at it again, " says I. "You must be makin' a hit for fair. "

"Precisely what I've always hoped might happen, —to be stared at in public, " says Zenobia. "I'm greatly obliged to him, I'm sure. You are quite certain, though, that it isn't someone just behind me? "

I whispers that there's no one behind her but a fat woman munchin' chocolates and rubberin' back to see if Hubby ain't through gettin' his drink.

"There! He's takin' his glasses down, " says I. "Know the party, do you? "

"Not at this distance, " says Zenobia. "No, I shall insist that he is an unknown admirer. "

By that time, though, I'd got a better view myself. And—say, hadn't I seen them ruddy cheeks and that gray hair and them droopy eyes before? Why, sure! It's what's-his-name, the old guy who blew into the Corrugated awhile ago, my absentee boss—Ballard!

Maybe I'd have told Zenobia all about him if there'd been time; but there wa'n't. Another flash of the lights, and we was watchin' the last act, where this gutter-bred Pygmalion sprouts a soul. And when it's all over of course we're swept out with the ebb tide, make a scramble for our taxi, and are off for home. Then as we gets to the door I has the sudden hunch about eats.

"There's a joint around on Sixth-ave., " says I, lettin' Aunt Zenobia in, "where they sell hot dog sandwiches with sauerkraut trimmin's. I believe I could just do with one about now. "

"What an atrocious suggestion at this hour of the night!" says she. "Torchy, don't you dare bring one of those abominations into the house—unless you have enough to divide with me. About four, I should say."

"With mustard?" says I.

"Heaps!" says she.

Three minutes later I'm hurryin' back with both hands full, when I notices another taxi standin' out front. Then who should step out but this Ballard party, in a silk hat and a swell fur-lined overcoat.

"Young man," says he, "haven't I seen you somewhere before?"

"Uh-huh," says I. "I'm your private sec."

"Wha-a-at?" says he. "My—oh, yes! I remember. I saw you at the Corrugated."

"And then again at the show to-night," says I.

"To be sure," says he. "With a lady, eh?"

I nods.

"Lives here, doesn't she?" asks Ballard.

"Right again," says I. "Goin' to call?"

"Why," says he, "the fact is, young man, I—er—see here, it's Zenobia Hadley, isn't it?"

"Preble," says I. "Mrs. Zenobia Preble."

"Hang the Preble part!" says he. "He's dead years ago. What I want to know is, who else lives here?"

"Only her and Sister Martha and me, " says I.

"Martha, eh? " says he. "Still alive, is she? Well, well! And Zenobia now, is she—er—a good deal like her sister? "

"About as much as Z is like M, " says I. "She's a live one, Aunt Zenobia is, if that's what you're gettin' at. "

"Thank you, " says he. "That is it exactly. And I am glad to hear it. She used to be, as you put it, rather a live one; but I didn't quite know how——"

"Kyrle Ballard, is that you? " comes floatin' out from the front door. "If it is, and you wish to know anything more about Zenobia Hadley, I should advise you to come to headquarters. Torchy, bring in those sandwiches—and Mr. Ballard, if he cares to follow. "

"There! " says I to Ballard. "You've got a sample. That's Zenobia. Are you comin' or goin'? "

Foolish question! He's leadin' the way up the steps.

"Zenobia, " says he, holdin' out both hands, "I humbly apologize for following you in this impulsive fashion. I saw you at the theater, and——"

"If you hadn't done something of the kind, " says she, "I shouldn't have been at all sure it was really you. You've changed so much! "

"I admit it, " says he. "One does, you know, in forty years. "

"There, there, Kyrle Ballard! " warns Zenobia. "Throw the calendar at me again, and out you go! I simply won't have it! Besides, I'm hungry. Torchy is to blame. He suggested hot dog sandwiches. Take a sniff. Do they appeal to you, or have you cultivated epicurean tastes to such an extent that——"

"Ah-h-h-h!" says Ballard, bendin' over the paper bag I'm holdin'. "My favorite delicacy. And if I might be permitted to add a bottle or two of cold St. Louis — —"

"Do you think I keep house without an icebox?" demands Zenobia. "Stop your silly speeches, and let's get into the dining-room."

Some hustler, Zenobia is, too. Inside of two minutes she's shed her wraps, passed out plates and glasses, and we're tacklin' a Coney Island collation.

"I had been wondering if it could be you," says Ballard. "I'd been watching you through the glasses."

"Yes, I know," says Zenobia. "And we had quite settled it that you were a strange admirer. I'm frightfully disappointed!"

"Then you didn't know me?" says he. "But just now — —"

"Voices don't turn gray or change color," says Zenobia. "Yours sounds just as it did — well, the last time I heard it."

"That August night, eh?" suggests Mr. Ballard, suspendin' operations on the sandwich and leanin' eager across the table.

He's a chirky, chipper old scout, with a lot of twinkles left in his blue eyes. Must have been some gay boy in his day too; for even now he shows up more or less ornamental in his evenin' clothes. And Zenobia ain't such a bad looker either, you know; especially just now, with her ears pinked up and her eyes sparklin' mischievous. I don't know whether it's from takin' massage treatments reg'lar, or if it just comes natural, but she don't need to cover up her collar bone or wear things around her neck.

"Yes, that night," says she, liftin' her glass. "Shall we drink just once to the memory of it?"

Which they did.

"And now," goes on Zenobia, "we will forget it, if you please."

"Not I," says Ballard. "Another thing: I've never forgiven your sister Martha for what she did then. I never will."

Zenobia indulges in a trilly little laugh. "No more has she forgiven you," says she. "How absurd of you both, just as though—but we'll not talk about it. I've no time for yesterdays. To-day is too full. Tell me, why are you back here?"

"Because seven armies have chased me out of Europe," says he, "and my charming Vienna is too full of typhus to be quite healthy. If I'd dreamed of finding you like this, I should have come long ago."

"Very pretty," says Zenobia. "I'd love to believe it, just for the sake of repeating it to Martha in the morning. She is still with me, you know."

"As saintly as ever?" asks Ballard.

"At thirty Martha was quite as good as she could be," says Zenobia. "There she seems to have stopped. So naturally her opinion of you hasn't altered in the least."

"And yours?" says he.

"Did I have opinions at twenty-two?" says she. "How ridiculous! I had emotions, moods, mad impulses; anyway, something that led me to give you seven dances in a row and stay until after one A. M. when I had promised someone to leave at eleven. You don't think I've kept up that sort of thing, do you?"

"I don't know," says Ballard. "I wouldn't be sure. One never could be sure of Zenobia Hadley. I suppose that was why I took my chance when I did, why I——"

"Kyrle Ballard, you've finished your sandwich, haven't you?" breaks in Zenobia. "There! It's striking twelve, and I make it a rule never to be sentimental after midnight. You and Martha wouldn't enjoy meeting each other; so you'll not be coming again. Besides, I've a busy week ahead of me. When you get settled abroad again, though, you might let me know. Good-night. Happy dreams."

And before Ballard can protest he's bein' shooed out.

"You'll take luncheon with me to-morrow," he calls back from his cab.

"Probably not," says Zenobia.

"Oh yes, you will, Zenobia," says he. "I'm a desperate character still. Remember that!"

She laughs and shuts the door. "There, Torchy!" says she. "See what complications come from combining hot dogs with Bernard Shaw. And if Martha should happen to get down before those bottles are removed—well, I should have to tell her all."

Trust Martha. She did. And when I finished breakfast she was still waitin' for Zenobia to come down and be quizzed. I don't know how far back into fam'ly hist'ry that little chat took 'em, or what Martha had to say. All I know is that when I shows up for dinner and comes downstairs about six-thirty there sits Martha in the lib'ry, rocking back and forth with that patient, resigned look on her face, as if she was next in line at the dentist's.

"Zenobia isn't in yet," says she. "We will wait dinner awhile for her."

Then chunks of silence from Martha, which ain't usual. At seven o'clock we gives it up and sits down alone. We hadn't finished our soup when this telegram comes. First off I thought Martha was goin' to choke or blow a cylinder head, I didn't know which. Then she takes to sobbin' into the consommé, and fin'lly she shoves the message over to me.

"Wh-a-at?" I gasps. "Eloped, have they?"

"I—I knew they would, " says Martha, "just as soon as I heard he'd been here. He—he always wanted her to do it. "

"Always? " says I. "Why, I thought he hadn't seen her for forty years or so. How could that be? "

"We-we-well, " sobs Martha, "I—I stopped them once. And she engaged to the Rev. Mr. Preble at the time! It was scandalous! Such a wild, reckless fellow Kyrle Ballard was too. "

"Wh-e-ew! " I whistles. "That was goin' some for Zenobia, wasn't it? How near did they come to doin' the slope? "

"She—she was actually stealing out to meet him, her things all on, " says Martha, "when—when I woke up and found her. I made her come back by threatening to call Mother. Engaged for two years, she and Mr. Preble had been, and the wedding day all set. He'd just got a nice church too, his first. I saved her that time; but now— —" Martha relapses into the sob act.

"The giddy young things! " says I. "Gone off on a honeymoon trip too! Say, that ain't such slow work, is it? Gettin' there a little late, maybe; but if there ever was a pair of silver sixties meant to be mated up, I guess it's them. Well, well! I stand to lose a near-aunt by the deal; but they get my blessin', anyway. "

As for Aunt Martha, she keeps right on thinnin' out the soup.

CHAPTER XIII

SIFTING OUT UNCLE BILL

Things happen to you quick, don't they, when the happenin' is good? Take this affair of Zenobia's. One day I'm settled down all comfy and solid with two old near-aunts who'd been livin' in the same place and doin' the same things for the last thirty years or so, and the next—well, off one of 'em goes, elopes with an old-time beau of hers that happens to show up here just because Europe is bein' shot up.

And then, before I've recovered from that jolt, comes this human surprise package labeled Dorsett, who blows breezy into the Corrugated. Fair-haired Vincent, who still holds my old place on the brass gate, brings in his card.

"William H. Dorsett? " says I. "Never heard of the party. Did he ask for Mutual Funding? "

"No, Sir, " says Vincent. "He asked for you, Sir. "

"How? " says I.

At which Vincent tints up embarrassed. "He said he wished to talk to a young fellow known as Torchy, Sir, " says he.

"Almost a description of me, ain't it? " says I. "Well, tow him in, Vincent, until I see if his map's any more familiar than his name. "

It wa'n't. He's a middle-aged gent, kind of tall and stoop-shouldered, with curly hair that's started to frost up above the ears. The raincoat he's wearin' is a little seedy, specially about the collar and cuffs; but he's sportin' a silver-mounted walkin'-stick, and has a new pair of yellow gloves stickin' from his breast pocket.

With a free and easy stride he follows Vincent's directions, sails over to my corner of the private office, pulls up a chair, and camps down by the desk without any urgin'. Also he favors me with a friendly smile that he produces from one corner of his mouth. Sort of a catchy smile it is too, and before we've swapped a word I finds myself smilin' back.

"Well! " says I. "You're introducin' what? "

"Just William H. Dorsett, " says he.

"You do it well, " says I.

He allows the off corner of his mouth to loosen up again, and for a second his deep-set brown eyes steady down as he gives me the once-over. Kind of an amused, quizzin' look it is, but more or less foxy. He crosses his legs and hitches up his chair confidential.

"I imagine you're rather used to handling big propositions here, " says he, takin' in the office mahogany, the expensive floor rugs, and everything else in a quick glance: "so I hope you won't mind if I present a small one. "

"In funding? " says I.

"It might very well come under that head, " says he. "Ever do much with municipal franchises, —trolleys, lighting, that sort of thing? "

"Nope, " says I; "nor racin' tips, church fair chances, or Danish lottery tickets. We don't even back new movie concerns. "

That gets a twinkle out of his restless eyes. "I don't blame you in the least, " says he. "I suppose there are more worthless franchises hawked around New York than you could stuff into a moving van. That's what makes it so difficult to get action on any real, gilt-edged propositions. "

"Such as you've got in your inside pocket eh? " says I.

"Precisely, " says he. "Mine are the worthwhile kind. Of course franchises are common enough. It's no trick at all to go into the average Rube village, 'steen miles from a railroad, and get 'em thrilled with the notion of being connected by trolley with Jaytown, umpteen miles south. Why, they'll hand you anything in sight! A deaf-mute could go out and get that sort of franchise. But to prospect through the whole cotton belt, locate opportunities where the dividends will follow the rails, pick out the cream of them all, get in right with the board of trade, fix things up with a suspicious town council, stall off the local capitalist who would like to hog all the profits himself, and set the real estate operators working for you tooth and nail—well, that is legitimate promoting; my brand, if you will permit me. "

"Maybe, " says I. "But the Corrugated don't——"

"I understand, " breaks in Mr. Dorsett. "Quite right too. But here I produce the personal equation. For five weary weeks I've skittered about this city, carrying around with me half a dozen of the ripest, richest franchise propositions ever matured. Bona-fide prospects, mind you, communities just yearning for transportation facilities, with tentative stock subscriptions running as high as two hundred thousand in some cases. They're schemes I've nursed from the seed up, as you might say. I've laid all the underground wires, seen all the officials that need seeing, planned for every right of way. Six splendid opportunities that may be coined into cash simply by pressing the button! And the nearest I can get to any man with real money to invest is a two-minute interview in a reception room with some clerk. All because I lack someone to take me into a private office and remark casually: 'Mr. So-and-So, here's my friend Dorsett, who's bringing us something good from the South. ' That's all. Why, only last week I actually offered to deliver a fifty-thousand-dollar franchise on a ten per cent. commission basis, provided I was given a beggarly two hundred advance for expenses—and had it turned down! "

"Ye-e-es, " says I. "The way some of them Wall Street plutes shrink from bein' made richer is painful, ain't it? But I don't see where I fit in. "

Mr. Dorsett pats me chummy on the shoulder and proceeds to show me exactly where. "You know the right people, " says he. "You're in with them. Very well. All I ask of you is the 'Here's Mr. Dorsett' part. I'll do the rest. "

"How simple! " says I. "And us old friends of about five minutes' standin'! Say, throw in your reverse or you'll be off the bridge. Who's been tellin' you I was such a simp? "

Mr. Dorsett smiles indulgent. "My error, " says he. "But I was hoping that perhaps you might —— Come, Torchy, hasn't it occurred to you that I would hardly come as an utter stranger? Who do you suppose now gave me your address? "

"The chairman of the Stock Exchange? " says I.

"Mother Leary, " says he.

"Eh? " says I, gawpin'.

"A flip of fate, " says he. "At my hotel I got to talking with the room clerk, and discovered that his name was Leary. It turned out that he was Aloysius, the eldest boy. Remember him, don't you? "

Seein' how I'd almost been brought up in the fam'ly when I was a kid, I couldn't deny it. Course I'd run more with Hunch than any of the other boys. We'd sold papers together, and gone into the A. D. T. at the same time. But there wasn't a Leary I didn't know all about.

"You must have boarded there too, " says I. "But if I ever heard your name, it didn't stick. "

"It may have been," says he, "that I was not using the Dorsett part of it just at that time. Business reasons, you understand. But the H in my name stands for Hines. What about William Hines, now?"

"Hm-m-m!" says I, starin' at him. Sure enough, that did have a familiar sound to it.

"Let's try it this way," says he: "Uncle Bill Hines."

And, say, that got me! I expect I made some gaspy motions before I managed to get out my next remark. "You—you ain't the one that left me with Mother Leary, are you?" I asks.

Dorsett nods. "I'm a trifle late in explaining that carelessness," says he, "and I can only plead guilty to all your reproaches. But consider the circumstances. There I was, a free lance of fortune, down to my last dollar, and rich only in the companionship of a bright-eyed, four-year-old youngster who had been trusted to my care. You remember very little of that period, I suppose; but it is all vivid enough to me, even now,—how we tramped up and down Broadway, you chattering away, excited and happy, while I was wondering what I should do when that last dollar was gone.

"Then, just when things seem blackest, arrived opportunity,—the Birmingham boom. I ran across one of the boomers, who was struck with the brilliant idea that he could make use of my peculiar talents in making known the coming glories of the new South. But I must join him at once, that very day. And he waved yellow-backed bills at me. I simply had to drop you and go. Mother Leary promised to take care of you for three months, or until your—well, until someone else claimed you. I sent word to them both, at least I tried to, and rushed gayly down into Dixie. Perhaps you never heard of the bursting of that first Birmingham boom? It was an abrupt but very-complete smash. I came out of it owning two gorgeous suits of clothes, one silk hat, and an opulent-looking pocketbook, bulging with thirty-day options on corner lots. One of the clerks in our office staked me with carfare to Atlanta, where I got a job collecting tenement house rents.

"Since then I've been up and down. Half a dozen times I've almost had my fingers on the tail feathers of fortune: only to stumble into some hidden pit of poverty. And in time—well, time mends all things. Besides, I hardly relished facing Mother Leary. There was the chance too that you no longer needed rescuing. I'm not trying to excuse my breach of faith: I am merely telling you how it came about. You realize that, I trust? "

Did I? I don't know. I expect I was just sittin' there gazing stary at him. Only one thing was shapin' itself clear in my head, and fin'lly I states it flat.

"Say, " says I, "you—you ain't my reg'lar uncle, are you? "

Maybe I wa'n't as enthusiastic as the case called for. He springs that smile of his. "Hardly a flattering way to put it, " says he. "Would you be disappointed if I was? "

"Well, " says I, eyin' him up and down, "you don't strike me as such a swell uncle, you know. "

Don't faze him a bit, either. "Our near relatives are seldom quite satisfactory, " says he. "Of course, though, if I fail to suit——" He hunches his shoulders and reaches for his hat.

So he had it on me, you see. Suppose you was as shy on relations as I am, would you turn down the only one that ever showed up?

"Excuse me if I don't get the cues right, " says I; "but—but this has been put over a little sudden. Course I'll take Mrs. Leary's word. If she says you're my Uncle Bill, that goes. Anyway, you can give me a line on—on my folks, I suppose? "

Yes, he admits that he can; but he don't. And I will say for him that he states his case smooth enough, smilin' that catchy smile of his, and tappin' me friendly on the knee. But when he's all through it amounts to this: He needs the loan of a couple of hundred cash the worst way, and he wants to be put next to a few plutes that are in the market for new trolley franchises. If I can boost him along that way, it'll relieve his mind so much that he'll be in just the right mood to go into my personal hist'ry as deep as I care to dip.

"Gee! " says I. "But this raisin' a fam'ly tree comes high, don't it? Besides, I'd have to get Mother Leary's O. K. on you first, you know. "

"Naturally, " says he. "And any time within the next day or so will answer. Suppose I drop around again, or look you up at your quarters? "

"Better make it at the house, " says I. "Here's the street number. Some evenin' after seven-thirty. I—I'll be thinkin' things over. "

And as I watches him swing jaunty through the door I remarks under my breath to nobody in partic'lar: "Uncle Bill, eh? My Uncle Bill! Well, well! "

You can be sure too that my first move is to sound Mother Leary. She says he's the one, all right, and I gathers that she gave him the tongue-lashin' she'd been savin' up all these years. But I don't stop for details. If I've really had an uncle wished on me, it's up to me to make the best of it, or find out the worst. But somehow I ain't so chesty about havin' dug up a relation. I don't brag about it to Martha when I go home. In fact, Martha has fam'ly troubles of her own about now, you remember. I finds her weepy-eyed and solemn.

"They've been gone more than a week, " says she, "Zenobia and that reckless Kyrle Ballard. Pretty soon they will be coming back, and then——"

"Well, what then? " says I.

"I've been packing up to-day, " says she, swabbin' off a stray tear from the side of her nose. "I have engaged rooms at the Lady Louise. I suppose you will be leaving too. "

"Me? " says I.

It hadn't struck me that Aunt Zenobia's getting married was goin' to throw us all out on the street. But Aunt Martha had it doped diff'rent.

"Stay in the same house with that man? " says she. "Not I! And I am quite sure he will not want either of us around when he comes back here as Zenobia's husband. "

"If that's the case, " says I, "it won't take me long to clear out; but I guess I'll wait until I get the hint direct. You'd better wait too. "

Martha'd made up her mind, though. She says she'd go right then if it wa'n't for leavin' the servants alone in the house; but the very minute Sister Zenobia arrives she means to beat it. And sure enough next day she has her trunk brought down into the front hall and begins wearin' her bonnet around the house. It's a little weird to see her pokin' about dressed that way, and her wraps and rubbers laid out handy, as if she belonged to a volunteer hose comp'ny.

It was after the second day of this watchful waitin', and we're sittin' down to a six-forty-five dinner, when a big racket breaks loose out front. The bell rings four times rapid, Lizzie the maid almost breaks her neck gettin' to the door, and in breezes the runaway pair with all their baggage, chucklin' and chatterin' like a couple of kids. Some stunnin' Aunt Zenobia looks, for all her gray hair; and Mr. Ballard, in his Scotch tweed suit and with his ruddy cheeks, don't look a day over fifty. They're giggling merry over some remark of Lizzie's, and Zenobia calls in through the draperies.

"Hello, Martha—Torchy—everybody! " she sings out. "Well, here we are, back from that absurd boardwalk resort, back to—well, for the love of ladies! Martha Hadley, why in the name of nonsense are you eating dinner with your hat on? "

"Because, " says Martha, beginnin' to sniffle, "I—I'm going away. "

"But where? Why? " demands Zenobia.

And between sobs Martha explains. She includes me in it too.

"Then why aren't you wearing your hat also, Torchy? " asks Zenobia.

"Well, " says I, "I ain't so sure about quittin' as she is. I thought I'd stick around until I got the word to move. "

"Which you're not at all likely to get, young man, " says Zenobia. "And as for you, Martha, you should have better sense. Trapsing off to a hotel, at your time of life! Rubbish! And why, please? "

Aunt Martha nods towards Ballard.

"Well, you're just going to get over that nonsense, " says Zenobia. "Kyrle, you know what you promised when you told me you'd make up with Martha? Now is the appointed time. Do it! "

And Mr. Ballard, chuckin' his hat and overcoat on a chair, sails right in. I expect it was the last thing in the world Martha was lookin' for; for she sits there gazin' at him sort of stupid until he's done the trick. Uh-huh! No halfway business about it, either. He just naturally takes her chubby old face between his two hands, tilts up her chin, and plants a reg'lar final curtain smack where I'll bet it's been forty years since the lips of man had trod before.

First off Martha flops her arms and squeals. Then, when she finds it's all over and ain't goin' to be any continuous performance, she quiets down and stares at the two of 'em, who are chucklin' away merry.

"Please, Sister Martha, " says Ballard, "try to overlook that old affair of mine when I tried to cut out the Rev. Preble. I was rather irresponsible then, I'll own; but I have steadied down a lot, although for the last week or so—well, you know how giddy Zenobia is. But you will help us. We can't either of us spare you, you see. "

Torchy, Private Sec.

Maybe it was the jollyin' speech, or maybe it was the unexpected smack, but inside of five minutes Martha has shed her bonnet and we're all sittin' around the table as friendly and jolly as you please.

I suppose it was by way of makin' Martha feel comf'table and as if she was really part of the game that they got to reminiscin' about old times and the folks they used to know. I wa'n't followin' it very close until Martha gets to askin' Ballard about some of his people, and he starts in on this story about his nephew.

"Poor Dick!" says he, pushin' back his demitasse and lightin' up a big perfecto. "Now if he'd been my boy, things might have turned out differently. But my respected brother—well, you knew Richard, Martha. Not at all like me,—eminently respectable, a bit solemn, and tremendously stiff-necked on occasion. The way he took on about that red-headed Irish girl, for instance. Irene, you know. Why, you might have thought, to have heard him storm around, that she was a veritable sorceress, or something of the kind; when, as a matter of fact, she was just a nice, wholesome, keen-witted young woman. Pretty as a picture, she was, and as true as gold too,—a lot too good for young Dick Ballard, even if she was merely a girl in his father's office. You couldn't blame her for liking Dick, though. Everyone did—the scatter-brained scamp! And when my brother went through all that melodramatic folly of cutting him off with a thousand a year—well, we had our big row over that. That was when I took my money out of the firm. Lucky I did too. When the panic came I was safe."

"Let's see," says Zenobia, "Dick and the girl ran off and were married, weren't they?"

"Yes," says Ballard. "It's in the blood, you see. They went to Paris, to carry out one of Dick's great schemes. He had persuaded some of his friends, big real estate dealers, to make him their foreign agent. His idea was, I believe, to catch Western millionaires abroad and sell 'em Fifth-ave. mansions. Actually did land one or two customers, I think. But it was his wife's notion that turned out to be really practical,—leasing French and Italian villas to rich Americans. Something in that, you know, and if Dick had only stuck to it—but Dick never could. He got in with some mine promoters, and after that nothing would answer but that he must rush right back to Goldfield and look over some properties that were for sale dirt cheap. As though Dick would have been any wiser after he'd seen 'em! But his biggest piece of folly was in taking the little boy along with him."

"What! Away from his mother?" says Martha.

"Just like Dick," says Ballard. "They couldn't both leave the leasing business, and as she knew more about it than he did—well, that's the way they settled it. He persuaded her it would be a fine thing for the youngster. Huh! I came over on the same boat with them, and I want to tell you that little chap simply owned the steamer! Bright? Why, he was the cutest kid you ever saw, —red-headed, like his mother, and with his father's laugh. Spent most of his time on the bridge with the first officer, or down in the engine room with the chief. Dick never knew where he was half the time.

"He was for taking the boy out into the mining country with him too. I supposed he had until I got this frantic cable from Irene. They'd sent her word about Dick's sudden end, —he always did have a weak heart, you know, —and something about the high altitude got him. Went off like that. But Irene was demanding of me to tell her where the boy was. Of course I didn't know. I did my best to find him, hunted high and low. I traced Dick to Goldfield. No use. The boy was not with him when he went West. Where he had left him was a mystery that——"

Buz-z-z-z! goes the front doorbell, right in the middle of Mr. Ballard's story, and in comes Lizzie sayin' it's someone to see me. For a second I couldn't think who'd be huntin' me up here at this time of the evenin'. And then I remembered, —Dorsett.

"It—it's an uncle of mine," says I to Zenobia, "a reg'lar uncle."

"Why," says she, "I didn't know you had one."

"Me either," says I, "until the other day. He just turned up. Could I take him into the libr'y?"

"Of course," says Zenobia.

I was kind of sorry he'd come. I hadn't been so chesty over Uncle Bill at the office; but here, where things are sort of quiet and classy—well, I could see where he wouldn't show up so strong. Besides, I hadn't made up my mind just how I was goin' to turn down his proposition.

I towed him in, though. He was glancin' around the room approvin', and makin' a few openin' remarks, when the folks come strollin' out from the dinin'-room. I glances up, and sees Mr. Ballard just as he's about to pass the door. So does Dorsett. And, say, the minute them two spots each other things sort of hung fire and stopped. Dorsett he breaks short off what he's sayin', and Mr. Ballard comes to a halt and stands starin' in the room. Next I know he's pushed in, and they're facin' each other.

"Pardon me, Sir," says Ballard, "but didn't you cross with me on the *Lucania* once? And weren't you thick with Dick Ballard?"

Course I could see something coming right then; but I didn't know what it was. Mr. Dorsett's shifty eyes take another look at Ballard, and then he hitches uneasy in his chair.

"Rather an odd coincidence, isn't it?" says he. "Yes, I was on board that trip."

"Then you're one of the men I've been looking for a good many years," says Ballard. "You knew Dick very well, didn't you? Then perhaps you can tell me who he left that boy of his with when he went West?"

"Why, yes," says Dorsett, smilin' fidgety. "He—er—the fact is, he left him with me."

"With you, eh? " says Ballard. "I might have guessed as much. Well, Sir, where's the boy now? "

"Wha-a-at? " gasps Dorsett, lookin' from me to Mr. Ballard. "Where, did you say? "

"Yes, Sir, " comes back Ballard snappy. "Where? "

More gasps from Dorsett. But he's good at duckin' trouble. With a wink at me and a chuckle he remarks: "Torchy, suppose you tell the gentleman where you are? "

Well, say, it was some complicated unravelin' we did durin' the next few minutes, believe me; but after Zenobia and Martha had been called in, and Dorsett has done some more of his smooth explainin', we all begun to see where we were at.

"Torchy, " says Zenobia at last, "bring down from your room that little gold locket you've always had. "

And when Mr. Ballard has opened it and held the picture under the readin' light, he winds up the whole debate as to who's who.

"It's Irene, of course, " says he. "Poor girl! But she had her day, after all. Married a French army officer, you know, and for a while they were happy together. Then the war. He was dropped somewhere around Rheims, I believe. Then I heard of her doing volunteer work at a field hospital. She lasted a month or so at that—typhus, or a German shell, I don't know which. But she's gone too. "

And me, I stands there, listenin' gawpy, with my eyes beginnin' to blur. It's Zenobia, you might know, who notices first. She steps over and gathers me in motherly. Not that I needs it, as I know of, but—well, it was kind of good to feel her arm around me just then.

"We'll find out all about it later; won't we, Torchy? " she whispers.

Meanwhile Mr. Ballard has swung on Dorsett. "So you were trying to pose as Uncle Bill, were you? " he demands. "Well, Sir, you're just about the caliber of man Dick would choose to put his trust in! But I'll bet a thousand you were not finding it so easy to fool his boy here! Going, are you? This way, Sir. "

"At that, though, " says I, as the door shuts after Dorsett, "he had me guessin'. "

"Yes, " says Mr. Ballard, "he would, any of us. "

"And I don't see, " I goes on, "as I got any fam'ly left, after all. "

"You—you don't, eh, you young scamp? " says Mr. Ballard. "Well, as there's no doubt about your being my nephew's boy, I'd like to know why I don't qualify as a perfectly good great-uncle to you! "

"Why, that's so! " says I, grinnin' at him. "I—I guess you do. And, say, if you don't mind my sayin' so, you'll do fine! "

So what if Uncle Bill did turn out a ringer! He was more or less useful, even if he did gum up the plot there for a while. Uh-huh! Mighty useful! For there's nothin' phony about my new Uncle Kyrle, take it from me!

CHAPTER XIV

HOW AUNTY GOT THE NEWS

Say, I expect it ain't good form to get chesty over your relations, specially when they're so new as mine; but I've got to hand it to Mr. Kyrle Ballard. After three weeks' tryout he shapes up as some grand little great-uncle, take it from me!

First off, you know, I had him card indexed as havin' more or less tabasco in his temper'ment, with a wide grumpy streak runnin' through his ego. And he is kind of crisp and snappy in his talk, I'll admit. Strangers might think he was a grouch toter. But that's just his way. It's all on the outside. Back of that gruff, offhand talk and behind them bushy, gray eyebrows there's a lot of fun and good nature. One of the kind that's never seemed to grow up, Uncle Kyrle is, sixty-odd and still a kid; always springin' some josh or other, and disguisin' the good turns he does with foolish remarks. And to hear him string Aunt Martha along from one thing to another is sure a circus.

"Good morning, Sister Martha," says he, blowin' in to a late Sunday breakfast, all pinked up in the cheeks from a cold tub and a clean shave. "I trust that you begin the day with a deep conviction of sin?"

"Why, I—I suppose I do, Kyrle," says she, gettin' fussed. "That is, I try to."

"Good!" says Uncle Kyrle. "It is important that some one in this family should recognize that this is a sad and wicked world, with Virtue below par and Honest Worth going baggy at the knees. Zenobia here has no conviction of sin whatever. Mine is rather weak at times. So you, Martha, must do the piety for all of us. And please ring for the griddle cakes and sausage."

Then he winks at Zenobia, gives his grapefruit a sherry bath, and proceeds to tackle a hearty breakfast.

Torchy, Private Sec.

A few days after him and Zenobia got back from their runaway honeymoon trip he calls her to the front door. "There's a person out here who says he has a car for you, " says he.

"Nonsense! " says Zenobia. "Why, I haven't ordered a car. "

"The impudent rascal! " says Uncle Kyrle. "I'll send him off, then. The idea! "

"Oh, but isn't it a beauty? " says Zenobia, peekin' out. "Let's see what he says about it first. "

So they go out to the curb, while Uncle Kyrle demands violent of the young chap in charge what he means by such an outrage. At which the party grins and shows the tag on the steerin' wheel.

"Why! " says Zenobia. "It has my name on it. Oh, Kyrle, you dear man! I've a notion to hug you. "

"Tut, tut! " says he. "Such a bad example to set the neighbors! Besides, this young man may object. He has a Y. M. C. A. certificate as a first-class chauffeur. "

That's the way he springs on Aunt Zenobia an imported landaulet, this year's model, all complete even to monogrammed laprobes and a morocco vanity case in the tonneau. It's one of these low-hung French cars, with an eight-cylinder motor that runs as sweet as the purr of a kitten.

Then here Sunday noon he takes me one side confidential. "Torchy, " says he, "could you assist a poor but deserving citizen to retain the respect of his chauffeur! "

"Go on, shoot it, " says I.

"Don't be rash, young man, " says he, "for the situation is desperate. You see, Herman seems to think we ought to use the machine more than we do. Just to please him we have been whirled through thousands of miles of adjacent suburbs during the last week. Still Herman is unsatisfied. Would it be asking too much if I requested you to let him take you out for the afternoon?"

I gives him the grin. "Maybe I could stand it for this once," says I.

"Noble youth!" says he. "You deserve the iron cross. And should there be perchance anyone who could be induced to share your self-sacrifice——"

The grin plays tag with my ears. "How'd you guess?" says I.

Uncle Kyrle winks and pikes off.

So about two-thirty P. M. I'm landed at a certain number on Madison-ave. and runs jaunty up the front steps. I was hopin' Aunty would either be out or takin' her after-dinner nap. But when it comes to forecastin' her moves you got to figure on reverse English nine cases out of ten. And if ever you want a picture of bad luck to hang up anywhere, get a portrait of Aunty. Out? She's right on hand, as stiff and sour as a frozen dill pickle. Her way of greetin' me cordial as I'm shown into the drawin' room is by humping her eyebrows and passin' me the marble stare.

"Well, young man?" says she.

"Why," says I, "not so well as I was a couple of minutes—er—that it's a fine, spiffy afternoon, ain't it?"

"Spiffy!" says she, drawin' in her breath menacin'.

"Vassarese for lovely," says I. "But I don't insist on the word. By the way, is Miss Vee in?"

"She is," says Aunty. "This is not Friday evening, however."

"Ah, say!" says I. "Can't we suspend the rules and regulations for once? You see, I got a machine outside that's a reg'lar—well, it's some car, believe me! —and seein' how there couldn't be a slicker day for a spin, I didn't know but what you'd let Vee off for an hour or so."

"Just you and Verona?" demands Aunty, stiffenin'.

It was some pill to swallow, but after a few uneasy throat wiggles I got it down. "Unless," says I, "you—you'd like to go along too. You wouldn't, would you?"

Aunty indulges in one of them tight-lipped smiles of hers that's about as merry as a crack in a vinegar cruet. "How thoughtful of you!" says she. "However, I am not fond of motoring."

I don't know whether someone punctured an air cushion just then, or whether it was me heavin' a sigh of relief. "Ain't you?" says I. "But Vee's strong for it, and if you don't mind——"

"My niece is writing letters," says Aunty, "and asked not to be disturbed until after five o'clock."

"But in this case," I goes on, "maybe she'd sidetrack the letters if you'd send up word how——"

"Young man," says Aunty, settin' her chin firm, "I think you are quite aware of my attitude. Your persistent attentions to my niece are wholly unwelcome. True, you are no longer a mere office boy; but—well, just who are you?"

"Private sec. of Mutual Funding," says I.

"And a youth known as Torchy?" she adds sarcastic.

"Yes; but see here!" says I. "I've just dug up a——"

"That will do," she breaks in. "We have discussed all this before. And I've no doubt you think me simply a disagreeable, crotchety old person. Has it ever occurred to you, however, that you may have failed to get my point of view? Can you not conceive then that it might be somewhat humiliating to me to know that my maids suppress a smile as they announce—Mr. Torchy? Understand, I am not censuring you for being a nameless waif. No, do not interrupt. I realize that this is something for which you should not be held responsible. But can't you see, young man——"

"If I can't, " I cuts in, "I need an eye doctor bad. I'll tell you what I'll do about this name business, though. I'm going to issue a white paper on the subject. "

"A—a what? " says Aunty.

"Seein' you ain't much of a listener, " says I, "I'll submit the case in writin'. You win the round, though. And if it don't hurt you too much, you might tell Vee I was here. You can use a bichloride of mercury mouth wash afterwards, you know. "

Saying which, I does the young hero act, swings proudly on muh heel, and exits left center, leavin' Aunty speechless in her chair.

So Herman and me starts off all by our lonesome, swings into the Grand Boulevard and out through Pelham Parkway to the Boston Post Road. Deep glooms for me! Even the way we breezed by speedy roadsters don't bring me any thrills.

I was still chewin' over that zippy roast Aunty had handed me. Nameless waif, eh? Say, that's the rawest she'd ever stated it. Course I was fixed now to show her where she'd overdone the part; but somehow I couldn't seem to frame up any way of gettin' my fam'ly tree on record without seemin' to do it boastful. Besides, Aunty wouldn't take my word for Uncle Kyrle and all the rest. She'd want an affidavit, at least.

But I had made up my mind to have a talk with Vee. I hadn't had more'n a glimpse of her for weeks now, and while I might not feel like givin' her complete details of all that had happened to me recent, I thought I might drop an illuminatin' hint or so. Was I goin' to let a gimlet-eyed old dame with an acetic acid disposition block me off as easy as that?

"Herman," says I, "you can just drop me on Madison-ave. as we go down. And you better report at the house before you put up the machine. They may want to be goin' somewhere."

I'd heard Uncle Kyrle speak of promisin' to make a call on someone he'd met lately that he'd known abroad. As for me, I just strolls up and down two or three blocks, takin' a chance that Vee might drift out. But I sticks around near an hour without any luck.

"Huh!" says I to myself at last. "Might as well risk it again, and if I can't run the gate—well, swappin' a few more plain words with Aunty'll relieve my feelin's some, anyway."

With that I marches up bold and presses the button. "Say," says I to the maid, "don't tell me Aunty's gone out since I left!"

Selma shakes her head solemn as her mighty Swedish intellect struggles to surround the situation. "Meesis she dress by supper in den room yet," says she.

"Such sadness!" says I. "Maybe there's nobody but Miss Vee downstairs?"

"Ja," says Selma, starin' stupid. "Not nobody else but Miss Verona, no."

"You're a bright girl—from the feet down," says I, pushin' in past her. "Shut the door easy so as not to disturb Aunty, and I'll try to cheer up Miss Verona until she comes down. She's in the lib'ry, eh?"

Yep, I was doin' my best. We'd exchanged the greetin's of the season and was camped cozy in a corner davenport just big enough for two, while I was explainin' how tough it was not havin' her along for the drive, and I'd collected one of her hands casual, pattin' it sort of absent-minded, when—say, no trained bloodhound has anything on

Aunty! There she is, standin' rigid between the double doors glarin' at us accusin'.

"So you returned after all that, did you? " she demands.

"I didn't know but you might want to tack on a postscript, " says I.

"Young man, " says she, just as friendly as a Special Sessions Judge callin' the prisoner to the bar, "you are quite right. And I wish to say to you now, in the presence of my niece, that— —"

"Now, Aunty! Please! " breaks in Verona, shruggin' her shoulders expressive.

"Verona, kindly be silent, " goes on Aunty. "This young person known as Torchy has— —"

When in drifts Selma and sticks out the silver card plate like she was presentin' arms.

"What is it? " asks Aunty. "Oh! " Then she inspects the names.

For half a minute she stands there, glancin' from me to the cards undecided, and I expect if she could have electrocuted me with a look I'd have sizzled once or twice and then disappeared in a puff of smoke. But her voltage wa'n't quite high enough for that. Instead she turns to Selma and gives some quick orders.

"Draw these draperies, " says she; "then show in the guests. As for you, young man, wait! "

"Gee! " I whispers, as we're shut in. "I wish I knew how to draw up a will. "

Vee snickers. "Silly! " says she. "Whatever have you been saying to Aunty now? "

"Me?" says I. "Why, not much. Just a little chat about fam'ly trees and so on, durin' which she — —"

Then the arrival chatter in the next room breaks loose, and I stops sudden, starin' at the closed portières with my mouth open.

"Hello!" says I. "Listen who's here!"

"Who?" says Vee.

"That's so," says I. "You don't know 'em, do you? Well, this adds thickenin' to the plot for fair. Remember hearin' me tell of Aunt Zenobia and her new hubby? Well, that's 'em."

"How odd!" says Vee. "But—why, I've heard his voice before! It was at—oh, I know! The nice old gentleman who had the villa next to ours at Mentone."

"Ballard?" I suggests.

"That's it!" says Vee. "And you say he is — —"

"My Uncle Kyrle," says I. "My reg'lar uncle, you know."

"Why, Torchy!" gasps Vee, grabbin' me by the arm. "Then—then you — —"

"Listen!" says I. "Hear your Aunty usin' her comp'ny voice. My! ain't she the gentle, cooin' dove, though? Now they're gettin' acquainted. So this was where Uncle Kyrle spoke of callin'! Hot time he picked out for it, didn't he, with me here in the condemned cell? Say, what do you know about that, eh?"

Vee smothers another giggle, and slips one of her hands into mine. "Don't you care!" says she, whisperin'. "And isn't it thrilling? But what shall we do?"

"It's by me," says I. "Aunty told me to wait, didn't she? Well, let's."

Which we done, sittin' there sociable, and every now and then swappin' smiles as the conversation in the next room took a new turn.

Fin'lly Uncle Kyrle remarks: "You had your little niece with you then, didn't you?"

"Little Verona? Oh, yes, " says Aunty. "She is still with me. Rather grown up now, though. I must send for her. Pardon me. " And she rings for Selma.

Well, that queers the game entirely. Two minutes more, and Vee has been towed in for inspection and I'm left alone in banishment.

"Well, well! " I can hear Uncle Kyrle sing out. "Why, young lady, what right had you to change from a tow-headed schoolgirl into such a—Zenobia, please face the other way and don't listen, while I try to tell this radiant young person how utterly charming she has become. No, I can't begin to do the subject justice. Twenty or thirty years ago I might have had some success. Ah, me! Those gray eyes of yours, my dear, hold mischief enough to wreck a convention of saints. Ah, blushing, are you? Forgive me. I ought to know better. Let me tell you, though, I've a young nephew with a pair of blue eyes that might be a match for your gray ones. You must allow me to bring him up some day. "

And I'd like to have had a glimpse of Vee's face just then. About there, though, Aunty breaks in.

"A nephew, Mr. Ballard? " says she.

"Poor Dick's boy, " says he. "The one we hunted all over the States for after Dick took him on that wild goose chase from which he never came back. Let's see, you must have known the youngster's mother, —Irene Ballard. "

"That stunning young woman with the copper-red hair whom you introduced at Palermo? " asks Aunty. "Is—is she——"

"No," says Uncle Kyrle. "Poor Irene! She was always doing something for someone, you know, and when this big war got under way—well, she went to the front at the first call from the Red Cross. I might have known she would. I suppose she simply couldn't bear to keep out of it—all that suffering, and so much help needed. No more skillful or efficient hands than hers, I'll wager, Madam, were ever volunteered, nor any braver soul. She was pure gold, Irene."

"And," puts in Aunty, "she was—er——"

Uncle Kyrle nods. "In a field hospital, under fire," says he, "late last September. That's all we know. Where do you think, though, I ran across that boy of hers? Found him at Zenobia's; found them both rather, at a theater. Sheer luck. For if you'll pardon my saying it, that youth is a nephew I'm going to be proud of some of these days unless I am——"

Say, this was gettin' a little too personal for me. I'd been shiftin' around uneasy for a minute or two, and about then I decided it wouldn't be polite to listen any longer. So I make a dash out the side door into the hall, not knowin' just what to do or where to go. And I bumps into Selma wheelin' in the tea wagon. That gives me a hunch.

"Say, Bright Eyes," says I, pushin' a dollar at her, "take this and ditch that tea stuff for a minute, can't you? Harken! There's goin' to be a new arrival at the front door in about a minute, and you must answer the bell. No, don't indulge in that open-face movement. Just watch me close!"

With that I clips past the drawin'-room entrance, opens the front door gentle, and gives the button a good long push. Then I slides back and digs up a card case that Aunt Zenobia has presented me with only a couple of days ago.

"Here!" says I. "Get out your plate and pass one of these to the Missus. That's it. Push it right on her conspicuous. Now! On your way!"

She's real quick at startin', Selma is, when she's shoved brisk from behind. And as she goes through the doorway I stretches my ear to hear what Aunty will say to the new arrival. And, believe me, if I'd given her the lines myself, she couldn't have done it better!

"Mr. Richard Taber Ballard? " says she, readin' the card. Then she turns to Uncle Kyrle. "Why, this must be some——"

"Eh? " says he. "Did you hear that, Zenobia? Torchy, you young rascal, come in here and explain yourself! "

"Torchy! " gasps Aunty. "Did—did you say—Torchy? "

"Anybody callin' for me? " says I, steppin' into the room with a grin on.

And to watch that stary look settle in Aunty's eyes, and see the purple tint spread back to her ears, was worth standin' for all the rough deals I'd ever had from her. At last I had her bumpin' the bumps! Sort of dazed she inspects the card once more, and then glances at me. Do you wonder? Richard Taber Ballard! I ain't got used to it myself.

"Here he is, " says Uncle Kyrle jovial, draggin' me to the front, "that scamp nephew I was telling you about. The Richard is for his father, you know; the Taber he gets from his mother—also his red hair. Eh, Torchy? And this, young man, is Miss Verona. "

He swings me around facin' her, and I expect I must have acted some sheepish. But trust Vee! What does she do but let loose one of them ripply laughs of hers. Then she steps up, pulls my head down playful with both hands, and looks me square in the eyes.

"Why didn't you tell me before, Torchy, " says she, "that you had such a perfectly grand name as all that? "

"Huh!" says I. "A swell chance I've had to tell you anything, ain't I? But if the folks will excuse us for half an hour, I'll tell you all I know about a lot of things."

And, say, Aunty don't even glare after us as we slips through the draperies into the lib'ry, leavin' 'em to explain to each other how I come to be on hand so accidental. The only disturbance comes when Selma butts in pushin' the tea cart, and, just from force of habit, I makes a panicky breakaway. After she's insisted on loadin' us up with sandwiches and so forth, though, I slips my arm back where it fits the snuggest.

"Now, Sir," says Vee, "how are you going to hold your cup?"

"I'd be willin' to miss out on tea forever," says I, "for a chance like this."

CHAPTER XV

MR. ROBERT AND A CERTAIN PARTY

We was havin' a directors' meetin'. Get that, do you? *We*, you know! For nowadays, as private sec. and actin' head of Mutual Funding, I crashes into all sorts of confidential pow-wows. Uh-huh! Right in where they put a crimp in the surplus and make plots to slip things over on the Commerce Board! Oh my, yes! I'm gettin' almost respectable enough to be indicted.

Well, we'd just pared the dividend on common and was about breakin' up the session when Mr. Robert misses some figures on export clearances he'd had made up and was pawin' about on the table aimless.

"Didn't I see you stowin' that away in one of your desk pigeonholes yesterday? " I suggests.

"By George! " says he. "Think you could find it for me, Torchy? And, by the way, bring along my cigarettes too. You will find them in a leather case somewhere about. "

I locates the export notes first stab; but the dope sticks ain't in sight. I claws through the whole top of the desk before I fin'lly discovers, shoved clear into a corner, a thin old blue morocco affair with a gold catch. By the time I gets back he's smokin' a borrowed brand and tosses the case one side.

Half an hour later the meetin' is over. Mr. Robert sighs relieved, bunches up a lot of papers in front of him, and begins feelin' absent-minded in his pockets. Seein' which I pushes the leather case at him.

"Ah, yes, thanks, " says he, and snaps it open careless.

But no neat little row of paper pipes shows up. Inside is nothing but a picture, one of these dinky portraits on ivory—mini'tures, ain't they? It shows a young lady with a perky chin and kind of a quizzin' look in her eyes: not a reg'lar front row pippin', you know, but a fairly good looker of the highbrow type.

For a second Mr. Robert stares at the portrait foolish, and then he glances up quick to see if I'm watchin'. As it happens, I am, and blamed if he don't tint up over it!

"Excuse," says I. "Only leather case I could find. Besides, I didn't know you had any such souvenirs as this on your desk."

He chuckles throaty. "Nor I," says he. "That is, I'd almost forgotten. You see— —"

"I see," says I. "She's one of the discards, eh?"

Sort of jolts him, that does. "Eh?" says he. "A discard? No, no! I—er—I suppose, if I must confess, Torchy, that I am one of hers."

"Gwan!" says I. "You? Look like a discard, don't you? Tush, tush!"

The idea of him tryin' to feed that to me! Why, say, I expect there ain't half a dozen bachelors in town that's rated any higher on the eligible list than Mr. Bob Ellins. It's no dark secret, either. I've heard of whole summer campaigns bein' planned just to land Mr. Robert, of house parties made up special to give some fair young queen a chance at him, and of one enterprisin' young widow that chased him up for two seasons before she quit.

How he's been able to dodge the net so long has puzzled more than me, and up to date I'd never had a hint that there was such a thing for him as a certain party. So I expect I was gawpin' some curious at the picture.

"Huh!" says I, but more or less to myself.

"Not intending any adverse criticism of the young lady, I trust?" remarks Mr. Robert.

"Far be it from me!" says I. "Only—well, maybe the paintin' don't do her justice."

"Rather discreetly phrased, that," says he, chucklin' quiet. "Thank you, Torchy. And you are quite right. No mere painter ever could do her full justice. While the likeness is excellent, the flesh tones much as I remember them, yet I fancy a great deal has escaped the brush,—the queer, quirky little smile, for instance, that used to come at times in the mouth corners, a quick tilting of the chin as she talked, and that trick of widening the eyes as she looked at you. China blue, I think her eyes would be called; rather unusual eyes, in fact."

He seems to be enjoyin' the monologue; so I don't break in, but just stands there while he gazes at the picture and holds forth enthusiastic. Even after he's finished he still sits there starin'.

"Gee!" says I. "It ain't a hopeless case, is it, Mr. Robert?"

Which brings him out of his spell. He shrugs his shoulders, indulges in an unconvincin' little laugh, snaps the case shut, and then tosses it careless down onto the table.

"Perhaps you failed to notice the dust," says he. "The back part of the bottom drawer is where that belongs, Torchy—or in the waste basket. It's quite hopeless, you see."

"Huh!" says I as I turns to go. And this time I meant to get it across to him.

Honest, I couldn't figure why a headliner like Mr. Robert, with all his good bank ratin', good fam'ly, and good looks to back him, should get the gate on any kind of a matrimonial proposition, unless it was a case of coppin' a Princess of royal blood, and even then I'd back him to show in the runnin'. Who was this finicky party with the willow-ware eyes, anyway? Queen of what? Or was it wings she was demandin'?

"He seems to be enjoying the monologue; so I just stands there while he gazes at the picture and holds forth enthusiastic."

Say, I most got peeved with this unknown that had ditched Mr. Robert so hard. All that evenin' I mulls over it, wonderin' how long ago it had happened and if that accounted for him bein' so cagy in makin' social dates. Not that he's what you'd call skirt-shy exactly; but I've noticed that he's always cautious about bein' backed into a corner or paired off with any special one.

Course, not knowin' the details of the tragedy, it wa'n't much use speculatin'. And somehow I didn't feel like askin' for the whole story right out. You know—there's times when you just can't. I ain't any more curious than usual over this special case, either; but, seein' how many good turns Mr. Robert's done for me along the only-girl line, I got to wishin' there was some way I could sort of balance the account.

So when I stumbles across this concert folder it almost looks like a special act, with the arrow pointin' my way. I was payin' my reg'lar official Friday evenin' call. No, nothin' romantic. Just because Aunty's mellowed up a bit since I'm announced proper by the front door help as Mr. Ballard, don't get tangled up with the idea that she stands for any dark corner twosin'. Nothin' like that! All the lights are on full blast, Aunty's right there prominent with her crochet, and on the other side of the table is me and Vee. And I couldn't be behavin' more innocent if I'd been roped to the chair. All I was holdin' was a skein of yarn. Uh-huh! You see, Vee got the knittin' habit last winter, turnin' out stuff for the Belgians, and now she keeps right on; though who she's goin' to wish a pink and white shawl onto in this weather is a myst'ry.

"It's for a sufferer—isn't that enough? " says she.

"From what—chilblains on the ears? " says I.

"Silly! " says she. "There! Didn't I tell you to bend your thumbs? How awkward! "

"Who, me? " says I. "Why, for a first attempt I thought I was puttin' up a real classy performance. Say, lemme wind awhile, and let's see you try this yarn-jugglin' act. "

She won't, though; so it's me sittin' there playin' dummy, with my arms held out stiff and my eyes roamin' around restless.

Which is how I happen to spot this folder with the halftone cut on it. It's been tossed casual on the table, and the picture is wrong side to from where I am; but even then there's something mighty familiar about it. I wiggles around to get a better view, and lets half a dozen loops of yarn slip off at a time.

"Stupid!" says Vee, runnin' her tongue out at me.

"Didn't I tell you you'd do better by drapin' it over a chair back?" says I. "But say, time out while I snoop into something. Who's the girl with the press notice stuff?" and I points an elbow at the halftone.

"That?" says she. "Oh, some concert singer, I think. Let's see. Yes— Miss Elsa Hampton. She's to give a benefit song recital in the Plutoria pink room for the Belgian war orphans, tickets two dollars. Want to go?" And Vee flips the folder into my lap.

Gettin' the picture right side to, I lets out a whistle. No mistakin' that. "Sure I want to go," says I.

"Why?" says Vee.

"Well, for one thing," says I, "she has china blue eyes that widen out when they look at you, and a queer, quirky little smile that——"

"How thrilling!" says Vee. "You must know her very well."

"Almost that," says I. "Anyway, I know someone that did know her very well—once."

"Oh!" says Vee, forgettin' all about the yarn windin' and hitchin' her chair up close. "That does sound interesting. I hope it isn't a deep secret."

"If it wa'n't," says I, "what would be the fun in tellin' it to you?"

"Goody!" says Vee. "Who is the poor man who knew her once but doesn't any more?"

"Whisper!" says I. "It's Mr. Bob Ellins!"

"Wha-a-at!" gasps Vee. "Do you really mean it?"

I'd pulled a sensation, all right, and for the next half-hour she keeps me busy tryin' to explain the details of a situation I hadn't more'n half sketched out myself.

"Kept a miniature of her on his desk!" Vee rattles on. "And it hadn't been opened for ever so long, you say? What makes you think it hadn't?"

"Dusty," says I.

"Oh!" says Vee. "Just fancy! And she must have given it to him herself—an ivory miniature, you know. Was—was there another man, do you think, or just some silly misunderstanding? I wonder?"

"I hadn't got in that deep," says I.

"But suppose it was," says Vee, "only a misunderstanding, wouldn't it be lovely if we could find some way of—of—well, why don't you suggest something?"

Did I? Say, we was plottin' so lively there for a spell, with our heads close together, that I can't tell for a fact which it was did get the idea first.

But, anyway, when I'm busy at the Corrugated next mornin', openin' the first batch of mail and sortin' the junk from the important letters, I laid the mine. All I had to do was pick out an envelope postmarked Madison Square, ditch the art dealers' card that came in it, and substitute this song recital folder, opened so the picture couldn't be missed. And when I stacks the letters on Mr. Robert's desk I tucks that one in second from the top. Some grand little strategy that, eh?

Then I keeps my ear stretched for any remarks Mr. Robert may unload when he makes the great discovery. But, say, when you try dopin' out such a complicated party as Mr. Bob Ellins you've tackled some deep proposition. Nothin' emotional about him, and although I'm sittin' only a dozen feet off, half facin' his way too, I don't get even the hint of a smothered gasp. Couldn't even tell whether he'd seen the picture or not, and by the time I works up an excuse to drift over by his elbow he's halfway through the pile.

"Nothin' startlin' in the mornin' run, eh? " I throws out.

"Oh, yes, " says he. "Mallory reports that those St. Louis people have applied for another injunction. Ring up Bates, will you, and have him call a general council of our legal staff for two-thirty? "

"Right, " says I. "Er—anything else, Mr. Robert? "

He simply shakes his head and dives into another letter. At that, though, I was lookin' for him to sound me out sooner or later on the picture business; but the forenoon breezes by without a word. By lunchtime I'm more twisted than ever. Had he glanced at the halftone without recognizin' her? Or was he just keepin' mum? Not until I gets a chance to explore the waste basket did I get any line. The folder wa'n't there. Neither was it on his desk. And all the hints I threw out durin' the day he don't seem to notice at all. So I didn't have much to tell Vee over the 'phone that night.

"Couldn't get a rise out of him at all, " says I.

"But you're certain Miss Hampton is the one, are you? " says she.

"If she wa'n't, " says I, "why should he keep the folder? "

"That's so, " says Vee. "Then—then shall we do it? "

"I'm game if you are, " says I.

"All right, " says she, and I hears one of them ripplin' laughs of hers comin' over the wire. "It's to-morrow at half after three, you know. "

"I'll be on hand, " says I.

And, believe me, when I gets there and sees the swell mob collectin' in the pink ballroom, I'm some pleased with myself for gettin' that hunch to doll up in my frock coat and lavender tie. It's mostly a fluff audience; but there's enough of a sprinklin' of Johnnies and old sports so I don't feel too conspicuous.

Course I wa'n't lookin' forward to any treat. I ain't so strong for this recital stuff as a rule; but I was anxious to size up the young lady who'd thrown the harpoon into Mr. Robert so hard. Same way with Vee. So we edges through to a front seat and waits expectant.

And, say, what fin'lly glides out on the stage and bows offhand to the soft patter of kid gloves is only an average looker. She's simple dressed and simple actin'. No frills about Miss Hampton at all. Why, you might easy mistake her for one of the girl ushers!

"Pooh! " says Vee.

"Also pooh for me, " says I.

More or less easy and graceful in her motions Miss Hampton is, though, I got to admit, as she stands there chattin' with the accompanist and lettin' them big blue eyes of hers rove careless over the crowd in front. They ain't the stary, baby blue sort, you know. China blue describes 'em best, I guess; and they're the calm, steady kind that it's sort of restful and fascinatin' to watch.

Almost before we know it she's stepped to the front and started in on the programme. Italian folk songs is what is down on the card, and she leads off with that swingin' rollickin' piece, "Santa Lucia. " You've heard it, eh? That's some song, ain't it?

But, say, I never knew how much snap and go there was to it until I heard Miss Hampton trill it out. Why, she just tosses up that perky chin of hers and turns loose the catchy melody until you felt the warm waves splashin' and saw the moonlight dancin' across the bay! I don't know where or what this Santa Lucia thing is, but she most made me homesick to go back there. Honest! And if you think a set of odd-shaded blue eyes can't light up and sparkle with diff'rent expressions, you should have seen hers. When she finishes and springs that folksy, chummy sort of smile—well, take it from me, the hand she gets ain't any polite, halfway, for-charity's-sake applause. They just went to it strong, gloves or no gloves.

"Isn't she bully? " whispers Vee.

"Uh-huh! " says I. "We take back the pooh-poohs, eh? "

The next number was diff'rent, but just as good. At the finish of the fourth a wide old dame in the middle row unpins a cluster of orchids from her belt and aims 'em enthusiastic at the stage. Course they swats a dignified old boy three seats beyond me back of the ear; but that starts the floral offerings. I gets a quick nudge from Vee.

"Go on, Torchy, " she whispers. "Do it now! "

We hadn't been sure first off that we'd have the nerve to carry the thing that far; but we'd come all primed. So I yanks the tissue paper off a dozen long-stemmed American beauts that I'd smuggled in under my coat, Vee ties on the card, and I tosses the bunch so accurate it lands almost on Miss Hampton's toes.

Course any paid performer would have been tickled to death to have a crowd break loose like that; but Miss Hampton acts a bit dazed by it all. For a second or so she stands there gazin' sort of puzzled, bitin' her upper lip. Then she springs that quirky, good-natured smile of hers, bows a couple of times, and proceeds to help the accompanist gather up the flowers and stack 'em on the piano.

When she comes to our big bunch she swoops it up graceful, and is about to pile it with the rest when her eyes must have caught the card. Just as easy and natural as if she'd been at home, she turns it over and reads the name.

And, say, for a minute there I thought we had bust up the show. Talk about goin' pink! Why, you could see the strawb'rry tint spread over her cheeks and up into her ears! Blamed if her eyes don't moisten up too, and she sweeps over the audience with a quick nervous glance, like she was tryin' to single someone out! She don't seem to know what to do next. Once she turns as if she meant to beat it into the wings; but as the applause simmers down the pianist strikes up the beginning of an encore. So she had to stick it out.

Her voice is more or less shaky at the start; but pretty soon she strikes her gait again and sings the last verse better than she had before. Then comes an intermission, and when Miss Hampton appears again she's wearin' that whole dozen roses pinned over her heart. Vee nudges me excited when she spots it.

"See, Torchy? " says she.

"Guess we've started something, eh? " says I.

Just what it was, though, we didn't know. I didn't get cold feet either, until the concert is all over and the folks begun swarmin' around the stage to pass over the hot-air congratulations.

But Miss Hampton wa'n't content to stand there quiet and take 'em. She seems to have something on her mind, and the next thing I knew she was pikin' down the steps right towards the middle aisle.

"Gee! " says I, grabbin' Vee by the arm. "Maybe she saw who passed 'em up. Let's do the quick exit. "

We was gettin' away as fast as we could too, squirmin' through the push, when I looks over my shoulder and discovers that Miss Hampton is almost on our heels.

"Good-night! " says I.

Torchy, Private Sec.

Believe me, I was doin' some high-tension thinkin' about then, tryin' to frame up an alibi, when she reaches over my shoulder and holds out her hand to someone leanin' against a pillar. It's Mr. Robert.

"How absurd of you, Robert!" says she.

"Eh! I—I beg pardon?" I hears him gasp out.

And, say, I expect that's the first and only time I've ever seen him good and fussed. Why, he's flyin' the scarlatina signal clear to the back of his neck!

"The roses, you know," she goes on. "So nice of you to remember me. I—I thought you'd forgotten. Thank you for them."

"Roses?" says he husky, starin' stupid at the bunch.

Then he turns his head a bit, and his eyes light on me, strugglin' to slip behind a tall female party who's bein' helped into her silk wrap. I must have looked guilty or something; for he shoots me a crisp, knowin' glance.

"Oh, yes—the—the roses," I hears him go on. "It was silly of me, wasn't it? I—I'll explain some time, if I may."

"Oh!" says she. "Of course you may, if they really need explaining."

Which was the last we heard, as Vee had found an openin' into the corridor and was dashin' out panicky. You can bet I follows!

"Did—did you ever?" pants Vee as we gets out to the carriage entrance. "Now we have done it, haven't we?"

"And I'm caught with the goods on, I guess," says I.

"Just fancy!" says she. "Mr. Robert was there all the time. I wonder what he will——"

"Pardon me, you pair of mischief makers," says a voice behind, "but I haven't quite decided."

It's Mr. Robert!

"Hel-lup!" says I gaspy.

"Do I understand," he goes on, "that one of my cards went with those roses?"

"Yep," says I prompt. "Little idea of mine. I—I wanted to see what would happen."

"Really!" says he sarcastic. "Well, I trust that my part of the performance was quite satisfactory to you." And with that he wheels and marches off.

"Whiffo!" says I, drawin' in a long breath. "But he is grouched for fair, ain't he!"

All the sympathy I gets from Vee, though, is a chuckle. "Don't you believe a word of it," says she. "Just wait!"

CHAPTER XVI

TORCHY TACKLES A SHORT CIRCUIT

There was no use discountin' the fact, or tryin' to smooth it over. I was in Dutch with Mr. Robert—all because Vee and I tried to pull a little Cupid stunt for his benefit. I'd invested six whole dollars in that bunch of roses we'd passed up to Miss Hampton, too! And just because we thought it would be a happy hunch to tie in his card with 'em, he goes and gets peevish.

Not that he comes right out and roasts me for gettin' gay. Say, that would have been a relief; but he don't. He just lugs around a dignified, injured air and gives me the cold eye. Say, that's the limit, that is! Makes me feel as mean and little as a green strawb'rry on top of a bakery shortcake.

Three days I'd had of it, mind you, with never a show to put in any defense, or plead guilty but sorry, or anything like that. And me all the time hoping it would wear off. I expect it would too, if someone could have throttled Billy Bounce. Course nobody could, or it would have happened long ago. Havin' no more neck than an ice-water pitcher has been Billy's salvation all through his career.

Maybe you don't remember my mentionin' him before; but he's the roly-poly club friend of Mr. Robert's who went with us on that alligator shootin' trip up the Wiggywash two winters ago. Hadn't shown up at the Corrugated General Offices for months before; but here the other afternoon he breezed in, dumps his 220 excess into a chair by the roll-top, mops the heavy dew from various parts of his full-moon face, and proceeds to get real folksy.

At the time I was waitin' on the far side of the desk for Mr. Robert to O. K. a fundin' report, and there was other signs of a busy day in plain sight; but Billy Bounce ain't a bit disturbed by that. He'd come in loaded with chat.

"Oh, I say, Bob, " he breaks out, after a few preliminary joshes, "who do you suppose I ran across up in the Fitz-William palm room the other night? "

"A head waiter, " says Mr. Robert.

"Oh, come! " says Billy. "Give a guess. "

"One of your front-row friends from the Winter Garden? " asks Mr. Robert.

"No, a friend of yours, " says Billy. "That blue-eyed warbler you used to be so nutty over—Miss Hampton. Eh, Bob? How about it? " With which he reaches over playful and pokes Mr. Robert in the ribs.

I expect he'd have put it across just as raw if there'd been a dozen around instead of only me. That's Billy Bounce. About as much delicate reserve, Billy has, as a traffic cop clearin' up a street tangle.

"Indeed! " says Mr. Robert, flushin' a bit. "Clever of you to remember her. I—er—I trust she was charmed to meet you again? "

"The deuce you do! " comes back Billy. "Anyway, she wasn't as grouchy about it as you are. Say, she's all right, Miss Hampton is; a heap too nice for a big ham like you, as I always said. "

"Yes, I believe I recall your hinting as much, " says Mr. Robert; "but if you don't mind I'd rather not discuss——"

"You'd better, though, " says Billy. "You see, I thought I had to drag you into the conversation. Asked her if she'd seen you lately. And say, old man, she's expecting you to call or something. Lord knows why; but she is, you know. Said you'd probably be up to-night. As much as asked me to pass on the word. Eh, Bob?

"Well, I've done it. S'long. See you at the club afterwards, and you can tell me all about it. "

He winks roguish over his shoulder as he waddles out, leavin' Mr. Robert starin' puzzled over the top of the desk, and me with my mouth open.

And the next thing I know I'm gettin' the inventory look-over from them keen eyes of Mr. Robert's. "You heard, I suppose? " says he.

"Uh-huh, " says I, sort of husky.

"And I presume you understand just what that means? " he goes on. "I am expected to call and explain about those roses. "

"Well? " says I. "Why not stand pat? Sendin' flowers to a young lady ain't any penal offense, is it? "

"As a simple statement of an abstract proposition, " says Mr. Robert, "that is quite correct; but in this instance the situation is somewhat more complicated. As a matter of fact, I find myself in a deucedly awkward position. "

"That's easy, " says I. "Lay it to me, then. "

Mr. Robert shakes his head. "I've considered that, " says he; "but sometimes the bald truth sounds singularly unconvincing. I'm sure it would in this case. If the young lady was familiar with all the buoyant audacity of your irrepressible nature, perhaps it would be different. No, young man, I fear I must ask you to do your own explaining. "

"Me? " says I, gawpin'.

"We will call on Miss Hampton about four-thirty, " says he.

And say, Mr. Robert has stacked me up against some batty excursions before now; but this billin' me for orator of the day when he goes to look up an old girl of his is about the fruitiest performance he'd ever sprung.

Torchy, Private Sec.

I don't know when I've ever seen him with a worse case of the fidgets, either. Why, you'd 'most think he was due to answer a charge of breakin' and enterin', or something like that! And you know he's some nervy sport, Mr. Robert—all except when it's a matter of skirts. Then he's more or less of a skittish party, believe me!

But at four-thirty we went. It wa'n't any joy ride we had, either. All the way up Mr. Robert sits there fillin' the limousine with gloom thick enough to slice. I tried chirkin' him up with a few frivolous side remarks; but they don't take, and I sighs relieved when we're landed at the apartment hotel where Miss Hampton lives.

"Say," I suggests, "you ain't goin' to lead me in by the ear, are you?"

"I'm not sure but that would be an appropriate entrance," says he. "However, it might appear a trifle theatrical."

"What's the programme, anyway?" says I, as we boards the elevator. "Do you open for the defense, or do I?"

"Hanged if I know!" he almost groans out. "I wish I did."

"Then let's stick around outside in the corridor here," says I, "until we frame up something. Now how would it do if——"

"You're to explain, that's all!" says he, steppin' up and pushin' the button.

It's a wonder too, from the panicky way he's actin', he don't shove me ahead of him for a buffer as we goes in. But he has just enough courage left to let me trail along behind.

So it's him gets the cordial greetin' from the vision in blue net that floats out easy and graceful from the window nook.

I couldn't see why it wa'n't goin' to be just as awkward for her, meetin' him again so long after their grand smash, or whatever it was; but, take it from me, there ain't any fussed motions about Miss

Hampton at all. Them big china blue eyes of hers is steady and calm, her perky chin is carried well up, and in one corner of her mouth she's displayin' that quirky smile he'd described to me.

"Ah, Robert!" says she. "So good of you to——"

Then she discovers me and breaks off sudden.

I'm introduced reg'lar and formal, and Mr. Robert adds: "A young friend of mine from the office."

"Oh!" says Miss Hampton, liftin' her eyebrows a little.

"I brought him along," blurts out Mr. Robert, "to tell you about how you happened to get the roses."

"Really!" says she. "How considerate of you!"

And if Mr. Robert hadn't been actin' so much like a poor prune he'd have quit that line right there. But on he blunders.

"You see," says he, "I've asked Torchy to explain for me."

"Ye-e-es?" says she, bitin' her upper lip thoughtful and glancin' from one to the other of us. "Then—then you needn't have bothered to come yourself, need you?"

Say, that was something to lean against, wa'n't it? You could almost hear the dull thud as it reached him.

"Oh, I say, Elsa!" he gets out gaspy. "Of course I—I wished to come, too."

"Thank you," says she. "I wasn't sure. And now that you've brought him, may I hear what your young friend has to say, all by myself?"

She even springs another one of them twisty smiles; but her head nods suggestive at the door. I expects I starts a grin; but one glimpse of Mr. Robert's face and it fades out. He wa'n't happy a bit. For a minute he stands there lookin' sort of dazed, as if he'd been hit with a lead pipe, and with his neck and ears tinted up like a raspb'rry sundae.

"Very well, " says he, and does a slow exit, leavin' me gawpin' after him sympathetic.

Not for long, though. My turn came as soon as the latch was clicked.

"Now, Torchy, " says she, chummy and encouragin', as she slips into an old-rose armchair and waves me towards another.

I'm still gazin' at the door, wonderin' if Mr. Robert has jumped down the elevator shaft or is takin' it out on the lever juggler.

"Ah, say, Miss Hampton! " says I. "Why throw the harpoon so hasty when he was doin' his best? "

"Was he? " says she. "Then his best isn't very wonderful, is it? "

"But you didn't give him a show, " says I. "Course it was a dippy play of his, luggin' me along, as I warned him. Believe me, though, he meant all right. There ain't any more yellow in Mr. Robert than there is in my tie. Honest! Maybe he don't show up brilliant when he's talkin' to ladies; but I want to tell you he's about as good as they come. "

"Indeed! " says she, widenin' her eyes and chucklin' easy. "That is what I should call an unreserved indorsement. But about the roses, now? "

Well, I sketched the plot of the piece all out for her, from findin' her miniature accidental in Mr. Robert's desk, to the day of the concert, when she got the bunch with his card tied to it.

"I'll admit it was takin' a chance, " says I; "but you see, Miss Hampton, when I was joshin' him as to whose picture it was he got so enthusiastic in describin' you— —"

"Did he, truly? " she cuts in.

"Unless I don't know a Romeo gaze when I see one, " says I. "And then, when I figures out that if you'd given him the chuck it might have been through some mistaken notion, why—well, come to talk it over with Vee, we thought— —"

"Pardon me, " says Miss Hampton, "but just who is Vee? "

"Eh? " says I, pinkin' up. "Why, in my case, she's the only girl. "

"Ah-ha! " says she. "So you—er— —"

"Uh-huh! " says I. "I've come near bein' ditched myself. And Mr. Robert he's helped out more'n once. So this looked like my cue to hand back something. We thought maybe the roses would kind of patch things up. Say, how about it, Miss Hampton? Suppose he hadn't boobed it this way, wouldn't there be a show of— —"

"You absurd youth! " says she, liftin' both hands protestin', but failin' to smother that smile.

And say, when it's aimed straight at you so you get the full benefit, that's some winnin' smile of hers—sort of genuine and folksy, you know! It got me. Why, I felt like I'd been put on her list of old friends. And I grins back.

"It wa'n't a case of another party, was it? " says I.

She laughs and shakes her head.

"Or an old watch-dog aunt, eh? " I goes on.

"Whatever made you think of that? " says she.

"You ought to see the one that stands guard over Vee, " says I. "But how was it, anyway, that Mr. Robert got himself in wrong with you? "

"How? " says Miss Hampton, restin' her perky chin on one knuckle and studyin' the rug pattern. "Why, I think it must have been—well, perhaps it was my fault, after all. You see, when I left for Italy we were very good friends. And over there it was all so new to me, — Italian life, our villa hung on a mountainside overlooking that wonderful blue sea, the people I met, everything, —I wrote to him, oh, pages and pages, about all I did or saw. He must have been horribly bored reading them. I didn't realize until—but there! We'll not go into that. I stopped, that's all. "

"Huh! " says I.

"So it's all over, " says she. "Only, when I thought he had sent the roses, of course I was pleased. But now that he has taken such pains to prove that he didn't——"

She ends with a shoulder shrug.

"Say, Miss Hampton, " I breaks in, "you leave it to me. "

"But there isn't anything to leave, " says she, "not a shred! Sometime, though, I hope I may meet your Miss Vee. May I? "

"I should guess! " says I. "Why, she thinks you're a star! We both do. "

"Thank you, Torchy, " says she. "I'm glad someone approves of me. Good-by. " And we shakes hands friendly at the door.

It was long after five by that time; but I made a break back to the office. Had to get the floor janitor to let me in. I was glad, though, to have the place to myself.

What I was after was a peek at some back letter files. Course I wa'n't sure he could be such a chump; but, knowin' somethin' about his habits along the correspondence line, I meant to settle the point.

Torchy, Private Sec.

And, fishin' out Mr. Robert's personal book, I begun the hunt. I had the right dope, too.

"The lobster!" says I.

There it was, all typed out neat, "My Dear Miss Hampton." And dictated! Much as ten lines, too! It starts real chatty and familiar with, "Yours of the 16th inst. at hand," just like he always does, whether he's closin' a million-dollar deal or payin' a tailor's bill. He goes on to confide to her how the weather's beastly, business on the fritz, and how he's just ordered a new sixty-footer that he hopes will be in commission for the July regattas.

A hot billy-doo to a young lady he's supposed to be clean nutty over, one that had been sittin' up nights writin' on both sides of half a dozen sheets to him! I found four or five more just like it, the last one bein' varied a little by startin', "Yours of the 5th inst. still at hand." Do you wonder she quit?

If this had been a letter-writin' competition, I'd have thrown up both hands; but it wa'n't.

I'd seen Mr. Robert gazin' mushy at that picture of her, and I'd watched Miss Hampton when she was tellin' me about him. Only they was short-circuited somewhere. And it seemed like a blamed shame.

Half an hour more and I'd located Mr. Robert at his club.

He ain't very enthusiastic, either, when one of the doormen tows me into the corner of the loungin' room where he's sittin' behind a tall glass gazin' moody at nothin' in particular.

"I suppose you told her all about it!" says he.

"And then a few," says I.

"Well?" says he sort of hopeless.

"Verdict for the defense, " says I. "I didn't even have to produce the florist's receipt. "

"Then that's settled, " says he, sighin'.

"You couldn't have made the job more complete if you'd submitted affidavits, " says I. "And if you don't mind my sayin' so, Mr. Robert, when it comes to the Romeo stuff, you're ten points off, with no bids. "

Course that gets a squirm out of him, like I hoped it would. But he don't blow out a fuse or anything. "Naturally, " says he, "I am charmed to hear such a frank estimate of myself. But suppose I am simply trying to avoid the—the Romeo stuff, as you put it? "

"Gwan! " says I. "You're only kiddin' yourself. Come now, ain't you as strong for Miss Hampton as ever? "

He stiffens up for a second; but then his shoulders sag. "Torchy, " says he, "your perceptions are altogether too acute. I admit it. But what's the use? As you have so clearly pointed out, this little affair of mine seems to be quite thoroughly ended. "

"It is if you let things slide as they stand, " says I.

"Eh? " says he, sort of eager. "You mean that she—that if——"

"Say, " I breaks in, "do you want it straight from a rank amateur? Then here goes. You don't gen'rally wait to have things handed to you on a tray, do you? You ain't that kind. You go after 'em. And the harder you want 'em the quicker you are on the grab. You don't stop to ask whether you deserve 'em or not, either. You just stretch your fingers and sing out, 'Hey, that's mine! ' And if somebody or something's in the way, you give 'em the shoulder. Well, that's my dope in this case. You ain't goin' to get a young lady like Miss Hampton by doin' the long-distance mope. You got to buck up. Rush her off her feet! "

"By Jove, though, Torchy, " says he, bangin' his fist down on the table, "I believe you're right! And I do want her. I've been afraid to say it, that's all. But now——"

He squares his shoulders and sets his jaw solid.

"That's the slant! " says I. "And the sooner the quicker, you know. "

"Yes, yes! " says he, jumpin' up. "Tonight! I—I'll write to her at once. "

"Ah, squiffle! " says I, indicatin' deep disgust.

Mr. Robert gazes at me astonished. "I beg pardon! " says he.

"Don't be a nut! " says I. "Excuse me if I seem to throw out any hints, but maybe letter writin' ain't your long suit. Is it? "

"Why, " says he, "I'm not sure, but I had an idea I could——"

"Maybe you can, " says I; "but from the samples I've seen I should have my doubts. You know this 'Yours of the steenth just received' and so on may do for vice-presidents and gen'ral managers; but it's raw style to spring on your best girl. Take it from me, sizzlin' sentiments that's strained through a typewriter are apt to get delivered cold. "

"But I'm not good at making fine speeches, either, " he protests.

"You ain't exactly tongue-tied, though, " says I. "And you ain't startin' out on this expedition with both arms roped behind you, are you? "

For a minute he stares at me gaspy, while that simmers through the oatmeal.

Then he chuckles. "Torchy, " says he, givin' me the inside-brother grip, "there's no telling how this will turn out, but I—I'm going up! "

Torchy, Private Sec.

I stayed long enough to see him start, too.

Then I goes home, not sure whether I'd set the scene for an ear cuffin', or had plugged him in on a through wire.

CHAPTER XVII

MR. ROBERT GETS A SLANT

It's all wrong, Percy, all wrong. Somebody's been and rung in a revise on this Romeo dope, and here we find ourselves tryin' to make the Cupid Express on a canceled time-card. What do I mean—we? Why, me and Mr. Robert. Ah, there you go! No, not Miss Vee. She's all right—don't worry. We're gettin' along fine, Vee and me; that is, so far as we've gone. Course there's 'steen diff'rent varieties of Vee; but I'm strong for all of 'em. So there's no room for tragedy there.

But when it comes to this case of Mr. Robert and a certain party!

You see, after I've sent him back to Miss Hampton loaded up with all them wise hints about rushin' her off her feet, and added that hunch as to rememberin' that he has a pair of arms—well, I leave it to you. Ain't that all reg'lar? Don't they pass it out that way in plays and magazines? Sure! It's the hero with the quick-action strong-arm stuff that wins out in the big scene. So why shouldn't it work for him?

I could tell, though, by the rugged set of his jaw as he marches into the private office next mornin', that it hadn't. I expect maybe he'd just as soon not have gone into the subject then, with me or anyone else; but so long as he'd sort of dragged me into this fractured romance of his I felt like I had a right to be let in on the results. So I pivots round and springs a sympathetic grin.

"Did you pull it?" says I.

He shrugs his shoulders kind of weary. "Oh, yes," says he. "I—er—I pulled it."

"Well?" says I, steppin' over and leanin' confidential on the roll-top.

"Torchy," says he, "please understand that I am in no way censuring you. You—you meant well."

"Ah, say, Mr. Robert!" says I. "Not so rough. I only gave you the usual get-busy line, and if you went and— —"

"Wasn't there some advice," he breaks in, "about using my arms?"

"Eh?" says I, gawpin' at him. "You—you didn't open the act by goin' to a clinch, did you?"

He lets his chin drop and sort of shivers. "I'm afraid I did," says he.

"Z-z-z-zingo!" I gasps.

"You see, the part of your suggestions which impressed me most was something to that effect, as I recall it. And then—oh, the deuce take it, I lost my head! Anyway, the next I knew she was in my arms, and I—I was— —" He ends with a shoulder shrug and spreads out his hands. "I thought you ought to know," he goes on, "that it isn't being done."

"But what then?" says I. "Did she hand you one?"

"No," says he. "She merely slipped away and—and stood laughing at me. She hardly seemed indignant: just amused."

"Huh!" says I, starin' puzzled. "Then she ain't like any I ever heard of before. Now accordin' to dope she'd either— —"

"Miss Hampton is not a conventional young woman," says he. "She made that quite plain. It seems, Torchy, that your—er—that my method was somewhat crude and primitive. In fact, I believe she pointed out that the customs of the Stone Age were obsolete. I was given to understand that she was not to be won in any such manner. Perhaps you can imagine that I was not thoroughly at ease after that."

And, honest, I'd never seen Mr. Robert when he was feelin' so low.

"Gee!" says I. "You didn't quit at that, did you?"

"Unfortunately no," says he. "Our caveman tactics having failed, I tried the modern style—at least, I thought I was being modern. The usual thing, you know."

"Eh?" says I. "Both knees on the rug and the reg'lar conservatory nook wilt-thou-be-mine lines?"

"I spoke my piece standing," says he, "making it as impassioned and eloquent as I knew how. Miss Hampton continued to be amused."

"Did you get any hint as to what was so funny about all that?" says I.

"It appears," says Mr. Robert, "that impassioned declarations are equally out of date—early-Victorian, to quote Elsa exactly. Anyway, she gave me to understand that while my love-making was somewhat entertaining, it was hopelessly medieval. She very kindly explained that undying affection, tender devotion, and the protection of manly arms were all tommyrot; that she really didn't care to be enshrined queen of anyone's heart or home. She wishes to avoid any step that may hinder the development of her own personality. You—er—get that, I trust, Torchy?"

"Clear as mush," says I. "Was it just her way of handin' you the blue ticket?"

"Not quite," says Mr. Robert. "That is, I'm a little vague as to my exact status myself. I assume, however, that I've been put on probation, as it were, until we become better acquainted."

"And you're standin' for that, Mr. Robert!" says I.

He hunches his shoulders. "Miss Hampton has taught me to be humble," says he. "I don't pretend to understand her, or to explain her. She is a brilliant and superior young person. She has, too, certain advanced ideas which are a bit startling to me. And yet, even when she's hurling Bernard Shaw or H. G. Wells at me she—she's fascinating. That quirky smile of hers, the quick changes of expression that flash into those big, china-blue eyes, the sudden lift of her fine chin, —how thoroughly alive she is, how well poised! So I—well, I want her, that's all. I—I want her!"

"Huh!" says I. "Suppose you happened to get her? What would you——"

"Heaven only knows!" says he. "The question seems rather, what would she do with me? Hence the probation."

"Is this going to be a long-distance tryout," says I, "with you reportin' for inspection every other Tuesday?"

He says it ain't. Miss Hampton's idea is to shelve the matrimony proposition and begin by seein' if they can qualify as friends. She shows him how they'd never really seen enough of each other to know if they had any common tastes.

"So I am to go with her to a few concerts, art exhibits, lectures, and so on," says he, "while she has consented to try a week-end yachting cruise with me. We start Saturday; that is, if I can make up a little party. But I don't just know whom to ask."

"Pardon me if I seem to hint," says I, "but what's the matter with brother-in-law Ferdie and Marjorie, with Vee and me thrown in for luck?"

"By Jove!" says he, brightenin' up. "Would you? And would Miss Vee?"

"Maybe we could stand it," says I.

"Done, then!" says he. "I'll 'phone Marjorie at once."

And you should have watched Mr. Robert for the next few days. Talk about consistent trainin'! Why, he quits goin' to the club, cuts out his lunch-hour, and reports at the office at eight-thirty. Not for business, though: Bernard Shaw. Seems he's decided to specialize in Shaw.

Honest, I finds him one noon with a whole tray of lunch gettin' cold, and him sittin' there with his brow furrowed up over one of them batty plays.

"Must be some thrillin', " says I.

"It's clever, " says he; "but hanged if I know what it's all about! I must find out though—I must! "

He didn't need to state why. I could see him preparin' to swap highbrow chat with Miss Hampton.

Meanwhile he barely takes time to 'phone a few orders about gettin' the cruisin' yawl ready for the trip. I hear him ring up the Captain, tell him casual to hire a cook and a couple of extra hands, provision for three or four days, and be ready to sail Saturday noon. Which ain't the way he usually does it, believe me! Why, I've known him to hold up a directors' meetin' for an hour while he debated with a yacht tailor whether a mainsail should be thirty-two foot on the hoist, or thirty-one foot six. And instead of shippin' up cases of mineral water and crates of fancy fruit, he has them blamed Shaw books packed careful and expressed to Travers Island, where the boat is.

We was to meet there about noon; but it's after eleven before Mr. Robert shuts his desk and sings out to me to come along. We piles into his roadster and breezes up through town and out towards the Sound. Found the whole party waitin' for us at the club-house: Vee and Marjorie and Miss Hampton, all lookin' more or less yachty.

"Hello! " says Mr. Robert. "Haven't gone aboard yet? "

"Go aboard what, I'd like to know? " speaks up Marjorie.

"Why, the *Pyxie*, " says he. "See, there she is anchored off—well, what the deuce! Pardon me for a moment. "

With that he steps over to a six-foot megaphone swung from the club veranda and proceeds to boom out a few remarks.

"*Pyxie* ahoy! Hey, there! On board the *Pyxie*! " he roars.

No response from the *Pyxie*, and just as he's startin' to repeat the performance up strolls one of the float tenders and hands him a note which soon has him gaspy and pink in the ears. It's from his fool captain, explainin' how that rich uncle of his in Providence had been taken very bad again and how he had to go on at once. The message is dated last Wednesday. Course, there's nothing for Mr. Robert to do but tell the crowd just how the case stands.

"How absurd—just an uncle! " pouts Marjorie. "Now we can't go cruising at all, and—and I have three pairs of perfectly dear deck shoes that I wanted to wear! "

"Really! " says Mr. Robert. "Then we'll go anyway; that is, if you'll all agree to ship as a Corinthian crew. What do you say? " And he glances doubtful at Miss Hampton.

"I'm sure I don't know what that means, " says she; "but I am quite ready to try. "

"Oh, let's! " says Vee, clappin' her hands. "I can help. "

"And Ferdie is a splendid sailor, " chimes in. Marjorie. "He's crossed a dozen times. "

"Then we're off, " says Mr. Robert.

And inside of ten minutes the club launch has landed us, bag and baggage, on the *Pyxie*.

Torchy, Private Sec.

She's a roomy, comf'table sort of craft, with a kicker engine stowed under the cockpit. There's a couple of staterooms, plenty of bunks, and a good big cabin. We leaves the ladies to settle themselves below while Mr. Robert inspects things on deck.

"Plenty of gasoline, thank goodness! " says he. "And the water butts are full. We can touch at Greenwich for supplies. Now let's get sail on her, boys. "

And it was rich to see Ferdie, all gussied up in yellow gloves, throwin' his whole one hundred and twenty-three pounds onto a rope. Say, about all the yachtin' Ferdie and me had ever done before was to stand around and look picturesque. But this was the real thing, and it comes mighty near bein' reg'lar work, take it from me.

But by the time the girls appeared we had yanked up all the sails that was handy, and the *Pyxie* was slanted over, just scootin' through the choppy water gay and careless, like she was glad to be tied loose.

"Isn't this glorious? " exclaims Miss Hampton, steadying herself on the high side and glancin' admirin' up at the white sails stretched tight as drumheads.

I expect that should have been Mr. Robert's cue to shoot off something snappy from Bernard Shaw; but just about then he's busy cuttin' across in front of a big coastin' schooner, and all he remarks is:

"Hey, Torchy! Trim in on that main sheet. Trim in, you duffer! Pull! That's it. Now make fast. "

Nothin' fancy about Mr. Robert's yachtin' outfit. He's costumed in an old pair of wide-bottomed white ducks some splashed with paint, and with his sleeves rolled up and a faded old cap pulled down over his eyes he sure looks like business. I could see Miss Hampton glancin' at him sort of curious.

But he don't have time to glance back; for we was zigzaggin' up the Sound, dodgin' steamers and motor-boats and other yachts, and he was keepin' both eyes peeled. Every now and then too something had to be done in a hurry.

"Ready about!" he'd call. "Now! Hard alee! Leggo that jib sheet—you, Ferdie. Slack it off. Now trim in on the other side. Flatter. Oh, haul it home!"

And I expect Ferdie and me wa'n't any too much help.

"Why, I never knew that yachting could be so exciting," says Miss Hampton. "It's really quite a game, isn't it?"

"Especially with a green crew," says Mr. Robert.

"But what a splendid breeze!"

"It'll be fresh enough by the time we open up Captain's Island," says he. "Just wait!"

Sure enough, as we gets further up the Sound the harder it blows. The waves got bigger too, and begun sloppin' over the bow, up where Ferdie was managin' the jib.

"Oh, I say!" he sings out. "I'm getting all splashed, you know."

"Couldn't he have an umbrella?" asks Marjorie.

"Please," puts in Vee, "let me handle the jib sheets. I've sailed a half-rater, and I don't mind getting wet, not a bit."

"Then for the love of soup go forward and send Ferdie aft!" says Mr. Robert. "Quick now! I'm coming about again. Hard alee!"

"How wonderful!" says Miss Hampton as she watches Vee juggle the ropes skillful. "I wish I could do that!"

"Do you? " says Mr. Robert eager. "Perhaps you'll let me teach you how to sail. Would you like to try the wheel? Here! Now this way puts her off, and the other brings her up. See? "

"N-n-not exactly, " says Miss Hampton, grippin' the spokes gingerly.

It wa'n't any day, though, for a steerin' lesson. Most of the time the deck was on quite a slant, which seems to amuse Miss Hampton a lot.

"How odd! " says she. "We're sailing almost on edge, aren't we? Isn't it glorious! "

Mr. Robert don't seem to be so enthusiastic. He keeps watching the sails and the water and rollin' the wheel constant.

"I suppose we really ought to get some of this canvas off her, " says he. "Ferdie, could you help tie in a reef? "

"I—I don't know, I'm sure, " says Ferdie. "I think perhaps——"

"This wouldn't be a thinking job, " says Mr. Robert. "Of course I might douse the mainsail altogether and run under jib and jigger; but—no, I guess she'll carry it. Ease off on that main sheet a trifle, Torchy. "

We was makin' a straight run for it now, slap up the Sound—and believe me we was breezin' along some swift! Vee had come back with the rest of us, her hair all sparkled up with salt spray and her eyes shinin', and shows me how to coil up the slack of the sheet like a doormat. On and on we booms, with the land miles away on either side.

"But see here! " protests Ferdie. "I thought we were to stop at Greenwich for provisions. "

"Make in there against this head wind? " says Mr. Robert. "Not today. "

It's comin' in heavy puffs now, and the sky is cloudin' up some. Two or three times Mr. Robert heads the *Pyxie* up into it and debates about takin' in the mainsail. Then he decides it would be better to square off and make for some cove he knows of on the north shore of Long Island. So we let out the sheet a bit more and go plungin' along.

Must have been about four o'clock when it got to blowin' hardest. A puff would hit us and souse the bow under, with the spray flyin' clear over us. We'd heel until the water was runnin' white along the lee deck from bow to stern. Then it would let up a bit, and the yacht would straighten and sort of shake herself before another came.

"I think we'll have to slack away on our peak and spill some of this over the gaff, " says Mr. Robert. "Torchy, stand by that halyard, and when I give the word — —"

Cr-r-r-rack! It come mighty abrupt. For a minute I can't make out what has happened; but when I sees the mast stagger and go lurchin' overboard, sail and all, I thought it was a case of women and children first.

"Oh, dear! How dreadful of you, Robert! " wails Ferdie. "We're wrecked! Help! Help! "

"Oh, dry up, Ferdie! " says Mr. Robert. "No hysterics, please. Can't we lose a mast or so without gettin' panicky? Just a weak turnbuckle on the weather stay, that's all. Here, Vee, take the wheel, will you, and see if you can keep her headed into it while we chop away this wreckage. Torchy, you'll find a couple of axes over the forward lockers. Get 'em up. Lively, now! "

We hacked away reckless, choppin' through wire stays and ropes, until we has it all clear. Then we trims in the jigger and gets away from it. Two minutes later and we've got the engine started and are wallowin' along towards land. It was near six before we made the cove and anchored in smooth water behind a little point.

Meanwhile the girls had gone below to explore the galley, and when we fin'lly makes everything snug, and trails on down into the cabin to see how they're comin' on, what do we find but the table all set and Marjorie fillin' the water glasses. Also there's a welcome smell of food driftin' about.

"Well, well! " says Mr. Robert. "Found something to eat, did you? What's the menu? "

"Smothered potatoes with salt pork, baked beans, hard-tack, and coffee, " says Marjorie. "Here it comes. "

And, say, maybe that don't sound so thrillin' to you, but to me it listens luscious.

"By Jove! " says Mr. Robert, after he's sampled the layout. "Who's the cook! "

Vee says it was Miss Hampton.

"Wha-a-at? " says he, starin'. "Not really? "

Miss Hampton comes back at him with that quirky smile of hers. "Why the intense surprise? " says she.

"But I didn't dream, " says Mr. Robert, "that you ever did anything so—er——"

"Commonplace? "

"Early-Victorian, " he corrects.

"Cook? " says she. "Oh, dear, yes! I can wash dishes, too. "

"Can you? " says he. "I'm fine at wiping 'em. "

"Such conceit!" says she.

"Then I'll prove it," says he, "right after dinner."

"I'll help you, Robert," says Marjorie.

"My dear sister," says he, "please consider the size of the *Pyxie's* galley."

So, as there didn't seem to be any more competition, after we'd finished everything in sight we left the two of 'em joshin' away merry, doin' the dishes. Later on, while Ferdie's pokin' around, he makes a discovery.

"Oh, I say, Bob," he calls down, "there's a box up here that hasn't been opened. Groceries, I think. Come have a look at it."

Mr. Robert he takes one glance and turns away disgusted. "No," says he. "I know what's in there. No use at all on this trip." Then, as he passes me he whispers: "I say, when you get a chance, chuck that box overboard, will you?"

I nods, grinnin', and explains confidential to Vee.

And half an hour or so afterwards, ten perfectly good volumes of Bernard Shaw splashed overboard.

Next we sends Ferdie to take a peek down the companionway and report.

"They're looking at a chart," says he.

"Same side of the table," says I, "or opposite?"

"Why, they're both on one side."

"Huh!" says I, nudgin' Vee. "That highbrow line might work out in time, but for a quick get-together proposition I'm backin' the dishpan."

CHAPTER XVIII

WHEN ELLA MAY CAME BY

Believe me, this job of bein' private sec. all day and doublin' as assistant Cupid after hours may be entertainin' and all that, but it ain't any drowsy detail. Don't leave you much time for restin' your heels high or framin' up peace programmes. Course, the fact that Vee is in with me on this affair between Mr. Robert and Miss Hampton is a help. I ain't overlookin' that.

And after our mix-up yachtin' cruise, when we lost a mast and Bernard Shaw overboard the same day, it looked like we'd got everything all straightened out. Why not? Mr. Robert seems to have decided that his lady-love wa'n't such a confirmed highbrow as he'd suspected, and he was doin' the steady comp'ny act constant and enthusiastic, just the way he does everything he tackles, from yacht racin' to puttin' a crimp in an independent. In fact, he wa'n't doin' much else.

"Where's Robert? " demands Old Hickory, marchin' out of his private office and glarin' at the closed roll-top.

"I expect he's takin' the afternoon off, " says I, maybe grinnin' a bit.

"Huh! " says the boss. "The second this week! I thought that fool regatta was over. "

"Yes, sir, it is, " says I. "Besides, he didn't enter. "

"Oh! " says Mr. Ellins. "Then it isn't a case of a sixty-footer! "

"The one he's tryin' to manage now is about five-foot six, " says I.

"Eh? " says Old Hickory, workin' his eyebrows. "That Miss Hampton again? "

I nods.

"Torchy," he goes on, "of course I've no particular right to be informed, being only his father, but—er—about how much longer should you say that affair would run before it comes to some sort of climax? In other words, how is he getting on?"

"The last I knew," says I, "he was comin' strong. Course, he made a couple of false starts there at the send-off, but now he seems to have struck his gait."

"Really!" says Old Hickory. "And now, solely in the interest of the Corrugated Trust, could you go so far as to predict a date when he might reasonably be expected to resume business activities?"

I chews that over a minute, and runs my fingers thoughtful through my red thatch.

"Nope," says I. "If I was any such prize guesser as that, I'd be down in Wall Street buckin' the market. Maybe after Sunday, though, I might make a report one way or the other."

"Ah! You scent a crisis, do you?" says he.

"It's this way," says I. "Marjorie's givin' a little week-end house party for 'em out at her place, and—well, you know how that's apt to work out at this stage of the game."

"You think it may end the agony?" says he.

"There'll be a swell chance for twosin'," says I. "Marjorie's plannin' for that."

"I see," says Mr. Ellins. "Undisturbed propinquity—a love charm that was old when the world was young. And if Marjorie is managing the campaign, it's all over with Robert."

Torchy, Private Sec.

That was my dope on the subject too, after I'd seen the layout of her first skirmish. There was just half a dozen of us mobilized at this flossy suburban joint Saturday afternoon, but from the start it was plain that four of us was on hand only to keep each other out of the way of this pair. Course, Vee and I hardly needs to have the cue passed. We were satisfied to hunt up a veranda corner of our own and stick to it.

But Brother-in-law Ferdie, with that doubleply slate roof of his, needs watchin' close. He has a nutty idea that he ought to be sociable, and he no sooner spots Mr. Robert and Miss Elsa Hampton, chattin' cozy in a garden nook, than he's prompted to kick in and explain to 'em all about the Latin names of the surroundin' vines and shrubbery. Which brings out business of distress from Marjorie. So one of us has to go shoo him away.

"Why—er—what's the matter? " says he, blinkin' puzzled, after he's been led off.

"You was makin' a noise like a seed catalogue, that's all, " says I. "Chop it, can't you? "

Ferdie only stares at me through his thick window-panes and puts on an injured air. Half an hour later, though, he's at it again.

"You tell him, Torchy, " sighs Marjorie. "Try to make him understand. "

So I makes a strong stab.

"Look, " says I, towin' him off on a thin excuse. "That ain't any convention they're holdin' out there. So far as they know, it's just a happy chance. If they're let alone the meetin' may develop tender moments. Anyway, you might give 'em a show, and if they want you bad they can run up a flag. See? There's times, you know, when two is bliss, but a third is a blister. Get me? "

I expect he did, in a way. The idea filters through sort of slow, but he finally decides that, for some reason too deep for him to dig up, he ain't wanted mixin' around folksy.

So from then on until dinnertime our couple had all the chance in the world. Looked like they was doin' noble, too; for every once in a while we could hear that ripply laugh of hers, or Mr. Robert's hearty chuckle—which should have been good signs that they was enjoyin' each other's comp'ny. We even had to send out word it was time to doll up for dinner.

But an affair like that is like a feather balanced on your nose. Any boob is liable to open a door on you. In this case, all was lovely and serene until Marjorie gets this 'phone call. I hears her summonin' Vee panicky and sketchin' out the details.

"It's Ella May Buell! " says she. "She's down at the station. "

Seems that Miss Buell was a boardin'-school friend who was about to cash in one of them casual blanket invitations that girls give out so reckless—you know, the Do-come-and-see-me-any-time kind. And, with her livin' down in Alabama or Georgia somewhere, maybe it looked safe at the time. But now she was on her way to the White Mountains for a summer flit, and she'd just remembered Marjorie for the first time in three years.

"Goodness! " says Marjorie, whisperin' husky across the hall. "Someone ought to go right down to meet her. I can't, of course; and Ferdie's only begun to dress. "

"Ask Torchy, " suggests Vee.

And, as I'm all ready except another half hitch to my white tie, I'm elected. Three minutes more and I'm whizzin' down in the limousine to receive the Southern delegate. And say, when I pipes the fairy in the half-masted skirt and the zippy Balkan bonnet, I begins bracin' myself for what I could see comin'.

One of these pouty-lipped, rich-tinted fairies, Ella May is, wearin' a baby stare and chorus-girl ear-danglers. Does she wait to be hunted up and rescued? Not her! The minute I drops out of the machine, she trips right over and gives me the hail.

"Are you looking for me? " says she. "I hope you are, for I've been waiting at this wretched station for ages. "

"If it's Miss Buell, I am, " says I.

"Of course I'm Miss Buell, " says she. "Help me in. Now get my bags. They're inside, Honey. "

"Inside what? " I gasps.

"Why, the station, " says she. "And give the man a quarter for me — there's a dear. "

Talk about speed! Leave it to the Dixie girls of this special type. I used to think our Broadway matinée fluffs was about the swiftest fascinators using the goo-goo tactics. But say, when it comes right down to quick action, some of these cotton-belt belles can throw in a high gear that makes our Gwendolyns look like they was only hittin' on odd cylinders. Ella May was a sample. We was havin' our first glimpse of each other, but in less 'n forty-five seconds by the watch she'd called me honey, dearied me twice, and patted me chummy on the arm. And we hadn't driven two blocks before she had me snuggled up in the corner like we was old friends.

"Tell me, Honey, " says she, "what is dear old Marjorie's hubby like? "

"Ferdie! " says I. "Why, he's all right when you get to know him. "

"Oh! " says she. "That kind! But aren't there any other men around? "

"Only Mr. Robert Ellins, " says I.

"Really! " says she, her eyes widenin'! "Bob Ellins! That's nice. I met him once when he came to see Marjorie at boarding school. I was such an infant then, though. But now — —"

She dives into her vanity bag and proceeds to retouch the scenic effects on her face.

"Don't waste it, " says I. "He's sewed up—a Miss Hampton. She's there, too. "

"Pooh! " pouts Miss Buell. "Who cares? She doesn't keep him in a cage, does she? "

"It ain't that, " says I; "but his eyesight for anyone else is mighty poor. "

"Oh, is it? " says she, sarcastic and doubtful. "We'll see about that. But, anyway, I'm beginning to be glad I came. Can you guess why? "

"I'm a wild guesser, " says I. "Shoot it. "

"Because, " says she, "I think I'm going to like you rather well. "

More business of cuddlin', and a hand dropped careless on my shoulder. We were still more 'n a mile from the house, and if I was to do any blockin'-off stunt, it was high time I begun. I twists my head around and gazes at the careless hand.

"Excuse me, sister, " says I, "but before this goes any further I got to ask a question. Are your intentions serious? "

"Why, the idea! " says she. "What on earth do you mean? "

"I only want to be sure, " says I, "that you ain't tryin' to trifle with my young affections. "

She stiffens at that and goes a little gaspy. Also she grabs away the hand.

"Of all the conceit!" says she. "Anyone might think that—that——"

"So they might," says I. "Of course, it's sweet to be picked out this way; but it's a little sudden, ain't it? You know, I'm kind of young and——"

"I've a great mind to box your ears!" breaks in Ella May.

"In that case," says I, "I couldn't even promise to be a brother to you."

"Wretch!" says she, her eyes snappin'.

"Sorry," says I, "but you'll get over it. It may be a little hard at first, but in time you'll meet another who will make you forget."

That last jab had her speechless, and all she could do was run her tongue out at me. But it worked. After that she snuggled in her own corner, and when we lands at the house she's treatin' me with cold disdain, almost as if I'd been a reg'lar brother. There's no knowin', either, what report Marjorie got. Must have been something interestin', for when she finally comes down after steerin' Miss Buell to her room, she gives me the knowin' wink.

Ella May gets even, though. She holds up dinner forty-five minutes while she sheds her travelin' costume for an evenin' gown. And it's some startlin' creation she springs on us about the time we're ready to bite the glass knobs off the dinin'-room doors. She's a stunner, all right, and she sails down with that baby stare turned on full voltage.

You'd most thought, though, with all the hints me and Marjorie had dropped, and her seein' Mr. Robert and Miss Hampton chattin' so busy together, that she'd have hung up the net and waited until she struck better huntin' grounds. But not Ella May. Here was a perfectly good man; and as long as nobody had handcuffs on him, or hadn't guarded him with barbed wire, she was ready to take a chance.

Just how she managed it I couldn't say, even if it was done right under my eyes; but when we starts in for dinner she's clingin' sort of playful to one side of Mr. Robert, chatterin' a steady stream, while Miss Hampton is left to drift along on the other, almost as if she was an "also-ran."

Mr. Robert wa'n't havin' such a swell time that meal, either. About once in three or four minutes he'd get a chance to say a few words to Miss Hampton, but most of the time he was busy listenin' to Ella May. So was the rest of us, in fact. Not that she was sayin' anything important or specially interestin'. Mainly it's snappy personal anecdotes—about Ella May, or her brother Glenn, or Uncle Wash Lee, the Buell fam'ly butler. Or else she's teasin' Mr. Robert about not rememberin' her better, darin' him to look her square in the eyes, and such little tricks.

Say, she was some whirlwind performer, take it from me. I discovers that everybody was "Honey" to her, even Ferdie. And you should have seen him tint up and glance panicky at Marjorie the first time she put it over on him.

As for Miss Hampton, she appears to be enjoyin' the whole thing. She watches Miss Buell sparkle and roll her eyes, and only smiles sort of amused. For what Ella May is unlimberin' is an attack in force, as a war correspondent would put it—an assault with cavalry, heavy guns, and infantry. And, for all his society experience, Mr. Robert don't seem to know how to meet it. He acts sort of dazed and helpless, now and then glancin' appealin' across to Sister Marjorie, or around at Miss Hampton.

All that evenin' the attack goes on, Ella May workin' the spell overtime, gettin' Mr. Robert to let her read his palm, pinnin' flowers in his buttonhole, and keepin' him cornered; while the rest of us sits around like cheap deadheads that had been let in on passes.

And next mornin', when Mr. Robert makes a desperate stab to duck right after breakfast, only to be captured again and led into the garden, Marjorie finally gets her mad up.

"Really, " says she, "this is too absurd! Of course, she always was an outrageous flirt. You should have seen her at boarding school—with the music professor, the principal's brother, the school doctor. Twice they threatened to send her home. But after I've told her that Robert was practically engaged to Miss Hampton—well, it must be stopped, that's all. Ferdie, can't you think of some way? "

"Eh? " says Ferdie. "What? How? "

That's the sort of help he contributes to this council of war Marjorie's called on the side terrace.

And all Vee will do is to chuckle. "It's such, a joke! " says she.

"But it isn't, " says Marjorie. "Do you know where Elsa Hampton is at this minute? In the library, reading a magazine—alone! And she and Robert were getting on so nicely, too. Torchy, can't you suggest something? "

"Might slip out there with a rope and tie her to a tree while Mr. Robert makes his escape, " says I.

A snicker from Vee.

"Please! " says Marjorie. "This is really serious. I can't explain to Elsa. But what must she think of Robert? I've simply got to get rid of that girl somehow. She's one of the kind, you know, who would stay and stay until——"

"Hello! " says I, glancin' out towards the entrance-gates. "What sort of a delegation is this? "

A tall, loppy young female in a sagged skirt and a faded pink shirtwaist is driftin' up the driveway, towin' a bow-legged three-year-old boy by one hand and luggin' a speckle-faced baby on her hip.

"Oh! " says Marjorie. "That scamp of a Bob Flynn's Katie again. "

Seems Flynn had been one of Mr. Robert's chauffeurs that he'd wished onto Ferdie a year or so back on account of Flynn's bein' married and complainin' he couldn't support his fam'ly in the city. If he could get a place in the country, where the rents wa'n't so high and his old chowder-party friends wa'n't so thick, Flynn thought he might do better. He had steadied down for a while, too, until he took a sudden notion to slope and leave his interestin' fam'ly behind.

"She's coming to ask if we've heard anything of him, " goes on Marjorie. "I've a good notion to send her straight to Robert. "

"Say, " says I, havin' one of my thought-flashes, "wait a minute. We might—do I understand that the flitting hubby's name was Robert? "

Marjorie nods.

"And will you stand for anything I can pull off that might jar Ella May's strangle-hold over there! "

"Anything, " says Marjorie.

"Then lend me this deserted fam'ly for a few minutes, " says I. "I ain't had time to sketch out the plot of the piece exactly, but if you say so I'll breeze ahead. "

It was going to be a bit raw, I'll admit; but Marjorie has insisted that it's a desperate case. So, after a short confab with Mrs. Flynn and the kids, they're turned over to me.

"I ain't sure, ma'am, " says I, "that young Mr. Ellins can spare the time. He's pretty busy just now. But maybe I can break in long enough to ask him, and if he's heard anything—well, you can be handy. Suppose you wait here at the garden gate. No, leave it open, that way. "

I had 'em grouped conspicuous and dramatic; and, with Mrs. Flynn's straw lid tilted on one side, and the youngster whimperin' to be let loose among the flowers, and the baby sound asleep with its mouth open, the picture was more or less pathetic.

At the far end of the garden path was a different sort of scene. Ella May was making Mr. Robert hold one end of a daisy chain she was weavin', and she's prattlin' away kittenish when I edges up, scufflin' my feet warnin' on the gravel. She greets me with a pout. Mr. Robert hangs his head sort of sheepish, but asks hopeful:

"Well, Torchy?"

"She—she's here again, sir," says I.

"Eh?" says he, starin' puzzled. "Who is here?"

"S-s-s-sh!" says I, shakin' my head mysterious.

All of which don't escape Miss Buell. Her ears are up and her eyes wide open. "What is it?" she asks.

"If I could have a few words in private with you, Mr. Robert," says I, "maybe it would be——"

"Nonsense!" says he. "Out with it."

"Just as you like," says I. "Only, she's brought the kids with her this time. She says how she wants her Robert back."

"Wha-a-at!" he gasps.

"Couldn't keep her out," says I. "You know how she is. There they are, at the gate."

I don't know which was quicker to turn and look, him or Ella May. And just then Mrs. Flynn happens to be gazin' our way, pleadin' and expectant.

"Oh! " says Mr. Robert, laughin' careless. "Katie, eh? "

Miss Buell has jumped and is starin' at the group. Then, at that laugh of Mr. Robert's, she whirls on him.

"Brute! " says she. "I'm glad she's found you. "

With which she dashes towards the house and disappears, leavin' Mr. Robert gawpin' after her.

"Why, " says he, "you—you don't suppose she could have imagined that—that——"

"Maybe she did, " says I. "My fault, I expect. I could find her, though, and explain how it was. I'll bet that inside of five minutes she'd be back here finishin' the floral wreath. Shall I? "

"Back here? " he echoes, kind of vague. Then he comes to.

"No, no! " says he. "I—I'd rather not. I want first to—— Where is Miss Hampton, Torchy? "

Well, I gives him full directions for findin' her, slips Mrs. Ryan the twenty he sends her instead of news from hubby, and then goes in, to find that Ella May is demandin' to be taken to the next train. We saw that she caught it, too, before she changed her mind.

"By George! " Mr. Robert whispers confidential to me, as the limousine rolls off with her in it, "if I could insure against such risks as that, I would take out a policy. "

"You can, " says I. "Any justice of the peace or minister will fix you up for life. "

Does that sink in? I wouldn't wonder. Anyway, from the hasty glimpse I caught of him and Miss Hampton strollin' out in the moonlight that night, it looked that way.

Torchy, Private Sec.

So I did have a bulletin for Old Hickory Monday mornin'.

"It's all over but the shoutin', " says I.

CHAPTER XIX

SOME HOOP-LA FOR THE BOSS

I must say it wa'n't such a swell time for Mr. Robert to be indulgin' in any complicated love affair. You know how business has been, specially our line. And our directors was about as calm as a bunch of high school girls havin' hysterics. Jumpy? Say, some of them double-chinned old plutes couldn't reach for a glass of ice water without goin' through motions like they was shakin' dice.

It's this sporty market that had got on their nerves. You know, all these combine rumors—this bunk about Germany buyin' up plants wholesale, and the grand scrabble to fill all them whackin' big foreign orders, with steamer charters about as numerous as twin baby carriages along Riverside Drive. Why, say, at one time there you could have sold us ferryboats or garbage-scows, we was so hungry for anything that would carry ocean freights.

And, of course, with Old Hickory Ellins at the helm, the Corrugated Trust was right in the thick of it. About twice a week some fool yarn was floated about us. We'd sold out to Krupps and was goin' to close; we'd tied up with Bethlehem; we'd underbid on a flock of submarines and was due for a receivership—oh, a choice lot of piffle!

But a few of them nervous old boys, who was placid enough at annual meetin's watchin' a melon bein' cut, just couldn't stand the strain. Every time they got fed up on some new dope from the Wall Street panic peddlers, they'd come around howlin' for a safe and sane policy. I stood it until here the other mornin' when a bunch of soreheads showed up before nine o'clock and proceeds to hold an indignation meetin' in front of my desk.

"Gwan! " says I. "Nobody's rockin' the boat but you. Go sit on your checkbooks. "

They just glares at me.

Torchy, Private Sec.

"Where is Old Hickory?" one of 'em wants to know.

"About now," says I, "Mr. Ellins would be finishin' the last of three soft-boiled eggs. He'll show up here at nine-forty-five."

"Mr. Robert Ellins, then?" demands another.

"Say, I'm no puzzle editor," says I. "Maybe he'll be here to-day and maybe he won't."

"But we couldn't find him yesterday, either," comes back an old goat with tufts in his ears.

"That's a way he has these days," says I.

No use tryin' to smooth things over. It's Mr. Robert they'd been sore on all along, suspectin' him of startin' all the wild schemes just because he's young. I'd heard 'em, after they'd moved into the directors' room, insistin' that he ought to be asked to resign. And what they was beefin' specially about to-day was because of a tale that a Chicago syndicate had jumped in and bought the *Balboa*, a 10,000-ton Norwegian freighter that we was supposed to have an option on. It was the final blow. That satisfied 'em they was being sold out, and their best guess was that Mr. Robert was turnin' the trick.

I was standin' by, listenin' to the general grouch develop, and wonderin' how long before they'd organize a lynchin' committee, when I hears the brass gate slam, and into the private office breezes Mr. Robert himself, lookin' fresh and chirky, his hat tilted well back, and swingin' a bamboo walkin'-stick. When he sees me, he springs a wide grin and grabs me by the shoulders.

"Torchy, you sunny-haired emblem of good luck!" he sings out. "What do you think! I've—got—her!"

"Eh!" says I. "The *Balboa*?"

"The *Balboa* be hanged! " says he. "No, no! Elsa—Miss Hampton, you know! She's mine, Torchy; she's mine! "

"S-s-s-sh! " says I, noddin' towards the other room. "Forget her a minute and brace yourself for a run-in with that gang of rag-chewers in there. "

Does he? Say, without even stoppin' to size 'em up, he prances right in amongst 'em, free and careless.

"Why, hello, Ryder! " says he, handin' out a brisk shoulder-pat. "Ah, Mr. Larkin! Mr. Busbee! Well, well! You too, Hyde? Hail, all of you, and the top of the mornin'! Gentlemen, " he goes on, shakin' hands right and left without noticin' how reluctant some of the palms came out, "I—er—I have a little announcement to make. "

"Humph! " snorts old Busbee. "Have you? "

"Yes, " says Mr. Robert, smilin' mushy. "I—er—the fact is, I am going to be married. "

"The bonehead! " I whispers husky.

Old Lawson T. Ryder, the one with the bushy white eyebrows and the heavy dewlaps, he puffs out his cheeks and works that under jaw of his menacin'.

"Really! " says he. "But what about the *Balboa*? Eh? "

"Oh! " says Mr. Robert casual. "The *Balboa*? Yes, yes! Didn't I tell someone to attend to that? A charter, wasn't it? Torchy, were you——"

I shakes my head.

"Perhaps it was Mr. Piddie, then, " says he. "Anyway, I thought I asked——"

"Here's Piddie now, sir, " says I. "Looks like he'd been after something. "

He's a wreck, that's all. His derby is caved in, his black cutaway all smooched with lime or something, and one eye is tinted up lovely. In his right fist, though, he has a long yellow envelope.

"The charter! " he gasps out dramatic. "*Balboa!* "

And, by piecin' out more jerky bulletins, it's clear that Piddie has pulled off the prize stunt of his whole career. He'd gone out after that charter at lunchtime the day before, been stalled off by office clerks probably subsidized by the opposition, spent the night hangin' around the water-front, and got mixed up with a dock gang; but, by bein' on hand early, he'd caught one of the shippin' firm and closed the option barely two hours before it lapsed. And as he sinks limp into a chair he glances appealin' at Mr. Robert, no doubt expectin' to be decorated on the spot.

"By George! " says Mr. Robert. "Good work! But you haven't heard of my great luck meantime. Listen, Piddie. I am to be married! "

I thought Piddie would croak.

"Think of that, gentlemen, " cuts in old Busbee sarcastic. "He is to be married! "

But it needs more 'n a little jab like that to bring Mr. Robert out of his Romeo trance. Honest, the way he carries on is amazin'. You might have thought this was the first case on record where a girl who'd said she wouldn't had changed her mind. And, so far as any other happenin's was concerned, he might have been deaf, dumb, and blind. The entire news of the world that mornin' he could boil down into one official statement: Elsa had said she'd have him! Hip, hip! Banzai! Elsa forever! He flashed that miniature of her and passed it around. He nudges Lawson T. Ryder playful in the short ribs, hammers Deacon Larkin on the back, and then groups himself, beamin' foolish, with one arm around old Busbee and the other around Mr. Hyde.

Maybe you know how catchin' that sort of thing is? It's got the measles or barber's itch beat seven ways. That bunch of grouches just couldn't resist. Inside of five minutes they was grinnin' with him, and when I finally shoos 'em out they was formin' a committee to shake each other down for two hundred per towards a weddin' present.

I finds it about as much use tryin' to get Mr. Robert to settle down to business as it would be teachin' a hummin'-bird to sit for his photograph. So I gives up, and asks for details of the big event.

"When does it come off?" says I.

"Oh, right away," says he. "I don't know just when; but soon—very soon."

"Home or church?" says I.

"Oh, either," says he. "It doesn't matter in the least."

"Maybe it don't," says I, "but it's a point someone has to settle, you know."

"Yes, yes," says he, wavin' careless. "I've no doubt someone will."

He was right. Up to then I hadn't heard much about Miss Hampton's fam'ly except that she was an orphan, and I expect Mr. Robert had an idea there wa'n't any nosey relations to butt in. But it ain't three days after the engagement got noised around that a cousin of Elsa's shows up, a Mrs. Montgomery Pulsifer—a swell party with a big place in the Berkshires.

Seems she'd been kind of cold and distant to Miss Hampton on account of her bein' a concert singer; but, now that Elsa has drawn down a prize like Robert Ellins, here comes Mrs. Pulsifer flutterin' to town, all smiles and greatly excited. Where was the wedding to be? And the reception? Not in this stuffy little hotel suite, she hopes! Why not at Crag Oaks, her place near Lenox? There was the dearest little ivy-covered church! And a perfectly charming rector!

Then Sister Marjorie is called in. Sure, she was strong for the frilly stuff. If Brother Robert had finally decided to be married, it must be done properly. And Mrs. Pulsifer's country house would be just the place. Only, she had an idea that their old fam'ly friend, the Bishop, ought to be asked to officiate. The perfectly charming rector might assist.

"Why, to be sure! " says Mrs. Pulsifer. "The Bishop, by all means. "

Anyway, it went something like that; and the first thing Mr. Robert knows, they've doped out for him a regulation three-ring splicefest with all the trimmin's, from a gold-braided carriage caller to a special train for the Newport guests. And, bein' still busy with his rosy dreams, Mr. Robert don't get wise to what's been framed up for him until here Saturday afternoon out at Marjorie's, when they start to spring the programme on him.

"Why, see here, sis, " says he, "you've put this three weeks off! "

"The bridesmaids' gowns can't be finished a day sooner, " says Marjorie. "Besides, the invitations must be engraved; you can't get a caterer like Marselli at a moment's notice; and there is the organ to be installed, you know. "

"Organ! " protests Mr. Robert. "Oh, I say! "

"You don't expect the Lohengrin March to be played on drums, I hope, " said Marjorie. "Do be sensible! You've been best man times enough to know that— —"

"Great Scott, yes, " says Mr. Robert. "But really, sis, I don't want to go through all that dreary business—dragging in to the wedding-march, with everyone looking solemn and holding their breath while they stare at you! Why, it's deadly! Gloomy, you know; a relic of barbarism worthy of some savage tribe. "

"Why, Robert! " protests Marjorie.

"But it is, " he goes on. "Haven't I pitied the poor victims who had to go through with it? Think of having to run that gauntlet—morbidly curious old women, silly girls, bored men—and trying to keep step to that confounded dirge. Wedding march, indeed! They make it sound more like the march of the condemned. *Tum-tum-te-dum!* Ugh! I tell you, Marjorie, I'm not going to have it. Nor any of this stodgy, grewsome fuss. I mean to have a cheerful wedding. "

"Humph! " says Marjorie. "I suppose you would like to hop-skip-and-jump down to the altar? "

"Why not? " asks Mr. Robert.

"Don't be absurd, Robert, " says she. "You'll be married quite respectably and sanely, as other people are. Anyway, you'll just have to. Mrs. Pulsifer and I are managing the affair, remember. "

"Are you? " says Mr. Robert, lettin' out the first growl I'd heard from him in over a week.

I nudges Vee and we exchanges grins.

"The groom always takes on that way, " she whispers. "It's the usual thing. "

I was sorry for the Boss, too. He'd been havin' such a good time before. But now he goes off with his chin down and his brow all wrinkled up. Course we knew he'd go straight to Elsa and tell her his troubles. But I couldn't see where that was goin' to do him any good. You know how women are about such things. They may be willin' to take a chance along some lines, but when it comes to weddin's and funerals they're stand-patters.

So Sunday afternoon, when I gets a 'phone call from Mr. Robert askin' me to meet him at Miss Hampton's apartment, and he adds that he's decided to duck the whole Crag Oaks proposition and do it his own way, I demands suspicious:

"But how about Miss Elsa?"

"She feels just as I do about it," says he. "Come up. She will tell you so herself."

And she does.

"I think it's the silly veil to which I object most," says she. "As if anyone ever did see a blushing bride! Why, the ordeal has them half scared to death, poor things! And no wonder. Yes, I quite agree with Robert. Weddings should be actually happy affairs—not stiff, gloomy ceremonies cumbered with outworn conventions. I've seen women weep at weddings. If I should catch one doing that at mine, I should be tempted to box her ears. Really! So we have decided that our wedding must be a merry one. That is why, Torchy, we have sent for you."

"Eh?" says I, gawpin'.

"You are to be best man," says Mr. Robert, clappin' me on the back.

"Me?" I gasps. "Ah, say!"

"Your Miss Verona," adds Elsa, "is to be my only bridesmaid."

"Well, that helps," says I. "But how—where——"

"It doesn't matter," says Mr. Robert. "Anywhere in the State—or I can get a Connecticut or New Jersey license. It shall be wherever you decide."

"Wha-a-at?" says I.

Mr. Robert chuckles.

"As best man, " he goes on, "we appoint you general manager of the whole affair; don't we, Elsa? "

She nods, smilin'.

"With full powers, " says she.

"We'll motor out somewhere, " adds Mr. Robert. "You and Miss Vee take the limousine; we will go in the roadster. If Marjorie and Ferdie wish to come along, they can join us in their car. "

"How about a dominie? " says I. "Do I pick up one casual along the road? "

"Oh, I forgot the Reverend Percy, " says Mr. Robert. "He's consented to quit that East Side settlement work of his for a day. You'll have to take him along. Now, how soon may we start? To-morrow morning, say? "

"Hel-lup! " says I. "I'm gettin' dizzy. "

"Then Tuesday, " says he, "at nine-thirty sharp. "

"But say, Mr. Robert, " says I, "just what——"

"Only make it as merry as you know how, " he breaks in. "That's the main idea; isn't it, Elsa? "

Another nod from Elsa.

"Robert has great faith in you as a promoter of cheerful affairs, " says she. "I think I have, too. "

"That being the case, " says I, "I got to live up to my rep. or strip a gear. So here goes. "

With which I breezes out and pikes uptown to consult Vee.

"Did you ever hear anything so batty?" says I.

"Why, I think it's perfectly splendid fun," says Vee. "Just think, Torchy, you can do anything you choose!"

"It's the choosin' that's goin' to bother me," says I. "I'm no matrimonial stage manager. I don't even know where to pull the thing off."

"I've thought of just the place," says she. "Harbor Hill, the Vernon Markleys' place out on Long Island. They're in the mountains now, you know, and the house is closed; but——"

"You ain't thinkin' of borrowin' their garage for this, are you?" says I.

"Silly!" says she. "Mrs. Markley's open-air Greek theater! You must have seen pictures of it. It's a dream—white cement pergolas covered with woodbine and pink ramblers, and a wonderful stretch of lawn in front. It would be an ideal setting. She's a great friend of Aunty's. We'll just wire for her permission; shall we?"

"Listens good," says I. "But we got to get busy. Tuesday, you know. What about eats, though?"

"There's a country club only half a mile away," says she.

"You're some grand little planner," says I. "Now let me go plot out how to put the tra-la-la business into the proceedin's."

I had a hunch that part would come easy, too; but after a couple of hours' steady thinkin' I decided that as a joy producer I'd been overrated. The best I could dig out was to hunt up some music, and by Monday noon that was my total contribution. I'd hired a band. It's some band, though—one of these fifteen-piece dance-hall combinations that had just closed a Coney Island engagement and was guaranteed to tear off this affair in zippy style. I left word what station they was to get off at, and 'phoned for a couple of jitneys to meet 'em. For the rest, I was bankin' on my luck.

And right on schedule we makes a nine-thirty getaway—three machines in all; for, while Marjorie had thrown seventeen cat fits when she first heard that Brother Robert had renigged, she shows up with Ferdie at the last minute. Catch her missin' out on any kind of a weddin'!

"But just where, Robert, " she demands, "is this absurd affair to take place? "

"Haven't the least idea, " says he. "Ask Torchy. "

So I names the spot, gives the chauffeurs their route directions, and off we booms across the College Point ferry and out towards the far end of the north shore. The Reverend Percy turns out to be kind of a solemn, serious-minded gink. Seems he'd been in college with Mr. Robert, had rooms just across the hall, and accordin' to his tell them must have been lively days.

"Although I can't say, " he adds, "that at all times I enjoyed being pulled out of bed at 2 A. M. to act as judge of an ethical debate between a fuddled cab-driver and a star halfback who had been celebrating a football victory. I fear I considered Bob's sense of humor somewhat overdeveloped. Just like him, running off like this. I trust the affair is not going to be made too unconventional. "

I winks at Vee.

"Only an open-air performance, " says I, "with maybe a little cheerin' music to liven things up. His instructions are to have it merry. "

"Ah, yes! " says the Reverend Percy. "Quite so. I understand. "

Torchy, Private Sec.

If he did he was a better guesser than me. For I was more or less at sea. We hadn't more than whirled in through the stone gate-posts of Harbor Hill, too, than I begun to scent complications. For there, lined up in front of the house, are four other machines, with a whole mob of people around 'em.

"Why! " says Vee. "Who can they be? "

"Looks like someone had beaten us to it, " says I. "I'll go do some scoutin'. "

Course, one close-up look is all that's needed. It's a movie outfit. I'm just gettin' hot under the collar, too, when I discovers that the gent in charge is none other than my old newspaper friend, Whitey Weeks. I'd heard how he'd gone into the film game as stage director, but I hadn't seen him at it yet. And here he is, big as life, wearin' a suit of noisy plaids as usual, and bossin' this assorted bunch of screen favorites like he'd done it all his life.

"A little lively with those grease-paints now, ladies, " he's callin' out. "This isn't for a next spring release, you know. "

"Huh! " says I, strollin' up. "Got the same old nerve with you, eh, Whitey? "

"Well, well! " says he. "The illustrious and illuminating Torchy! Don't tell me you've just bought the estate? "

"Would it matter to you who owned it, " says I, "if you wanted to use it bad? "

"Such cruel suspicions! " says he. "Sir, my permit! "

He's got it, straight enough—a note to the lodge-keeper, signed by Mrs. Vernon Markley, and statin' that the Unexcelled Film Company was to have the courtesy of the grounds any afternoon between the 15th and 25th.

"You see," explains Whitey, "we're staging an old English costume piece, and this Greek theater of Mrs. Markley's just fits in. Our president worked the deal for us. And we've got to do a thousand feet between now and five o'clock. Not in the same line, are you?"

And he glances towards our crowd, that's pilin' out of the cars and gazin' puzzled towards us.

"Do we look it?" says I. "No, what we was plannin' to pull off here was a weddin'. That's the groom there—my boss, Mr. Robert Ellins."

"Bob Ellins!" says Whitey. "Whe-e-ew!"

"Mrs. Markley must have forgot," says I. "Makes it kind of awkward for us, though."

"But see here," says Whitey. "A real wedding, you say? Why, that's odd! That's our stunt, with merry villagers and all that stuff. Now, say, why couldn't we—— Let's see! Do you suppose Mr. Ellins would mind if——"

I got the idea in a flash.

"He won't mind anything," says I, "so long as he can be married merry. He's leavin' that to me—the whole act."

"By Jove!" says Whitey. "The very thing, then. We'll—— But who else is this arriving? Look, coming in, two motor-buses full!"

"That's our band," says I.

"Great!" says Whitey. "Rovelli's, too! Say, this is going to be a bit of all right! Have him form 'em on between those cedars, out of range. Now we'll just get your folks into costume, let our company trail along as part of the wedding procession, and shoot the dear public the real thing, for once. What do you say?"

Torchy, Private Sec.

Course, considerin' how Mr. Robert had shied at a hundred or so spectators, this lettin' him in on a film exchange circuit might seem a little raw; but it was too good a chance to miss. Another minute, and I'm strollin' over, lookin' bland and innocent.

"Any hitch? " says Mr. Robert. "Have we got to the wrong place? "

"Not much, " says I. "This is the right place at the right time. Didn't you tell me to go as far as I liked, so long as I made it merry? "

"So I did, Torchy, " he admits.

"Then prepare to cut loose, " says I. "This way, everybody, and get on your weddin' clothes! "

For a second or so Mr. Robert hangs back. He glances doubtful at Miss Hampton. But say, she's a good sport, she is.

"Come along, Robert, " says she. "I'm sure Torchy has planned something unique. "

I didn't dispute her. It was all of that. First we groups the ladies on the south veranda behind a lot of screens, and herds the men around the corner. Then we unpacks them suitcases of Whitey's and distributes the things. Such regalias, too! What Mr. Robert draws is mostly two colored tights, spangled trunks, a gorgeous cape, peak-toed shoes of red leather, and a sword. Maybe he didn't look some spiffy in it!

You should have seen Ferdie, though, with a tow-colored wig clapped down over his ears and his spindle shanks revealed to a cold and cruel world in a pair of faded pink ballet trousers. For the Reverend Percy they dug out a fuzzy brown bathrobe with a hood, and tied a rope around his waist. Me, I'm dolled up in green tights and a leather coat, and get a bugle to carry.

How frisky a few freak clothes make you feel, don't they? Mr. Robert begins cuttin' up at once, and even Ferdie shows signs of wantin' to indulge in frivolous motions, if he only knew how. The reg'lar movie people gets the idea this is goin' to be some kind of a lark, and they joins in, too. When the ladies appeared they sure looked stunnin'. Miss Hampton has on a fancy flarin' collar two feet high, and a skirt like a balloon; but she's a star in it just the same. Sister Marjorie, who's a bit husky anyway, looks like a human hay-stack in that rig. And Vee—well, say, she'd be a winner in any date costume you could name.

Meanwhile Whitey has posted his camera men in the shrubbery, where they can get the focus without bein' seen, and has rounded us up for a little preliminary coachin'.

"Remember, " says he, "what we're supposed to be doing is a wedding, back in the days of Robin Hood, with all the merry villagers given a day off. So make it snappy. We want action, lots of it. Let yourselves go. Laugh, kick up your heels, let out the hi-yi-yips! Now, then! Are you ready? "

"Wait until I start the band, " says I. "Hey, there, Mr. Rovelli! Music cue! Something zippy and raggy. Shoot it! "

Say, I don't know how them early English parties used to put it over when they got together for a mad, gladsome romp on the greensward, but if they had anything on us they must have been double-jointed. For, with Mr. Robert and Miss Hampton skippin' along hand in hand, Vee and me keepin' step behind, a couple of movie ladies rushin' the Reverend Percy over the grass rapid, and the other couples with arms linked, doin' fancy steps to a jingly fox-trot—well, take it from me, it was gay doin's.

And when we'd galloped around over the lawn until we'd bunched for the weddin' picture in front of this Greek theater effect, the Reverend Percy had barely breath enough left to go through his lines. He does, though, with Mr. Robert addin' joshin' remarks; and we winds up by givin' the bride and groom three rousin' cheers and peltin' 'em with roses as they makes a run through the double line we forms.

Torchy, Private Sec.

Yep, that was some weddin', if I do say it. And the sit-down luncheon I'd ordered at the Country Club in Mr. Robert's name wa'n't any skimpy affair, even though we did spring an extra number on 'em offhand. For the boss insists on goin' just as we are, in our costumes, and luggin' along all the movie people. The reckless way he buys fizz for 'em, too!

And, by the time the party breaks up, Whitey Weeks is so full of gratitude and enthusiasm and other things that he near bubbles over.

"Torchy, " says he, wringin' my hand fraternal, "you have given my company the time of their lives. They're all strong for you. And, say, I've got a thousand feet of film that's simply going to knock 'em cold at the first-run houses. Any time I can— —"

"Don't mention it, " says I. "Specially about that film. The boss don't know yet that you had the camera goin'. Thought it was only rehearsin', I guess. All he's sure of now is that he's been married merry. And if he ever forgets just how merry, for a dime he can go take a look and refresh his mem'ry, can't he? But I'm bettin' he never forgets. "

THE END